Publisher's Foreword

Back in the 90s, Mike Schoenborn contributed occasional articles to our magazine, *Canadian Master Point*, each one a gem. Usually, they would recount, more or less truthfully, some insane-sounding but fascinating bridge escapade that had happened about twenty years before. The Shoe would always apologize for his faulty memory of the actual deals: 'The spots are mostly right,' he would say, 'but I'm not totally certain who had the ◇4 on the third hand.'

I've been trying to get the Shoe to collect more of his ramblings into a book for many years. About ten years ago, he actually sent me one chapter, but after that nothing happened for several weeks. Then I got an email: 'Boy, this is a lot of work!' (That's the expurgated version.) Eventually, he summoned up the resolve to get going again, and you are holding the result in your hands. Inside its pages, you will meet a cast of characters worthy of Damon Runyon or even Victor Mollo. And the usual publisher's disclaimer, 'Any resemblance to real persons, living or dead, is purely coincidental', is not operative here. Everyone in this book is very real; they include the best man and maid of honor at my wedding, several of the guests, and many of Linda's and my bridge partners, some more serious than others. It was the Shoe himself, in a Regional open pairs in Detroit, who helped me earn the last few points I needed to become a Life Master all those years ago.

Hart House still exists, as does its bridge club, and for all I know the downtown YMCA still runs a duplicate game too. Alas, Kate's and the Metro Club are no more, but they too were as real as the players in these stories. Fran's is still around too, although the Yonge-Eglinton location around the corner from Kate's has been closed. So you can look at this book one of two ways: as a fascinating look back at the bridge scene in Toronto in the 60s and 70s, or as a bridge 'coming-of-age' story that takes its hero from fooling around at the afternoon duplicates to playing for Canada in a world championship. Either way, you have a treat in store. And you may never bid or play quite the same way again.

You have been warned.

Ray Lee
June 2014

BRIDGE ON A
Shoestring

Michael Schoenborn

Master Point Press • Toronto, Canada

...born

...ages

Master Point Press
331 Douglas Ave.
Toronto, Ontario, Canada
M5M 1H2 (416)781-0351
Email: info@masterpointpress.com

Websites:	www.masterpointpress.com
	www.teachbridge.com
	www.bridgeblogging.com
	www.ebooksbridge.com

Library and Archives Canada Cataloguing in Publication

Schoenborn, Michael, author
    Bridge on a shoestring / written by Michael Schoenborn.

Issued in print and electronic formats.
ISBN 978-1-77140-012-1 (pbk.).—ISBN 978-1-55494-604-4 (pdf).--
ISBN 978-1-55494-490-3 (epub).--ISBN 978-1-55494-741-6 (mobi)

    1. Contract bridge. 2. Bridge players--Ontario--Toronto.
I. Title.
GV1282.3.S36 2014   795.41'5   C2014-900578-4
                                             C2014-900579-2

We acknowledge the financial support of the Government of Canada through the Book Publishing Industry Development Program (BPIDP) for our publishing activities.

Editor	Ray Lee
Copyeditor/layout	Sally Sparrow
Cover and interior design	Olena S. Sullivan/New Mediatrix

1 2 3 4 5 6 7   18 17 16 15 14
PRINTED IN CANADA

Contents

Introduction

This book was originally intended to cover fifty years of fun and seriousness at the bridge table in the Toronto, Canada area, from 1962 to 2012. However, there was so much material that I had to stop half way. The locations are real, described as they were in the 1960s and 1970s. Pretty much all the hands and auctions are real although some players have been changed to fit the story. The characters are based on real people. Well-known players get their real names.

I regret that I could not convert all the people who put up with me as a partner/critic into characters in this book. I am particularly sad to have no stories about John Gowdy: I just didn't write them down. Also, I shamelessly sourced hands from old issues of *What's Trump*, a short-lived magazine that was the brainchild of Bob Haines, of Metro Bridge Club fame. Among his contributors, I relied heavily on Andy Altay's writeups of Canadian Intercollegiate bridge and on John Sabino's priceless stories.

These are the real people behind some of the major characters:

Eric the Half Bee: in real life, an engineer, Eric Rankine. Full of goodwill and enthusiasm, his intelligence was not always transferable to bridge. He was the source of many excellent dinners during my starving student days.

Colonel Bulldozer: is based on Fred Lerner, the only partner from those early days who still plays with me. A great player who is routinely underrated, maybe because of his unfailingly sunny disposition. His loud, happy laughter can regularly be heard across the room, whether he is winning or not. Fred acquired his name playing regularly with his equally good-natured wife, Margaret (Mrs. Four Notrump), who more or less schooled Fred in auctions that use Blackwood in the early rounds of the bidding.

The Albatross: Although it certainly fit, this was never actually used as a nickname for David Bryce, a lawyer and my first serious partner. He was an excellent player and director, whom I ribbed mercilessly about butchering hands on which he went into prolonged trances. His other famous blunders included twelve exposed cards on a single hand in the Spingold. The real Albatross was Eric Landau.

The Bambino: John Sabino, a great talent and in his younger days, a devastatingly creative mind at the bridge table. I played a game of duplicate with him the first day he played, and he was pretty much perfect. Once, we won a duplicate game by bidding three notrump on every hand.

The Hummingbird: John Cunningham, regional genius at the invention of bizarre, useful bidding treatments. On a good day, one of the best players I ever saw in action.

The Victim: Doug Dearborn, my partner for three months, during which time I went from 100 masterpoints to Life Master. An exceptional card player, with an uncanny sense for what was happening at the table, Doug specialized in impossible plays, such as inducing a shift holding three small opposite three small when the ace or king was led, by calling for the highest card from dummy. The opponents never could figure out what he was up to, but they knew it had to be something and they weren't going to fall for it.

The Tree: Katie Thorpe, at the time that the book takes place, a law student learning how (not?) to play bridge. Subsequently, a successful internationalist for Canada. Katie always seemed to have something to spare in the bidding, and was famous for tabling 'Thorpe dummies'.

The Old Guy: Harry Rombach, whom I met when he was in his mid-eighties. A survivor of the Ukrainian pogroms, he laughed at the Canadian government for giving him so much money that he could live well and still go to the racetrack three times a week. Harry's sight was failing, so he occasionally called for the three of clubs from dummy when it was the three of spades. A bad player who never seemed to get a bad result.

The Owl: Harry Abel, a rotund bespectacled student of the game who never rose further than being the terror of little old ladies in club games. Harry, unlike many of us, was prepared to work for a living, and occupied himself variously as a cab driver and a process server. He was also an assistant to Don 'Moo' Cowan in his entertainment agency, where among other duties he got to drive the occasional stripper to her performance at some private function.

Bozo: Dominic di Felice, who originally brought me the forcing club canapé system and took us to within a whisker of qualifying to represent Canada when we lost a heartbreaking 1975 Canadian Team Championship in the finals.

Big Bird: Harmon Edgar, who has been called the World's Largest Rookie, in bridge and in life, but aren't we all? Helped to continue to develop the forcing club canapé system. Missed a few easy plays, but made more impossible good plays than anyone else I've met.

The Snowman: based on Bruce Raichman, who had the delightful quality of dressing and talking like a serious human being while implementing a few ideas at least as warped as my own.

Flashy: Roy Coleman, who sailed with my brother and me. He really did play only six hands of bridge in his lifetime and the chapter about bridge on Toronto Island chronicles the results.

The Shoe: Loosely based on me, as if those who know me were ever fooled. In 1987, I reached the Bermuda Bowl as promised (and finished sixth).

My original title for this book was *The Wrong Play at the Right Time*. Then, of course, my ideas were merely considered some kind of idiotic diversion. Now, I see leading players quite often making these "wrong" plays, with excellent success. It's still not a bad title, even now when I, like everyone else, have become slavishly devoted to making the right play.

It is 1987, and the scene is set in Ocho Rios, Jamaica. Eight teams are in contention for the Bermuda Bowl, emblematic of the world championship of bridge. One of them is Canadian. Our imaginary camera zooms in on the North-South pair, surely the legendary Murray and Kehela… but no. Instead of a suave, gentlemanly, cigar-smoking duo, we see two tall, thin, badly-dressed individuals. They rejoice in the Runyonesque sobriquets of Big Bird and The Shoe. One of them still looks much like the student he was twenty years ago when his bridge odyssey began, when as a rookie who spent every waking moment playing and thinking about bridge, he vowed that one day, he would play for Canada in this great event. As Jerry Garcia might have mused, it has been a long, strange trip…

1

The Hart House Bridge Club

In the 1960s, as now, the Hart House Bridge Club was located at the downtown campus of the University of Toronto, where it had operated since the Great Depression. It had originally been run by the legendary Percy 'Shorty' Sheardown, one of the greatest bridge players who ever lived. Shorty by that time had moved on to manage Toronto's rubber bridge club, the St. Clair, one of the few places in the city where one could play the game for money.

Hart House was a dark, castle-like structure built by the Masseys (of Massey-Ferguson fame) after World War I, and roughly modelled on the Oxford and Cambridge Unions in England. It had an art gallery, a music room, a debates room, a library, a chapel, common rooms and extensive athletic facilities. You could eat at Hart House: there was a cafeteria for coffee, snacks and bridge games, and the Great Hall for actual dinners. The kitchen was universally known, prompting some wag to inscribe in the bathroom cubicle of the campus library the advice: "Please flush twice, it's a long way to the Hart House kitchens." Hart House also housed the campus clubs for innumerable activities, including bridge.

Perhaps I should introduce myself here. My name is Bill Miller and I am an older, solitary guy, with my children all grown up. I am fascinated by bridge and by human nature, and kibitzing allows me to indulge my two vices simultaneously. My contribution to the game is the Winning Butterfly, which accompanies me and lights on the shoulder of those I kibitz if they behave well. There was no better place for me than Hart House. The Hart House Bridge Club featured inexperienced bridge players with overactive imaginations, often vindicated by an excess of intelligence. Alcohol, as they would say today, "was involved". There were few real experts, except of course in their own minds.

The bridge club conducted regular Tuesday night duplicates, appropriately held in the debates room, with the added attraction that games were totally free. The director had hair that was both too long and badly cut, as well as a name nobody could spell, and a tendency to boastfulness and sarcasm. He was universally known as "the Shoe".

I had heard a few stories about the Shoe's eccentric theories and behavior, so it was with some trepidation I first wandered over to Hart House, introduced myself and asked if I might be permitted to kibitz. He skipped the part about being glad to meet me and said, "We'll call you 'Bungalow Bill'. That way you won't be confused with *The Kibitzer*, the Ontario Unit bridge magazine." I took that as a "yes" as far as the kibitzing was concerned, and so began the first day of many years of priceless entertainment.

The Shoe was a superb natural card player, and like many in his circle, he had little use for textbook bids and plays. The objective was to win, and have fun doing it, rather than to slavishly follow well-trodden paths. Shoe's inclinations prompted him to reinvent the game, rather than seeking assistance from experts. He particularly disdained the percentage play, reasoning that 52% for the drop against 50% for the finesse paid off one time in fifty, whereas any really good player, himself automatically included, could induce the opponents to make a mistake at least half the time. His goal was fittingly immodest: one day he would play in the Bermuda Bowl. What better place to begin such a journey than at the Hart House Bridge Club?

The first bridge hand that the Shoe ever submitted to *The Kibitzer* was rejected by its then editor, Sami Kehela, one of the few players who could legitimately lay claim to being possibly even better than Shorty. We have to presume that he considered the story too improbable to publish, or perhaps just not instructive. I can vouch for the hand because I watched it. Justice did not necessarily triumph.

Shoe was directing the Hart House game sitting at his usual spot, South at Table 1. He claimed that he had learned from the newspaper bridge columns that South always got the good hands. He picked up, at favorable colors:

♠ 8 6   ♡ —   ◊ 4   ♣ J 10 9 8 7 6 5 4 3 2

The Shoe's RHO opened four spades, and Shoe so desperately wanted to bid five clubs that he actually hesitated more than the required ten seconds before passing. His partner on this occasion had been introduced to me as Eric the Half Bee, and I had to wonder how he had ever met up with the Shoe. The Half Bee was an older, silver haired gentleman in a blue suit. Later, it transpired he was a successful engineer whose only shortcoming was a fanatic love of bridge. His success in life and intelligence had not, so far, been transferable to duplicate bridge.

The Half Bee would be bound to assume that a five club bid showed more than a jack. Worse than that from the Shoe's point of view, if a five club bid proved unsuccessful, the Half Bee would be sure to win the post-mortem discussion. He'd have enough opportunity to do that when he treated the Shoe to another dinner.

Reluctantly, the Shoe passed, as did LHO. The Half Bee doubled, RHO passed, and Shoe contributed a modest five clubs, confident that any blame had now safely been transferred to the Half Bee.

The five club bid seemed to bring the table to life: LHO bid five diamonds, the Half Bee five hearts, RHO five spades. This was surely what bidding up the line was all about! Once again, the Shoe wanted to bid on, but even he could see no way to justify it. After a pass by LHO, the Half Bee came to the rescue with a bid of five notrump. This was all the excuse Shoe needed: he could win any argument that might possibly ensue. If the heart bid had not promised club tolerance, surely the five notrump bid did? Anyway, holding all the low clubs, where was his hand entry? Accordingly, six clubs by the Shoe, double by LHO, all pass.

This was the entire deal:

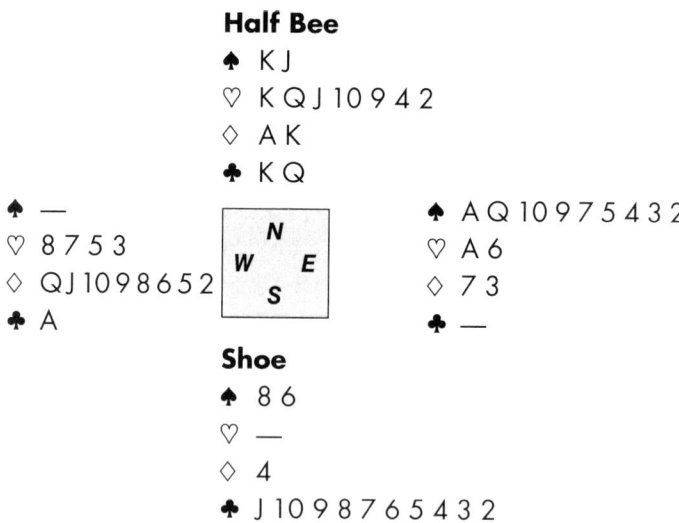

Half Bee
♠ K J
♡ K Q J 10 9 4 2
◇ A K
♣ K Q

♠ —
♡ 8 7 5 3
◇ Q J 10 9 8 6 5 2
♣ A

♠ A Q 10 9 7 5 4 3 2
♡ A 6
◇ 7 3
♣ —

Shoe
♠ 8 6
♡ —
◇ 4
♣ J 10 9 8 7 6 5 4 3 2

After the opening lead of the ◇Q, Shoe was in a position to make the hand regardless of the location of the ♡A: two rounds of diamonds pitching a spade, followed by a club lead, putting West in a position of yielding a heart trick or a ruff and discard at Trick 4!

In case anyone had overlooked the beauty of this hand, the Shoe expressed disappointment with the other two +1090 scores, which probably only occurred because he had the misfortune to find the ♡A with RHO. Shoe persisted with further analysis: even on a diamond lead, declarer in 6♠ would lose only four tricks for minus 800. Furthermore, 6♣ would not make from the Half Bee's hand, as the ♠A could be cashed. As far as I know, this was the first occasion when the Shoe noted that the hand would play at least a trick better from his side, an observation codified in Shoe's Second Rule of Bridge. If the ten-club hand was the original example, the following was proof positive:

♠5 ♡10 2 ◇A 3 2 ♣A K J 8 6 5 2

Rejecting a vulnerable gambling three notrump rebid, Shoe opened one spade. After a pass, the Half Bee raised to two spades, RHO doubled and Shoe bid three notrump. LHO passed, and the Half Bee was face-to-face with Shoe's First Rule of Bridge: *never* pull three notrump.

However, the Half Bee was wavering because he had stretched a bit for the 2♠ raise:

♠ 10 9 7 4   ♡ Q 7 6 5   ◇ Q 5 4   ♣ 10 7

After all, Shoe would still be declarer at spades, so Half Bee would be complying with the Second Rule if he bid four spades. Reluctantly, he decided that the First Rule must come first for a reason, so he passed. RHO exercised his table presence with another double, and when this came back to the Half Bee, he could restrain himself no longer and removed to four spades. RHO had a thing going now and doubled again. The Shoe removed to four notrump.

Even the Half Bee knew this was not Blackwood, and quailed inwardly at the discussion that would ensue if four notrump went one down. RHO doubled again, the Shoe redoubled and the Half Bee watched the events that ensued, not as a full-sized Half Bee, but more like a mosquito watching itself fly into a campfire. He wished he could be an even smaller insect, actually.

This was the whole deal:

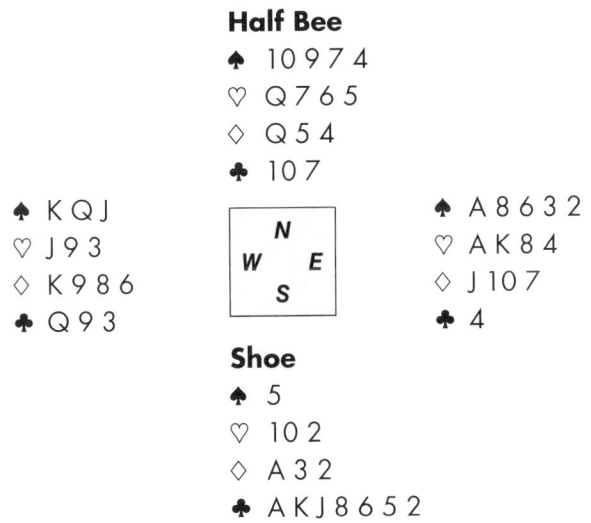

Half Bee
♠ 10 9 7 4
♡ Q 7 6 5
◇ Q 5 4
♣ 10 7

♠ K Q J
♡ J 9 3
◇ K 9 8 6
♣ Q 9 3

♠ A 8 6 3 2
♡ A K 8 4
◇ J 10 7
♣ 4

Shoe
♠ 5
♡ 10 2
◇ A 3 2
♣ A K J 8 6 5 2

The Half Bee was squirming needlessly about one down, as he might have inferred when the ♡3 was led and the Shoe thanked him politely for the dummy. The play was swift: small from dummy, ♡K from RHO, small from Shoe. The ♠3 was returned, won by LHO with the ♠J. Many routes now lead to six down, minus 3400, if the batteries in my calculator are still working (for example, cash two more spades and then lead the ♡J to squash the ten).

The opponents had other ideas, however. LHO returned the ♡9, which was ducked round to the Shoe's ten. Shoe now led the deceptive ◇3 toward dummy: small by LHO, ◇Q, small by RHO(!). LHO had now shown up with the ◇K, ♡J and spades headed by honor-jack. Surely RHO had *something* for the four doubles? Accordingly, ♣10 from dummy, small, small, queen! West was as confused as everyone else and, suspecting the Shoe of subterfuge, returned a diamond.

Shoe won, and began the avalanche of clubs, finally coming down to the good ♣2 and the not-so-good ◇2. In the two-card ending, LHO 'had to' hold the ♠KQ (the Shoe had bid spades, after all) and RHO 'had to' hold the major-suit aces. The Shoe was able to claim with the two minor-suit deuces. This is probably the occasion where the Shoe first developed a penchant for picturesque endings.

Nowadays, he would have logged up an immodest +1120, but in those days, the insult was only worth fifty, so the total was only +1070. The opponents moved on to the next table, so they missed Shoe's comment that the swing compared to down six had been nearly 4500 points. "Of course," he added to no one in particular, "had West led the nine of hearts, an obvious unblocking play, it could have been down seven, for minus 4000."

Of course, the Shoe got away with a lot of atrocious bidding because he discovered early that running his long suit produced unexpectedly good results. He was about to learn the word 'pseudo-squeeze'.

Half Bee
- ♠ 6
- ♡ A K Q J 9 5
- ◊ K J
- ♣ Q 6 3 2

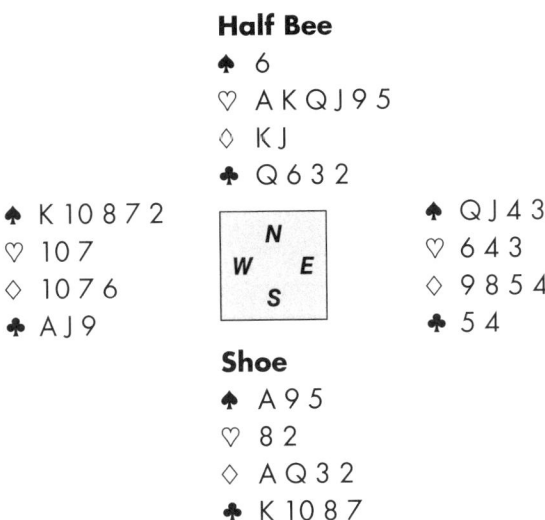

♠ K 10 8 7 2
♡ 10 7
◊ 10 7 6
♣ A J 9

♠ Q J 4 3
♡ 6 4 3
◊ 9 8 5 4
♣ 5 4

Shoe
- ♠ A 9 5
- ♡ 8 2
- ◊ A Q 3 2
- ♣ K 10 8 7

On this deal, after some auction like one heart – two clubs – three hearts with the opponents silent, the Shoe shamelessly hogged the hand from the Half Bee by bidding three notrump, which was emphatically for play, though far from the par spot. The Half Bee did not even consider removing three notrump.

Justice demanded that there be a spade lead. The Shoe made a *pro forma* duck, hoping for some miracle shift. Spades were continued and he couldn't cash his eleven winners due to the blockage in diamonds. He nonchalantly ran the hearts. East was persuaded that his little diamonds were worthless and pitched one. That was back to eleven tricks, a top board instead of a bottom, as all the normal people reached 4♡ making five.

Somewhere along the way, the Shoe began to experiment with preempting short suits. It began simply enough, on a deal where the opponents were two of those players who inveterately listened to auctions and, what was worse, believed them. Almost without thinking, the Shoe determined to send out false information. In the old days, Shoe was not all that subtle. Come to think of it, he's not all that subtle now. He held as dealer, at favorable vulnerability:

♠ 6 5 4 3   ♡ A 10 8 7 4   ◊ A 10 9 5   ♣ —

With a Listener on his left and the vulnerability right, the Shoe began the proceedings with an opening bid of three clubs. Presumably, the Half Bee had already learned about the dangers of raising non-vulnerable preempts, and also knew about Shoe's Third Rule: "Do not take a save unless you think you might make it."

LHO, the first Listener, bid a smooth three spades and the Half Bee contributed four hearts (!), which went pass, pass back to LHO. He tried four spades. An astonishing five hearts from the Half Bee, five spades by East. Shoe had two aces and five more hearts than promised, plus the surprise club control. He risked six hearts, doubled by LHO, redoubled by Shoe. The play was uninteresting, as the Half Bee held:

$$\spadesuit — \ \heartsuit K Q J 9 6 5 3 \ \diamondsuit J 4 2 \ \clubsuit 10 8 7$$

On the spade lead, the Half Bee ruffed, drew one round of trumps, ruffed black cards back and forth ending in his hand, and finally advanced a diamond to the ten, not caring where the honors were located. He explained that he was counting on his club fit when he bid to the five-level, and Shoe congratulated him on his play, suggesting he might soon qualify as a full bee. The Shoe managed also to point out, before the opponents fled the table, that the club preempt was essential to get the Half Bee off to a club lead, the only lead to beat 6♠.

2

Walking on the Wild Side

Bridge had come a long way since Culbertson, but in some ways, it was much the same. Goren had popularized Standard American bidding, the Acol group had done something similar in Europe. But now things were starting to loosen up, and systems were a fertile area for the imaginative and unfettered minds of the Young Turks. Of course, many bridge clubs, mindful of the comfort of their paying customers, placed restrictions on what could actually be played in their games.

The early sixties were the days when the Italian Blue Team had just begun to win one world championship after another. Some of the Italians were incredible card players, but nevertheless their bidding systems were given much of the credit for their successes: Roman Club, Neapolitan Club, and eventually, Blue Team Club. Everyone wanted to be just like them, except without doing the work. Complexity was work. Defense was work. Counting was work. With these parameters firmly in mind, the Shoe invented a system that promised to combine the forcing club with five-card majors, while leaving the entire two-level open for an assortment of preemptive bids that would make it less necessary to defend. He called it the Neapolitan Diamond or simply the Forcing Diamond. It looked like this:

1♣	any opening bid 11-16 HCP that did not fit elsewhere
1◇	17+ HCP control-asking
1M	11-16 HCP, at least five cards
1NT	15-17 HCP balanced
Two-bid	6-11 HCP: suit bid and next higher suit, at least nine cards
2NT	6-11 HCP, non-touching suits

Of course, the Shoe needed a victim who would learn this system and actually play it. For this honor, he selected the Albatross, a student from his university class. The Albatross was a gifted analyst and a quick study who instinctively played very well. Too much thought, however, tended to cause him to snatch defeat from the jaws of victory. If partner was going to make a mistake, it was even more annoying to have to wait a long time before he made it. It was for all these reasons, and more, that he had become known as the Albatross.

Shoe had made him famous for a hand where the Albatross received a small spade lead against a notrump game. (What was the Albatross doing playing notrump from his side in any event?) Holding ♠J109 in dummy opposite ♠AQ6 in the closed hand, the Albatross huddled inordinately to decide where to win the first trick, opting after some minutes for the closed hand, and deciding to overtake the jack with the queen for that purpose. That is what he did. Unfortunately, he had concentrated so hard that he had failed to notice that RHO had contributed the king to this trick. So it was that the Albatross had become the ultimate demonstration of the Shoe's Second Rule of Bridge. In case you have forgotten already, that's the one that says, "Everything plays at least a trick better from the Shoe's side." The Albatross would learn the system and Shoe would shamelessly hog the hands.

The Forcing Diamond was wonderful for the Hart House game, where people were even worse at bidding in competition than they were at uncontested auctions. I believe that now, years later, the idea of bidding as much as possible has become accepted as a fundamental tenet of successful bridge. Not so, back then. People idolized 'soundness'. Even worse, often the interval that elapsed between tournament success and an accusation of unfair advantage was too short to measure.

On in-between hands, it turned out to be particularly useful to show both suits before the opponents had bid. There was a hand in a rubber bridge game, of all places, where the Albatross opened two spades (spades and clubs) and the Shoe held:

♠ J 9   ♡ A Q J 10 9   ◇ A 10 9 8 5   ♣ 5

Right away, it became unnecessary to be tempted to look for a game, or even a fit. The hand belonged on defense, or at a low level for your side, so it was easy to pass. LHO balanced with a double and the eventual result was +1400 in three hearts doubled, with the added bonus of 100 honors.

Another early success featured a hand where the Shoe held:

♠ Q 10 3 2   ♡ 9 3   ◇ A K 10 9 6 2   ♣ 8

The Albatross opened two hearts, showing hearts and spades. Shoe jumped to the optimistic four spades, just making, with the opponents on for three notrump with their six club tricks.

Eventually, the Albatross and the Shoe took the system to a tournament. I was expected to watch. It was their luck to start against a member of the Unit conventions committee, and a Life Master to boot. You have to picture the Shoe, no shrinking violet, and the Albatross, a lawyer and future tournament director, filling in their convention card under the watchful eye of this committee member. Inevitably, he progressed from watching to bold, active condescension. He introduced himself, cited his credentials (including the Life Master bit), and proceeded to explain in the most minute detail exactly how amateurish and useless the system was. Shoe responded with a kindly smirk. As they used to say on his report card, "Does not relate well to authority." Oblivious to the smirk, the committee member forged ahead, assuring them that with time and increased maturity, they would certainly switch to Standard American.

"Is this a way to treat new players?" the Shoe coyly inquired. But those were the days when new players were cherished not for their future participation, but for the two top boards they were likely to give you right now. Shoe was still mumbling for all to hear, something about having to do the best they could with their immature system, when he took out the cards from the first board. In second chair he picked up:

♠ K 10   ♡ Q 3   ◇ K Q J 10 9   ♣ K Q J 9

RHO, the Conventions Guy, passed. The Shoe had 17 high-card points, no aces, but too nice for one notrump, so the he tried the forcing one diamond (17+) asking for controls. After a pass, the Albatross responded one notrump, showing two controls (ace = 2, king = 1). In this case, it had to be an ace, though on other hands it could have been two kings. The Albatross perked up in his seat, as his chances of becoming declarer had just improved dramatically. Of course, from the Shoe's point of view, notrump was not so great with all those missing aces, unless the Albatross could furnish two heart stoppers and a second spade stopper. Also, Shoe had to consider his own Second Rule of Bridge. If hands played at least a trick better from his side, they must play at least a trick worse from the Albatross' side. That virtually proved that notrump could not be the right spot. Shoe rebid two diamonds, raised to three by the Albatross.

With the Albatross having no biddable major, three notrump would need a miracle. Shoe passed and this was the entire deal:

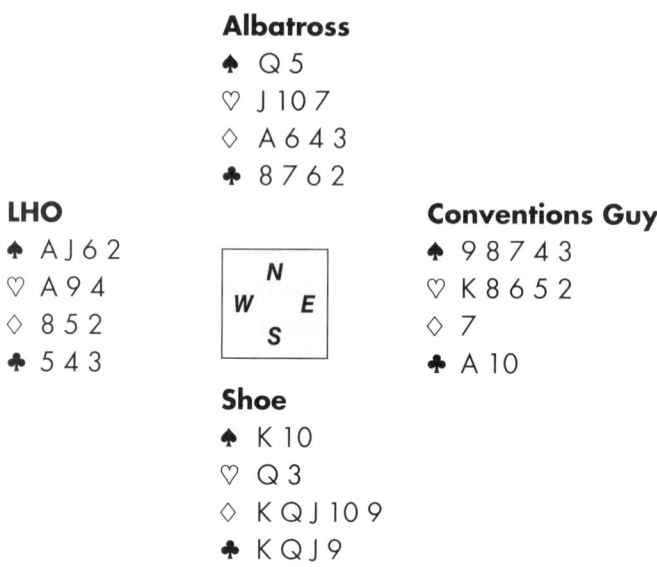

Albatross
♠ Q 5
♡ J 10 7
◇ A 6 4 3
♣ 8 7 6 2

LHO
♠ A J 6 2
♡ A 9 4
◇ 8 5 2
♣ 5 4 3

Conventions Guy
♠ 9 8 7 4 3
♡ K 8 6 5 2
◇ 7
♣ A 10

Shoe
♠ K 10
♡ Q 3
◇ K Q J 10 9
♣ K Q J 9

The fun did not really start until after the Shoe had made three diamonds and had embarked on a comprehensive discussion with himself on the merits of the system. The strong bidding had kept the opponents out of the auction when they could have made three of either major. In notrump, the Albatross would make seven tricks if the defense went after hearts but only six tricks if they chose spades. I was waiting for Shoe to fashion a sentence that casually inserted the word "immature" into the conversation, but he remained unimaginatively satisfied with belaboring the point that all these good things had happened because of the system. Then, almost as if he had just noticed it at that very moment, he added that had the opponents been playing the system, the Conventions Guy would have opened two hearts and they would have declared three spades or defended some number of notrump doubled.

As in the theater, the Shoe's asides tended to be audible to everyone in the room. He permitted himself an aside at that point, turning to me and venturing "Bungalow, does this mean our system has been upgraded from immature to lucky?" I knew he'd got to "immature" eventually, but I glowered him back to the second board. That turned out, if anything, even worse than the first. The Albatross opened two hearts holding:

♠ K J 9 5 4   ♡ Q 4 3 2   ◇ 8 6   ♣ A 9

The request for an explanation came rather pointedly and Shoe indicated that the bid showed 6-11 high-card points with at least nine cards in the majors, both suits biddable. Eventually, the Conventions Guy overcalled a natural two notrump, raised to three by partner. Shoe did not have a lead problem as the entire deal was:

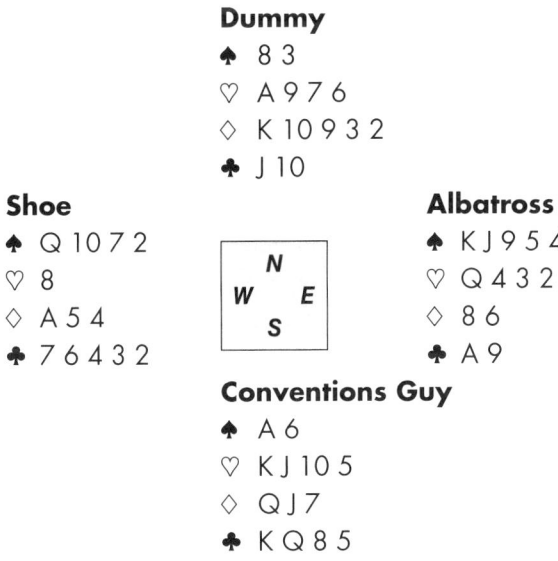

Dummy
♠ 8 3
♡ A 9 7 6
◇ K 10 9 3 2
♣ J 10

Shoe
♠ Q 10 7 2
♡ 8
◇ A 5 4
♣ 7 6 4 3 2

Albatross
♠ K J 9 5 4
♡ Q 4 3 2
◇ 8 6
♣ A 9

Conventions Guy
♠ A 6
♡ K J 10 5
◇ Q J 7
♣ K Q 8 5

On the automatic spade lead, three notrump was two down for +200. In case they missed it, the Shoe pointed out that his side could make three spades for +140 even on trump leads, which, needless to say, was not as good as three notrump two down. "Needless to say" pretty much guaranteed Shoe *would* say it, but still that was not enough.

Shoe could not help but observe that had the opponents been playing the system, dummy would have opened two diamonds

(6-11 points, diamonds and hearts), so that the opponents would have reached four hearts. The director was summoned as Shoe was beginning his dissertation on whether or not four hearts should make. Suddenly, the Conventions Guy had come to an appreciation of the unfair advantage possessed by his opponents because of their system. The prediction he had made at the outset came true in fifteen minutes flat, albeit not in the manner that had been forecast. The director ordered the Shoe and the Albatross to play Standard American for the rest of the event.

Exotic systems may have been out of favor with the ACBL, but they flourished at the Hart House Bridge Club. Since the games were held Tuesday evening, Tuesday afternoons were devoted to chicken wings and beer, typically at the Embassy or Bay-Bloor taverns. Ridiculous pet projects could turn into serious theoretical adventures after a pitcher of beer. One Tuesday, Shoe and I were drinking drafts with the Victim, a clean-cut nice-looking guy who looked like he had just walked out of the graduation pictures in your pre-1960s high school yearbook. My instincts said that one or probably both of his parents were schoolteachers.

The Victim had a natural talent for cards. He preferred poker, where he was the best I had ever seen. He also liked blackjack and gin rummy. Almost as an afterthought, he routinely beat up most of the serious bridge players. In addition, he blushed fiercely and looked generally nonplussed when others hustled him to play cards for money. He was forever being approached to play. Once, we were discussing bridge but leaving the pub to go to the Hart House game. Two total strangers approached us and asked if we played bridge. Before I could blow them off with our planned departure, the Victim stammered a shaky, "Yeah... you guys ever heard of Goren?" That, in turn, elicited: "Do you play bridge... for... *money*?"

Another day, we were in the Bay-Bloor when the Hummingbird arrived. The Bird struck you right away as a regular guy, both in appearance and in manner, but this was misleading. It does not do justice to the Hummingbird to say he was eccentric. Not only did that skip right over his immense natural bridge ability, it understated the quality of his eccentricity. Even the Shoe thought the Hummingbird was eccentric.

On that particular Tuesday, the Bird's project was to invent a system that would destroy the takeout double. Not only did he invent that system, he made it small enough to fit on a single cocktail napkin and labelled it the "Ugly Club":

1♣	6-12 HCP, majors
1◇	13+ HCP, majors
1♡	6-12 HCP, minors
1♠	13+ HCP minors
1NT	10-12 HCP balanced
2m	6-12 HCP, minor plus same color major
2M	6-12 HCP, major plus other color minor

That left a pass to show 0-5 HCP. They couldn't help it that Ferts[1] had not yet been invented, or they would surely have switched the pass and the one spade opening. Later, the Ugly Club was refined to include "single raise, artificial and forcing" but on that first night at Hart House, Shoe taught the Ugly Club to the Albatross as described. As usual, I kibitzed. No conventions committee here. The Victim and the Hummingbird each indoctrinated a partner and also sat North-South in a field of fifteen tables. Unleashing Ugly Club in its original terrifying simplicity and without further discussion, the three pairs came first, second and fourth.

Part of the fun of watching the Shoe was that occasionally he demonstrated that his bragging was not 100% unjustified. I liked the very first hand of the Ugly Club's debut at Hart House. He was dealer, vulnerable. The reader should know everything about Ugly Club that the Shoe knew when he picked up:

♠ J 10 9 8 7 5   ♡ J 5 3   ◇ A 10 9 6   ♣ —

The Shoe opened one club (6-12 HCP, majors). The bidding took off like a rocket.

---

1. Ferts (or 'fertilizer bids', a polite version of what many called them) are weak openings that are part of many systems where an initial pass shows a strong hand. These systems are designed more to disrupt the opponents' bidding than to be constructive.

West	Shoe	East	Albatross
	1♣*	1♡	2♡
3♡	pass	4♡	4♠
pass	?		

It seemed that the Albatross had the right to expect some spades on this auction, but was that enough to explain that he had come out in a vulnerable four spades without waiting to hear what Shoe had to say about four hearts? Perhaps the Shoe was also considering what might have impelled the Albatross to violate the Second Rule of Bridge, taking the play away from him, on the very first board of the night. What could the Albatross be showing? Looking only slightly intoxicated, Shoe jumped to six spades. This was the deal:

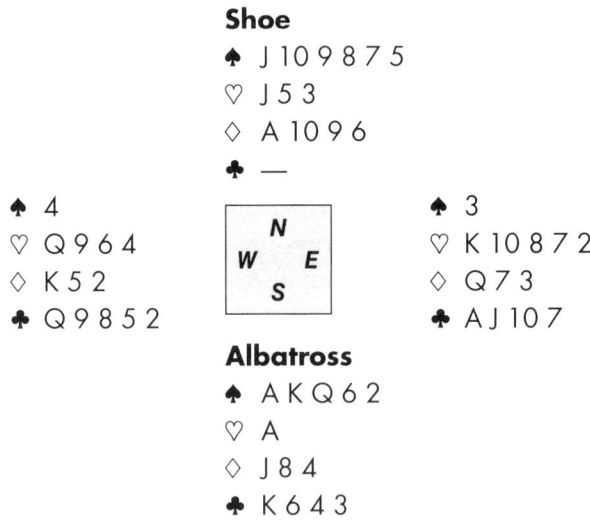

Shoe
♠ J 10 9 8 7 5
♡ J 5 3
◇ A 10 9 6
♣ —

♠ 4
♡ Q 9 6 4
◇ K 5 2
♣ Q 9 8 5 2

♠ 3
♡ K 10 8 7 2
◇ Q 7 3
♣ A J 10 7

Albatross
♠ A K Q 6 2
♡ A
◇ J 8 4
♣ K 6 4 3

What a system! Shoe had concluded there was at most one red-suit loser. The Ugly Club permitted him to open a vulnerable six-count, and then leap to slam on his "extras". The Albatross' hand was not ideal. How could it be? He was on play. Six spades was still cold.

The quest for progress could hardly end with the Ugly Club. For one thing, people still had to pass with 0-5 HCP. Shoe eagerly adopted the Neapolitan Shaft, which was part of the Hart House victim response to the Ugly Club. The Neapolitan Shaft actually made you bid on *every* hand:

1♣	17+ HCP, asks controls
1◇	6-12 HCP, more cards in the majors, raise only force
1♡	6-12 HCP, more cards in the minors, raise only force
1♠	0-12 HCP and one of
	i) longest suit minor, more cards in majors,
	ii) same as (i) with long major, more minors, or
	iii) 0-5 HCP, *any* distribution
1NT	13-16 HCP balanced
Pass	13-16 HCP unbalanced
2♣	6-12 HCP, clubs and hearts or diamonds and spades
2◇, 2♡, 2♠	6-12 HCP, suit and next higher
2NT	6-12 HCP, minors

This use of the one spade bid in the 1960s can probably lay claim to having been the first Fert.

Shoe did a test-run of the Neapolitan Shaft with the Tree at the YMCA Bridge Club on College Street in downtown Toronto, another place that had never heard of the conventions committee. The Tree was, at that time, a mere talented rookie who had acquired her name because of the manner in which she remained rooted to the spot catching a Frisbee. Later she was to become a highly successful Canadian international player, so apparently the Shoe was unable to ruin her completely.

It turned out to be not exactly *every* hand on which you opened. Playing opposite the long-suffering Tree and against a husband and wife pair destined for walk-on parts in this particular farce, Shoe was in third chair and held:

♠ Q 9 7 6 5 2   ♡ 8 7 4   ◇ J 9 4   ♣ 6

The Tree started proceedings with a pass and Shoe remembered to alert, explaining that pass showed an unbalanced hand of 13-16 HCP. Considerable discussion followed, including questions relating to mental health that Shoe, had he harbored any paranoid tendencies, might well have taken personally. Things ultimately threatened to get nasty during the more substantial debate about whether you could make a takeout double of a pass that showed an opening bid. Years later, the ACBL reported a similar debate as a great novelty.

Eventually, the wife passed and Shoe had a serious problem of his own. If the Tree's hand was unbalanced, she probably had short spades, or at least long clubs. Anyways, was he responding to a pass, or opening the bidding? That turned out not to matter, as he had a one spade bid either way. Then, he'd be odds-on to be rebidding over two clubs. It went against the grain to pass with good spades and nice distribution. On the other hand, his side held at most 19 HCP. Courageously suppressing the pain, the Shoe passed.

The Shoe's pass led to a discussion even more heated than the first. Shouldn't you have to play the same system in first and third chair? If so, how could you pass out a hand where both players had 13-16 points? If the second pass showed a really weak hand, didn't Shoe have to bid one spade to show 0-5 HCP? It took a while to convince the opponents that Shoe was really *responding* to the pass, so that the bids were natural. A cloud of heavy sarcasm began to condense around the word "natural". The Tree generously agreed that the word "natural" could be a bit misleading when describing actions taken by the Shoe.

It was only just and fair that the husband, in passout seat, should also have a problem:

♠ 10 4   ♡ A Q J   ◇ K 5   ♣ A K Q J 8 2

Maybe Mr. Passout should have considered a pass, thereby trumping the opening pass by issuing a pass with half the deck. It would surely have been the strangest passout in history, a story to tell his grandchildren when they were trying to complete their high school bridge course. On this hand, the Shoe would have passed just so he could make history, but Mr. Passout just could not bring himself to pass.

Three notrump stood out as the opening bid, but Mr. P would have the Tree's sound, unbalanced opening bid on lead to his left. Surely it included running spades? Mr. Passout was like the man who knew too much in the Hitchcock movie. His mind began to wander, troubled by questions like: Could a person really be sound and unbalanced at the same time? Three pairs of eyes stared expectantly in his direction. Who could possibly fault an opening bid of one club? Almost everybody, as it later transpired.

The Tree overcalled one diamond and suddenly the Shoe's dog had become a great hand. After a pass by Mrs. Passout, he responded one spade, barely resisting the temptation to jump shift into two spades. Over one spade, Mr. Passout tried to bail the water out of his sinking ship with a jump to three clubs, which was passed back to the Shoe. Shoe had enough to try three diamonds, and that became the final contract. The whole auction had been:

West	North	East	South
Mrs. Passout	Shoe	Mr. Passout	Tree
			pass*
pass	pass	1♣	1◊
pass	1♠	3♣	pass
pass	3◊	all pass	

The whole deal was:

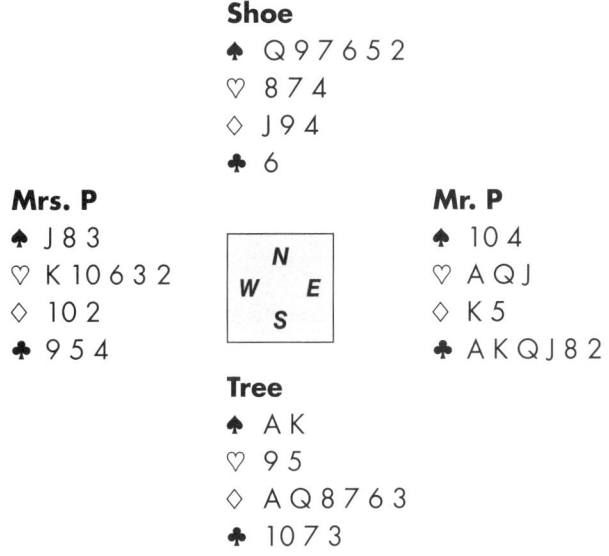

Shoe
- ♠ Q 9 7 6 5 2
- ♡ 8 7 4
- ◊ J 9 4
- ♣ 6

Mrs. P
- ♠ J 8 3
- ♡ K 10 6 3 2
- ◊ 10 2
- ♣ 9 5 4

Mr. P
- ♠ 10 4
- ♡ A Q J
- ◊ K 5
- ♣ A K Q J 8 2

Tree
- ♠ A K
- ♡ 9 5
- ◊ A Q 8 7 6 3
- ♣ 10 7 3

Mr. Passout won the opening club lead and used this golden opportunity to shift to a trump. Six trump tricks and six spade tricks added up to the rest of the tricks, making six. That was the signal for further discussion. Shoe criticized the Tree for treating the hand as unbalanced, adding that a notrump opening bid would have led to the superior spade partial. The Tree countered with the argument that spades can be held to three on repeated heart leads and that she had made +170 in diamonds. No one was really listening.

Mrs. Passout interrupted to berate Mr. Passout for opening the bidding but, other than the result, seemed to be at a loss for good reasons to pass 20 HCP with a solid six-card suit. Shoe helpfully jumped to Mr. Passout's defense by pointing out that notrump from his side would probably make five, as it would take an immediate cashout to hold him to four. On the other hand, he continued blithely, Mrs. Passout would go eight down in three notrump from her side if, on a low diamond lead, she rose with the king. Shoe was about to digress into an exposition of the Second Rule of Bridge, but the Director announced there were three minutes left in the round, and there was still another exciting board to be played. Keeping it short, the Shoe contented himself with the suggestion that anyone who could be playing a hand ten tricks worse than her partner should not be critiquing the bidding.

The second board proved that there is no justice and quite possibly, that there may be no grandchildren for Mr. and Mrs. Passout. In second chair, at favorable colors, Shoe opened two clubs, duly alerted. If you have been paying attention, you will recall that this bid shows 6-12 high-card points and a two-suiter, either in clubs and hearts or in diamonds and spades. The Tree held:

♠ 3 2   ♡ Q J 10 7 5 2   ◇ 4   ♣ A Q 9 8

Mr. Passout competed with a very hesitant two diamonds. The Tree naturally thought that this was one of partner's suits, so with vulnerable opponents she passed, hoping for further developments. Mrs. Passout raised to three diamonds, passed back to the Tree. Where were the spades? The Tree concluded partner had them, which meant he also had diamonds. She doubled and everyone passed. The whole auction had been:

Tree	Mrs. P	Shoe	Mr. P
	pass	2♣*	2◇
pass	3◇	pass	pass
dbl	all pass		

The Tree led the ♠3, little anticipating what an artistic card this would turn out to be, as this was the entire deal (hand rotated):

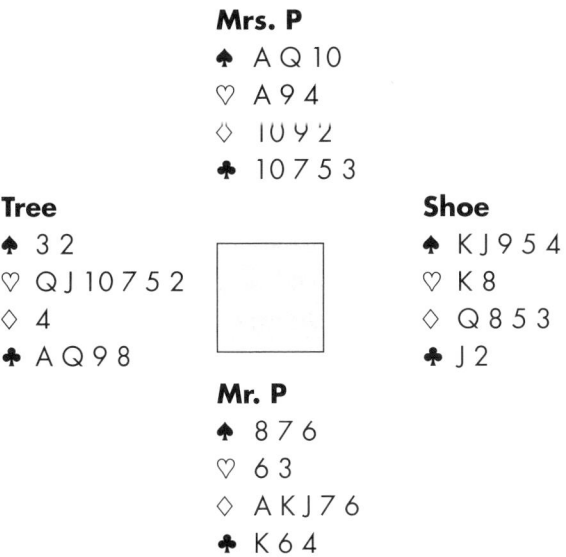

Mrs. P
♠ A Q 10
♡ A 9 4
◊ 10 9 2
♣ 10 7 5 3

Tree
♠ 3 2
♡ Q J 10 7 5 2
◊ 4
♣ A Q 9 8

Shoe
♠ K J 9 5 4
♡ K 8
◊ Q 8 5 3
♣ J 2

Mr. P
♠ 8 7 6
♡ 6 3
◊ A K J 7 6
♣ K 6 4

The ♠10 from dummy was won by Shoe's jack. He returned the inspired deuce of clubs through Mr. P.'s king, taken by the Tree's ace. Back came the deuce of spades: now doesn't that look as though the Tree is the one with five spades and four diamonds? Trying to salvage at least something, Mr. Passout finessed the queen, losing to the king. The ensuing spade ruff clarified the position in spades and diamonds. The Tree squandered Shoe's ♣J by cashing the ♣Q and then ruffing out dummy's ten. Mr. Passout worked out the diamond position but still had to lose a heart trick for down three, minus 800. The ensuing post-mortem is probably best left to the imagination.

As I have mentioned, the ACBL frowned on bidding creativity of this type, and so too did some of the local clubs. Fortunately, intercollegiate bridge did not ban these inspired bidding systems. That year, the Canadian Intercollegiates were held at Hart House and I was chief kibitzer. You can still find the writeup describing how the Shoe's team swept the event. Obviously, I had succeeded in bringing along the Winning Butterfly. The team game, I should add, was board-a-match scoring. Some way into a pretty nice game, the Shoe picked up:

♠ K 9 8 3   ♡ —   ◇ A K 5 2   ♣ A K J 9 8

His partner was one of the usual victims who could play the forcing diamond, probably Roy Hughes. The system dictated that the Shoe open one diamond, forcing, 17+ HCP. The vulnerable player on his left bid two spades, and it went pass, pass, back to the Shoe. Now what? I was rooting for him to find the pass, but the Shoe balanced two notrump for the minors. This felt like Mr. Passout all over again.

Balancing two notrump may have been the wrong thing to do, but as so often is the case, sinning makes your life considerably more interesting. Shoe's LHO continued to three hearts, partner bid four clubs and RHO bid four hearts. The Shoe found a pass and should have been suspicious when partner did not double the vulnerable four hearts, choosing instead to bid five clubs. RHO competed with five hearts and after two passes, partner doubled and led a trump. One of the most frightening dummies that the Shoe can recall turned up, as this was the deal:

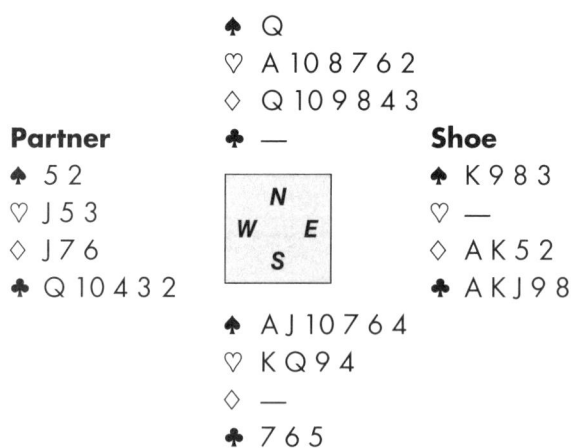

```
                    ♠  Q
                    ♡  A 10 8 7 6 2
                    ◇  Q 10 9 8 4 3
   Partner          ♣  —                Shoe
   ♠  5 2                                ♠  K 9 8 3
   ♡  J 5 3              N               ♡  —
   ◇  J 7 6          W       E           ◇  A K 5 2
   ♣  Q 10 4 3 2         S               ♣  A K J 9 8
                    ♠  A J 10 7 6 4
                    ♡  K Q 9 4
                    ◇  —
                    ♣  7 6 5
```

The unfortunate result was five hearts doubled making six, minus 1050. The Shoe had the gall to estimate this as a win, as partners rated to be doubled in four hearts, making six, or might even bid the slam. Sure enough, they did win the board, as the other table had this auction:

West	North	East	South
		1♠	pass
pass	2♡	dbl	3♡
pass	4♡	dbl	all pass

The last board was another success on an auction that was destined for failure, indeed one that was nominated for worst auction of the year. There were lessons in there somewhere, but it's difficult to articulate what they were. The Shoe presented the rotated deal with no comments for once, though he did furnish the annotations.

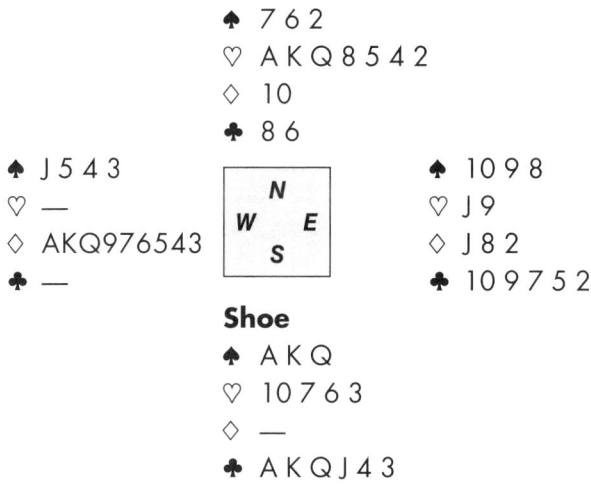

```
                    ♠ 7 6 2
                    ♡ A K Q 8 5 4 2
                    ◇ 10
                    ♣ 8 6
  ♠ J 5 4 3                              ♠ 10 9 8
  ♡ —                N                   ♡ J 9
  ◇ AKQ976543     W     E                ◇ J 8 2
  ♣ —                S                   ♣ 10 9 7 5 2

                    Shoe
                    ♠ A K Q
                    ♡ 10 7 6 3
                    ◇ —
                    ♣ A K Q J 4 3
```

Here was the auction, with annotations:

West	North	East	South(Shoe)
			1◇[1]
pass[2]	2♣[3]	pass	2NT[4]
pass[5]	4NT[6]	pass	pass[7]
double[8]	5♡[9]	pass	6♣[10]
6◇[11]	6♡	pass	7♡[12]
all pass			

1. 17+ HCP asks controls.
2. Rats, they stole my suit.
3. 3 controls (A=2, K=1).
4. Per our last discussion, this just showed slam interest.

5. They'll never play it here, will they?
6. I know we play delayed transfer bids, but what if partner forgets?
7. 4NT is a quantitative raise and we are missing an ace and a king.
8. If diamonds break, I can set this a million.
9. I should never have bid 4NT.
10. Whatever 6♣ shows, I have it. Why didn't I bid clubs sooner?
11. Maybe I should have passed 4NT.
12. Partner's controls must be the ace and king of hearts. There are no losers.

Seven hearts bid and made was another win, as partners escaped in five diamonds doubled, one down. Years later, the Shoe commented that nowadays a jump to three notrump over the forcing club identifies a solid suit. When he checks back to find out it's hearts, the grand slam becomes a lot easier to bid. On the other hand, you're not going to get the nine solid diamonds to pass if you open one club.

3

Short Suit Night at the Metro

Back in the late 1960s, as we shall see in the next chapter, the pre-eminent Toronto bridge club was Kate Buckman's, which ran seven days a week. There were many small clubs that held weekly games, and we have already encountered Hart House and the YMCA. The Metro Bridge Club served as a fascinating alternative to Kate Buckman's. It was operated on Friday nights on College Street West by the unique Bob Haines. Bob was never seen eating food, preferring clear alcoholic beverages. Nevertheless, every Friday, he prepared and served a delicious multi-course dinner at his home before game time, then reconvened there afterwards with a group for more food, post-mortem discussions and bidding quizzes. And drinks.

This was a perfect forum for penniless university students. Bob was a true bridge enthusiast, who greatly preferred exotic inventions to expert publications. The Shoe came to me, demanding information about the Metro Club. It seemed to be too good to be true: he wanted to see it for himself, so I volunteered to take him and the Victim along for a look.

When we arrived, the Hummingbird was conducting a little seminar on how to defend against the Ugly Club. You may recall from the last chapter that the Ugly Club was the system invented to destroy the takeout double. The gist of the defense to it was: double for penalties and overcall your short suit. Loosely speaking, it used exclusion bids. The question was how to compete holding normal overcalls. At the moment, one notrump was favored for that. The dissenters felt that using one notrump created new problems of its own: what to bid or lead if the opponents blasted to a high level, or worse, bid three notrump?

The Hummingbird's solution was to use *transfer* exclusion bids. In that system, a simple overcall would show one of two hands in the suit *above* the suit overcalled:

(i) A one-suiter in the next higher suit; or

(ii) A three-suiter excluding the next higher suit.

Toss in jump overcalls to show two-suiters and you could bid just about anything. The advantages of this system were postulated to include that the ambiguity would damage the ability of the opponents to evaluate their cards, to bid suits naturally or as cuebids, to locate fits or to bid notrump. Someone pointed out that such a system would work well against forcing club systems or short club systems.

The Shoe was mightily impressed and invited the Hummingbird to try out transfer exclusion bids in that night's duplicate game. Of course, I had to watch. They were rewarded on the very first board. The Shoe, South as always, heard West open one club, forcing. The Bird overcalled one diamond, showing either a one-suiter in hearts or a three-suiter without hearts. East doubled, showing a positive response. No surprise there, as Shoe held:

♠ 10 9 4 3 2 ♡ 8 6 5 3 ◇ Q J 6 ♣ 2

How did he always manage to be non-vulnerable for these hands? The Shoe ventured a jump to two hearts, doubled by West, redoubled by the Bird. Redouble was undiscussed, but it had to show the three-suiter. Shoe removed to two spades. Somebody doubled. The Bird had:

♠ K Q 8 7 ♡ 7 ◇ K 9 8 3 2 ♣ J 10 8

After two spades doubled made, the Shoe was compelled to enter upon a discussion about whether or not three hearts would have been preemptive. He soon got distracted by the need to observe that the opponents could make six hearts or seven clubs. That, in turn, led to another "interesting" question, though perhaps not for these particular opponents: would a heart bid by opponents have been natural or a cuebid?

Probably it was this early success that got the Bird caught up in the short-suit karma. A little while later, with no one vulnerable, he picked up:

♠ 6 ♡ — ◇ 10 9 2 ♣ A K Q 10 8 7 6 4 2

When RHO opened one heart, the Bird overcalled one spade! Opponents made things difficult for ordinary mortals, as the auction returned to the Bird as follows:

LHO	Shoe	RHO	Bird
		1♡	1♠(!)
3♡	3♠	4♡	?

Fortunately, the Bird was no ordinary mortal. He was, in the then-recent words of Jimi Hendrix, "experienced". The only thing *not* to do was to bid clubs. That was bound to elicit a spade preference from the Shoe, who probably hadn't pictured the actual hand. The Bird calmly rebid four spades on his singleton. At least he was ruffing in the short hand. True, if the opponents passed, he might have some rather unusual score like minus 350, but the opponents probably had a game. Also, if the opponents passed, the Bird and the Shoe would fall over each other to make a note of their names, as it seemed likely that they would never double anything as long as they lived.

Naturally, the opponents did double four spades. They also doubled five clubs "on momentum", allowing Shoe to pass to let the Bird work his own way out of this fine mess. This was the entire deal:

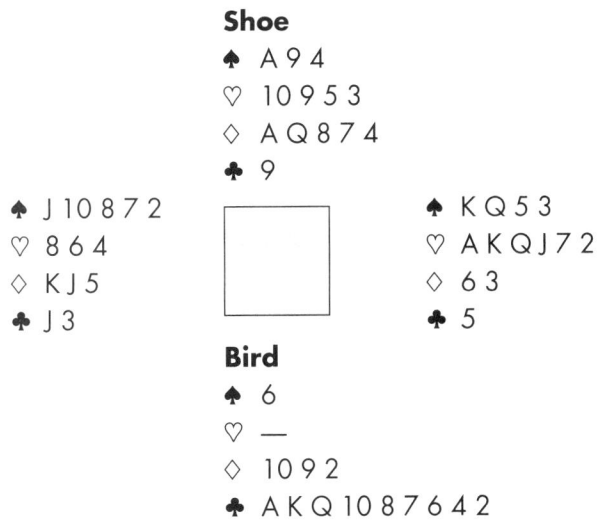

Shoe
♠ A 9 4
♡ 10 9 5 3
◇ A Q 8 7 4
♣ 9

♠ J 10 8 7 2
♡ 8 6 4
◇ K J 5
♣ J 3

♠ K Q 5 3
♡ A K Q J 7 2
◇ 6 3
♣ 5

Bird
♠ 6
♡ —
◇ 10 9 2
♣ A K Q 10 8 7 6 4 2

Unfortunately, the dummy had the all-important eight of diamonds, and the double diamond finesse worked, so five clubs doubled with two overtricks, +750, was not a good score. All the cleverness was rewarded with very few matchpoints.

The top score on the board belonged to the Bambino, who had paired up with the Victim. At their table, East opened "Skip bid, four hearts" on the Victim's right. The Victim hardly ever played bridge, being universally regarded as a world-class poker player. Good poker demanded an immediate jump to six clubs. If this action disregarded the skip bid warning, it also successfully masked the weakness of his hand. The Bambino figured that whatever the Victim's two losers were, he had them covered, so he raised to seven clubs, pausing to redouble when one of the opponents had the temerity to double. The double diamond finesse worked at their table, too, for a score of +1810 old-style scoring. Another triumph for the wrong bid.

Shoe and the Bird were continuing the great short-suit adventure. Eventually, they arrived at a table where a pair of young newlyweds was occupied with a learned dissertation on the subject of which of them was more stupid. Shoe surprised me by not volunteering any helpful contributions to the debate, possibly because he was new at the club and lacked information, but more likely because he was recording new quips to add to his repertoire. The young couple were far too engrossed in the debate to notice, far less to acknowledge, the arrival of Shoe and the Bird at their table, or anywhere in the world, for that matter.

Shoe really was on amazingly good behavior, so it was wait... wait... wait, withdraw the hand from the pocket... wait a little more... notice they were vulnerable and the opponents were not. Shoe sorted out the following:

♠ A J 9 8 5 4 3 2 ♡ 5 ◇ 3 ♣ Q 10 3

Finally, when the argument showed no sign of being resolved or even resolvable, he could wait no longer. Shoe asked, in a polite tone that the hearers might have considered sarcastic, if play might commence, or words to that effect. Dumb Wife, East, began with a surly bid of one heart. The Shoe, who had not failed to notice that the Bird had out-brillianced him on the spade overcall and that the opponents were perhaps a little distracted, decided to contribute to the divorce with an overcall of two diamonds. That was sure to get doubled and when he removed to two spades, the odds were terrific they'd take a moment to check the vulnerability and double again. That was the Shoe's story after the game, and he was sticking to it.

The analysis turned out to be wrong but the result was right. I greatly prefer that to the expert method: perfect analysis, wrong result. Also, it was a kind of retribution for the punishment the gods had visited on the Bird's earlier brilliance. Dumb Husband (West) obliged with an earth-shaking double of two diamonds, but Dumb Wife removed the double to two spades. Spades? Shoe looked visibly perturbed as he recalculated the number involved in his nice safe runout to two spades.

Eventually, the unhappy couple bid to four hearts. Dumb Husband was livid when this went two down after Shoe's lead of his singleton diamond. Dumb Husband insisted that he did not mind so much that he had seven diamonds to a hundred honors and that his dumb partner had removed the double with ace doubleton. Nor, he claimed slightly louder, did he mind that they were cold for six diamonds. What *really* annoyed him was that Dumb Wife did not know how to draw trumps. Instead, she led a low spade up to the singleton ♠K in dummy, no doubt failing to suspect the 8-0 spade split and intending to ruff some spades in dummy. The Hummingbird ruffed the ♠K and gave Shoe a diamond ruff on the way back.

Even Shoe now believed that there had to be positive karma for short suits that night. Little wonder that he was unable to resist a similar move on the next hand, especially as he was still playing against Dumb and Dumber. As was ordained, there was another loud double and another pull and another missed slam. As the couple left the table, the debate was still raging over who was the more stupid. The points on both sides of the debate had become exceptionally strong. No doubt the debate is still raging today.

In the post-mortem the Shoe met the Bambino, usually modest and self-effacing. Bambino claimed he had a better short-suit story from that evening's game. He heard the Victim open one spade, both vulnerable, and the next player doubled. The Bambino held:

♠ J 10 8　♡ A 2　◇ 9 8 7 3　♣ 10 9 6 2

The problem was: how to buy the hand in spades, preferably at the two-level but at least without going for a vulnerable number, when the opponents make three or four hearts. With this in mind, the Bambino bid two hearts (forcing). West went into the grandfather of all trances. Then he picked up the convention card and read it carefully on both sides. The message was loud, but was it clear? Finally, West passed and the Victim raised to three hearts in tempo.

The raise to three hearts ruined everything for the Bambino, who returned to three spades trying not to look too unhappy about it. The Victim raised himself to four spades, doubled by West. This was the deal:

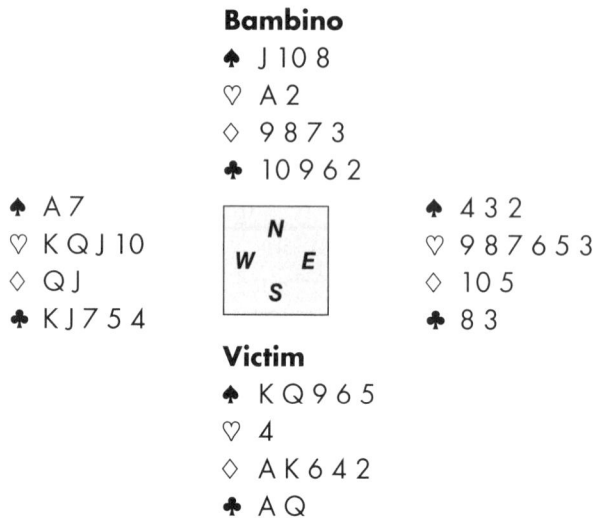

Bambino
♠ J 10 8
♡ A 2
◇ 9 8 7 3
♣ 10 9 6 2

♠ A 7
♡ K Q J 10
◇ Q J
♣ K J 7 5 4

♠ 4 3 2
♡ 9 8 7 6 5 3
◇ 10 5
♣ 8 3

Victim
♠ K Q 9 6 5
♡ 4
◇ A K 6 4 2
♣ A Q

The outcome was a very satisfactory making five, +990. The Victim had found the heart raise on his singleton heart, showing why he was universally feared as a poker player. The Victim thought nothing of this, saying that he, too, was entitled to be at the table. Or maybe we overestimated him: maybe he was on to the short suit karma, just like everyone else.

This success got the Bambino to reminiscing about other short-suit triumphs. Or, maybe not triumphs, if the opponents were even less reliable than you were. The Bambino held, in fourth chair, neither vulnerable:

♠ A Q 8 6 3   ♡ A Q 9 8 5   ◇ J 4   ♣ 8

His opponents looked wild, but the Bambino had never seen them in action. West opened two clubs, which East explained as strong and forcing. The Victim overcalled two spades and East passed. Already, the Bambino had a serious problem of whom to trust. It certainly seems there were far too many points and spades in this deck. Why should partner be the only one who gets to have any fun? The Bambino joined the fray with a bid of three clubs. This could have been anything from natural to a cuebid. Maybe two wrongs would make a right.

If this hand had taken place in a bidding contest, you'd have to say that on a scale of one to ten, the three club bid could have scored a zero. It might not have scored much on a scale of a thousand. Tonight, of course, there was a strong case of short-suit karma going on. So let's suppose that the Bambino cared nothing for impressing the critics and merely wanted to find out what would happen.

What happened was this: everybody passed! The whole auction had been:

West	Victim	East	Bambino
2♣	2♠!	pass	3♣!
all pass!			

This was the deal:

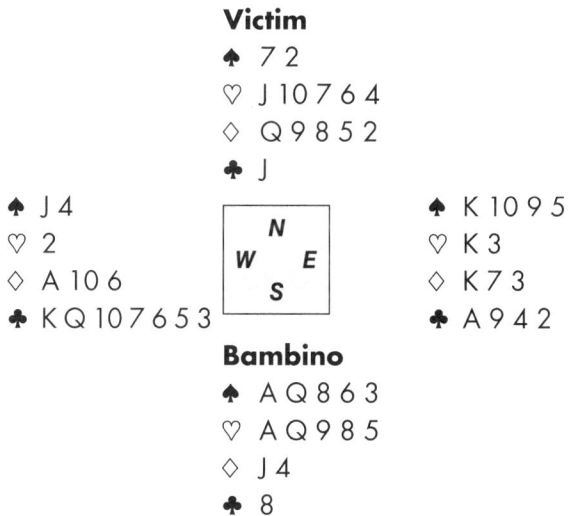

The ensuing discussion went something like this: West was obviously playing secret Precision, which was tough because in that year, Precision had not yet been invented or if it had been, no one knew about it. Maybe it wasn't that secret either: look at the hand East passed throughout when it must surely make slam opposite a strong, forcing two clubs. The Victim had obviously been planning a series of rescue redoubles unless he, too, knew about secret Precision. Your side makes four hearts on the lucky lie of the cards, but the other side makes four notrump from RHO's side.

Instead, here you were, playing three clubs on your 1-1 fit. The opponents lived up to their bidding by permitting a diamond trick and a spade ruff, so the result was four down, -200. This salvaged two matchpoints, beating the pair that could not beat the notrump game and the pair that defended one notrump making five for -210. A bad score, but who else gets to tell their grandchildren about the time they stole a spade ruff to get out for only four down in their 1-1 club fit?

All of this discussion encouraged the Bambino to skip the story of seven clubs redoubled and to launch directly into other tales of short-suit glories from days gone by.

"Speaking of short suits," the Bambino began, "against two dear little old ladies, we had a superior lead-inhibiting sequence. This time, my partner opened one club, which in our system describes a basically nondescript hand with at least four cards in one of the suits. The next hand doubled and I held:

♠ 2   ♡ A 10 9 4   ◊ A 8 7 6   ♣ A J 9 4

"If you play double advance lead-inhibiting cuebids, you have no problem. Accordingly, I bid: 'Two spades.' Next hand trembled slightly and enunciated in a firm tone: 'I double *that*.' Partner obliged with a 'forcing' pass and the Little Old Lady on my right leaped in with four hearts. I managed to find a double and the result of +1100 was, surprisingly, a cold top."

The audience was begging for more, so the Bambino continued on the topic of distributional hands. "There was the usual assortment of freak hands in a recent team game. My favorite occurred against the American Olympiad team, which was mopping us up for practice. I picked up:

♠ A K Q 10 9 7 5 3 2   ♡ —   ◊ A J 10 8   ♣ —

"I opened this delightful number with a bid of three hearts. I had in mind taking a save in four spades redoubled. To my surprise, everyone passed! I always knew Americans were reluctant to balance against any kind of preemptive action. It is no wonder they nearly always lose to the Italians. We gained several IMPs on this board as partners doubled seven spades and set it two tricks for +500. I went down only three for -300 as the opponents could not get a count on the trump suit. I never believe in being greedy at IMPs.

"Later in the same match, my partner and I happened upon an unusual use of the Unusual Notrump. With only the opponents vulnerable, the bidding proceeded as follows:

West	Partner	East	Bambino
		1♡	2NT
dbl	3NT	dbl	?

"I held:

♠ —   ♡ 9   ◇ K Q J 6 3 2   ♣ K Q 10 9 4 2

"It was obvious we didn't have much and I deduced my partner's bid of three notrump asked me to select my better minor. Obviously, my diamonds were better than my clubs, but as West could have the world, I elected to temporize with a bid of four hearts. 'Double' came in a loud voice from West, and then my partner produced the best bid of the event, a 'waiting' bid of four spades. This produced another double from opponents who were beginning to lose confidence in the auction, and I came up with my second unusual notrump of the auction: four notrump. I was hoping the opponents would think this was Blackwood.

"At this juncture, West requested a review of the auction, which we produced without a trace of laughter. He was uncertain what to do, but eventually he doubled. Partner redoubled, and I went into my Terence Reese-like analysis, ruling out this being ROP1. I noted, in passing, that if partner *did* have zero aces, the opponents probably had a grand slam. But wait! Partner had three times failed to pick a minor. Holding one minor-suit ace, wouldn't he have told me what to lead? He must have neither minor-suit ace, or *both* of them. If none, the ROP1 argument still applied, but if both, we make six of a minor and they make six of a major or go one down. To cater to the two-ace scenario, I decided to muddy the waters with a raise to five notrump. There was no risk that partner would construe this as that deadly Canadian invention, the grand slam force, as he could not hold two of the top three honors in either minor suit. Another double and partner remained stuck on redouble, so I decided to rescue to six clubs, doubled by West. Partner passed and East, in an annoyed tone, also passed. At this point, I found the master call of pass. Partner held:

♠ 7   ♡ 8 5   ♢ 9 8 7 5 4   ♣ 10 8 7 6 5

"I lost one heart, one diamond and one club for -300. Both major grand slams make, as I'm on lead against hearts. So does seven notrump, but we took away their valuable cuebidding room, and Blackwood as well. Our opponents, who held thousands of master points between them, folded up their cards and gazed at each other, not knowing quite what to say."

Throughout the Bambino's stories, I had watched a look of increasing admiration spread over the Shoe's face. One day, he and the Bambino would have to play a game. The partnership might turn out to be too much of a good thing, but whatever the outcome, I definitely wanted to be watching. Bob Haines said how nice it had been to meet the Victim and the Shoe, adding how much he had enjoyed their brilliant insights, and inviting them back for next week.

4

Kate's

It was not long after we first met at Hart House that the Shoe explained to me that I must visit Toronto's only other worthwhile bridge emporium, known formally as the **Kate Buckman Bridge Studio**, and informally as Kate's. Kate's was located on the third floor of 10 Eglinton Avenue East, at least until it burned down in the mid-1970s. This location put it diagonally across from the Eglinton subway station, an important feature for a student with neither a car nor a driver's licence. It was also around the corner from one of the three incarnations of Fran's, a Toronto institution that provided cheap food twenty-four hours a day. Equally essential were the daily afternoon duplicate bridge game, the $1.00 entry fee for students, and the absence of any restrictions on bidding conventions. This latter was likely because no one who played at Kate's had ever heard of any conventions beyond Stayman and Blackwood, as the big ethical debate of the day was whether you should be allowed to open a weak two-bid on any range except 6-12 high-card points. The Shoe, as it transpired, had more than a passing interest in that debate.

Kate Buckman herself was the proprietor, an older lady of unlimited patience and niceness. The Shoe always called her "Mrs. Buckman" and he always called the bridge club "Bucky's". He had been brainwashed that it was rude to call his elders by their first name, the name of the bridge club notwithstanding. Mrs. Buckman had brought with her from her previous bridge-club life, reputed to have been in Vancouver, a director who was a cross between an oppositional-defiant child and Attila the Hun. Loyalty forbade Mrs. Buckman from ever speaking a word of criticism about him. The only other permanent employee was Hanka, later a member of the Bucky's All Stars and winner of several sectional tournaments with that team. Hanka was a telephone marketer par excellence long before the job had been invented, and would work her lists ferociously to round up players for every game. Hanka also ruled over the money games — mostly bridge, but occasionally 'short cards', as games such as gin rummy were known. (The origin of this term is unclear — the Professor, David Silver, told me that the legendary Donny da Costa once told him that it referred to all games where your hand consisted of fewer than thirteen cards.) Last but not least, the kitchen was run by an entrepreneur with the improbable name of Cary Grant. There were rumors that in his spare time, he ran a diploma course on the subject of bankruptcy.

The Shoe assured me that there were people I would know at Bucky's, like the Hummingbird, the Bambino, the Albatross and the Victim. I would also meet the Owl, the Snowman and Colonel Bulldozer. Bulldozer had received his name from his wife's penchant for bidding Blackwood on the second round of the auction, coupled with the club's cult-like admiration for the bidding philosophy of the British bridge pioneer Colonel Buller: "If you have more, open higher." Both the Bambino and the Victim were paying their way through university playing in the money card game and the Shoe was hoping to join them as soon as the duplicate game was over.

According to the Shoe, the afternoon duplicate bridge featured a fantastic assortment of blue-haired ladies to prey upon. The Shoe preferred to play the afternoon games with the Hummingbird, whose imagination was almost unlimited. However, on the day I was being introduced around the afternoon duplicate game at Kate's, I was meeting women too old even for me to date, and I was watching Colonel Bulldozer sit down opposite the Shoe.

Bulldozer's good cheer knew no apparent bounds. He pointed out that on the first round, they would be matched up against the Owl, Kate's ranking "Player of the Month". He showed that he could match the Shoe for sheer volume of conversation, as he hurried to add that the Owl would have been Player of the Month in perpetuity, but he had interrupted his streak with a pilgrimage to Israel. Kate's had held a club championship in his honor on the eve of his departure, with the winner of the game to become the new "Owl". Of course, it was an impossible task, to become the new Owl. There was only one Owl: *the* Owl.

The Colonel continued his tale, saying that unfortunately for the Owl, his plane to Israel was delayed for a few days, so he had to explain to all the people who had feted his farewell why it was that he wasn't kibbutzing in Israel or coaching the Israeli national bridge team. The Colonel had been driving up to Kate's and saw the desolate Owl days later, still grounded in Toronto, dragging his heels up Avenue Road. Bulldozer slammed on the brakes, depositing a carload of bridge players on the windshield, threw open the door, leaped out into traffic, ran up to the Owl and, throwing his arms around him, cried out in his loudest voice, "Welcome to Israel!"

It is almost too cruel to recite what the Shoe did to the Owl that afternoon. The Shoe arrived at the table complaining that last night's party had been so strenuous he could hardly wake up. On the first hand, Bulldozer propelled the Shoe into six spades, never a good strategy unless the slam is 100%, as half the field will be in partscore, and the trump suit consisted of ♠AQ32 in dummy and ♠9864 in the Shoe's hand. There were no other losers. The Owl was sitting behind the dummy on Shoe's right. The Shoe won the opening lead in dummy and smoothly led a low spade toward the hand. The Owl flew with the king and, after the 3-2 trump break, the hand was over. The Shoe felt that it was his duty to inform the Owl and all others within earshot that he plays better in his sleep than the Owl does when he is wide awake.

The crime was compounded on the second hand. Apparently, the card gods are no nicer than the Shoe. Stayman and other gadgetry propelled the Owl to a pretty fair four spade contract. This was the deal:

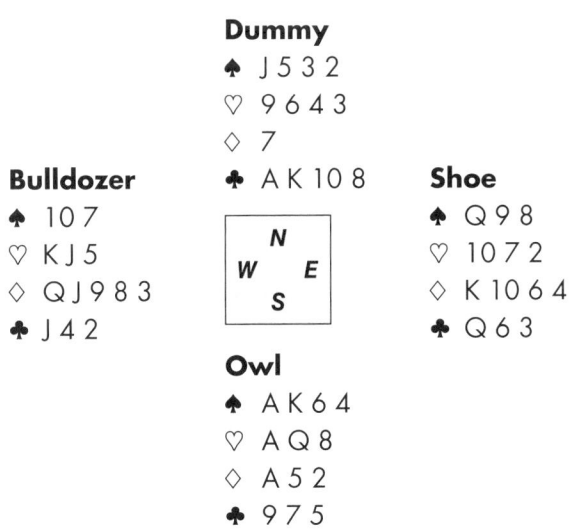

Dummy
♠ J 5 3 2
♡ 9 6 4 3
♢ 7
♣ A K 10 8

Bulldozer
♠ 10 7
♡ K J 5
♢ Q J 9 8 3
♣ J 4 2

Shoe
♠ Q 9 8
♡ 10 7 2
♢ K 10 6 4
♣ Q 6 3

Owl
♠ A K 6 4
♡ A Q 8
♢ A 5 2
♣ 9 7 5

The opening lead of the $\diamond$Q was won in the closed hand with the ace. After the Owl surveyed the prospects, he decided to lead the $\clubsuit$9 and float it, calling the eight from dummy. The Shoe ducked! The Owl could hardly believe his good fortune. He straightened up perceptibly and, squatting cross-legged on his chair, continued with one top trump, followed by another club. Bulldozer, who never looks as though he is paying close attention, rose with the jack, won by the Owl in dummy. The Owl returned to the hand with the other high trump and the queen did not appear. No problem, as he now took the marked finesse against the $\clubsuit$Q. Unfortunately for the Owl, the $\clubsuit$10 lost to the queen. The Shoe cashed the $\clubsuit$Q, leaving the Owl a ruff short in the dummy. He could take one red pitch, but the defense would get two heart tricks, or a heart and a diamond, down one. You didn't have to be Forquet to realize that almost all other roads lead to making four.

The Owl, of course, had to ask the Shoe how he found the duck. The Shoe, in a rare moment of honesty, admitted that it was the hangover that did it. He thought the Owl had called the ace from the dummy, not the eight. Then he added that he thought this would make an excellent bridge story, which he planned to call "The Owl Falls for a Duck".

A little later, the Shoe and the Colonel came upon the Snowman, in the days when this worthy was not yet directing at Kate's. After introducing me as Bungalow Bill Miller, inventor of the Winning Butterfly and chief kibitzer, the Shoe warned the Colonel comprehensively in the presence of both opponents that the Snowman was not to be trusted, as he was an exceptionally erratic bidder, plus he psyched a lot. The Shoe was dealer and held, at favorable vulnerability:

$\spadesuit$ K Q J 8 7 $\heartsuit$ 5 $\diamond$ 8 5 $\clubsuit$ Q 8 7 3 2

After the little diatribe about the Snowman, Shoe opened three hearts! Snowman doubled and Bulldozer raised to four with $\heartsuit$AQ102 and nothing else. Snowman's partner doubled and the Shoe removed to four spades, which got doubled, two down for three hundred. The field was in four hearts doubled the other way, somehow making.

The Snowman, who may be the only player with a disposition sunny enough to rival that of the Colonel, was filled with awe and admiration for the Shoe's auction. After the second hand, he furnished a bidding problem of his own. You hold:

$$\spadesuit A K Q J 10 8 7 5 4 2 \quad \heartsuit 10 2 \quad \diamondsuit - \quad \clubsuit 6$$

He asked all of us what we would open, and because we were early in the round, there was a rousing discussion that favored the simple four spade bid, but also gave kudos to the possibilities of one spade, three spades, five spades, Blackwood, a strong forcing two clubs, and pass. After the discussion finally died down, Snowman continued, "Okay, here's the real problem on the hand. Suppose you open one club, and the bidding proceeds three spades, pass, pass to you?" This hand remains famous to this day as "The Snowman Bidding Problem".

The game gradually petered out and it became obvious that Bulldozer and the Shoe were not going to get 100% of the matchpoints, nor were they going to lose. I missed the final hand answering the call of nature, and when I got back, everyone was sitting around waiting for the scores to be posted. The Shoe was bragging about the very hand I had missed. The Snowman had inserted himself into the group, undoubtedly seeking to find methods of perfecting his alleged erratic bidding. What better place than listening to the Shoe?

As he usually does on a daily basis, the Shoe announced that he had a story that couldn't be topped. The dealer, on Shoe's left, was a nice, white-haired old lady who opened with a complaint about how she never got any matchpoints off the Shoe, then passed. Two more passes came around to the Shoe who held, in fourth chair, vulnerable:

$$\spadesuit A J 9 6 5 \quad \heartsuit A \quad \diamondsuit A 9 7 3 \quad \clubsuit A 8 7$$

The Shoe opened one spade and was surprised, in an uncontested auction, to hear the Colonel raise to four. Continuing in the bulldozing spirit, the Shoe raised himself to the small slam. He then disclosed LHO's hand:

$$\spadesuit K 4 \quad \heartsuit K 6 3 \quad \diamondsuit K 8 4 2 \quad \clubsuit K 5 4 3$$

The Shoe cited this hand as proof positive that you have to open a bad 12-count. The audience debated this, arguing that an opening bid will force the Shoe to make the hand by disdaining the black-suit finesses, setting up the hearts with two ruffs while stripping the diamonds and then exiting in spades for the endplay in clubs. The Shoe changed the subject by asking everyone the proper lead from LHO's cards. There was no consensus, so Shoe disclosed the whole deal:

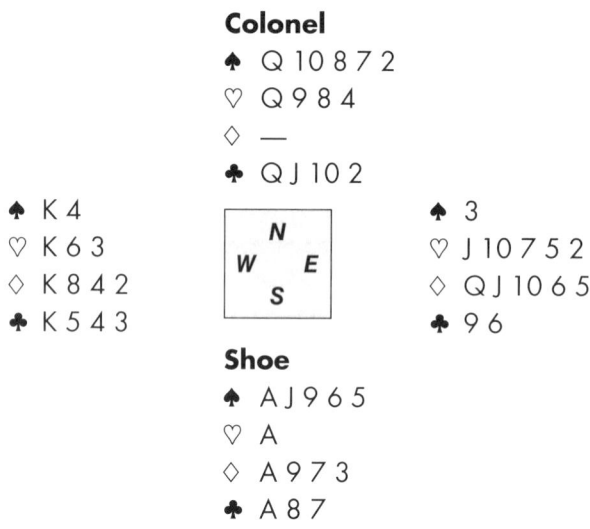

Colonel
♠ Q 10 8 7 2
♡ Q 9 8 4
◇ —
♣ Q J 10 2

♠ K 4
♡ K 6 3
◇ K 8 4 2
♣ K 5 4 3

♠ 3
♡ J 10 7 5 2
◇ Q J 10 6 5
♣ 9 6

Shoe
♠ A J 9 6 5
♡ A
◇ A 9 7 3
♣ A 8 7

It is obvious that after a club lead, the ♡Q can be established to pitch the other club. All the brilliant young players who opted for a trump from K4 had given away the contract without any struggle at all. On a red-suit lead, which was what happened at the table, declarer must read the position and endplay LHO, instead of taking the black finesses. The Shoe found the winning line of play because RHO did not cover the lead of the ♠Q from dummy. Never in her 100 years of bridge experience had RHO failed to cover an honor with an honor. So the Shoe dared them all to top that: all four kings behind the aces, and the slam is unbeatable.

The Snowman volunteered to top it and what's more, he intended to top it on that very hand. The Shoe bet him a beer he couldn't. The Snowman took the bet. At his table, the Snowman had reluctantly passed the hand with the four kings and then heard the Hummingbird raise himself to slam on the identical auction that had occurred at the Shoe's table. Now the Snowman was on lead with the nightmare hand. He took a while to sort through the unpalatable options and eventually decided that there was no good choice. Furthermore, the Hummingbird, always devilishly clever, would undoubtedly work out all the inferences from the hesitations. "Accordingly," announced the Snowman, "I was forced to invent the inference-destroying lead."

The Snowman had led the ◊K! The Bird won that in the closed hand, discarding a club from dummy. Cash the ♡A, ruff a diamond, ruff a heart, ruff a second diamond, ruff a second heart. Hmm, the king dropped from the Snowman. As expected, the Hummingbird duly took stock of the inferences: the Snowman had shown the ♡K and ◊KQ, maybe even the jack, so it was a cinch that for the original pass he couldn't have both black kings as well. The Bird had been presented with his choice of suicides, deciding which black finesse to take first.

Congratulations all around were offered to the Snowman, and we adjourned to Fran's for dinner, where the Shoe ordered the all-day breakfast and two beers, one of them for the Snowman.

Watching the Shoe in action at Kate's in the afternoon becomes a habit. One day early on, I am to watch him in action with the Hummingbird. Even though it should be the anticipated afternoon duplicate massacre, this game matters both to the Hummingbird and to the Shoe. Both are trying to win their entry fee to the 1967 Summer Nationals in Montreal, the prize for collecting the most masterpoints for the year at Kate's. The Bird is leading the Under-100 masterpoints division and the Shoe is second in the Open section.

Most players are in the other room taking in one of Kate Buckman's famous bridge lectures, but a few have stayed outside to get first crack at the free coffee. There is a new little old lady also sitting out the lecture. She is a tiny, mischievous-looking person who looks sixty-something years old. She might well be a cartoon out of Little Orphan Annie. There is someone with her, and she is holding forth on the virtues of Precision while the Shoe, the Bird and I sit there, fascinated.

The director, today the Snowman, walks in, turns to her and asks, "How ya doing, you old bat?" and she jumps up, threatening him with her fist and chasing him around the room, laughing "You devil, you." The Shoe is in love, and at the first legal opportunity inquires who the wonderful little old lady is. We are informed that she is Mrs. Anita A. Whaley, of the partnership of Whaley and Bailey, and that she is over 80 years old.

That first time he actually played against Mrs. Whaley, the Shoe was obviously trying to show off when he picked up:

$$\spadesuit A Q 109853 \quad \heartsuit A K 1092 \quad \diamondsuit 4 \quad \clubsuit —$$

How to impress a little old lady when you've never been introduced? The Shoe opened a weak two spades, 6-12 HCP. When the Bird bid two notrump (forcing), the Shoe found himself stuck for a rebid. Finally he settled on six hearts. The auction died there and a suspicious Mrs. Whaley led a spade. How could anyone have a weak two-bid in spades when they had enough hearts to bid a slam?

The Hummingbird tabled:

$$\spadesuit K J \quad \heartsuit Q J 76 \quad \diamondsuit A 1052 \quad \clubsuit A 76$$

Mrs. Whaley's partner trumped the opening spade lead, so there they were, making six hearts exactly with 14 top tricks in notrump and seven spades also laydown.

Oddly enough, no one in the whole field negotiated a slam on these cards, so it was a top board anyway. The beauty of matchpoints! That, of course, led to post-mortem questions about how they reached the slam and inevitably it became known that the Shoe had opened a weak two-bid on 13 HCP. In those days, the ACBL had strict rules against that, and Shoe was severely warned *never* again to open a weak two-bid except on 6-12 HCP. Naturally, two spades became the Shoe's opening of choice against Mrs. Whaley, whatever he held.

Another encounter with Mrs. Whaley was in the "B" League IMP teams at Bucky's. I was in attendance, watching the Shoe forcing Colonel Bulldozer to experiment with the Neapolitan Shaft. Mrs. Whaley was playing with a partner who might have been her mother. Early in the match, the older lady, holding a weak hand with short clubs, opened two clubs strong and forcing, then passed Mrs. Whaley's response. That action talked the Shoe out of a makeable game. Shoe could not resist asking how the lady had thought of the two club opening, and received the quick, cryptic reply: "I had to find out who had the clubs." For once, the Shoe was speechless.

It wasn't exactly revenge Shoe was looking for when he next picked up:

♠ K Q 10 9 8 4   ♡ 10 8   ◊ J 7 5 4 3   ♣

If you've remembered the system, you will know that in Neapolitan Shaft this was a two club opening, a weak two-suiter in either clubs and hearts or diamonds and spades. Mrs. Whaley overcalled two hearts, Bulldozer passed and Mrs. Whaley's mother raised uncomfortably to three hearts. Shoe took a rare, uncharacteristic huddle. Colonel Bulldozer would know by now that he held the spade-diamond hand. How to indicate the desire to play *and* the right defense? Shoe finally emerged with a pretty decent bid of four clubs. Mrs. Whaley carried on to four hearts. The Colonel doubled and led the ace of clubs. How sweet was that? This was the entire deal:

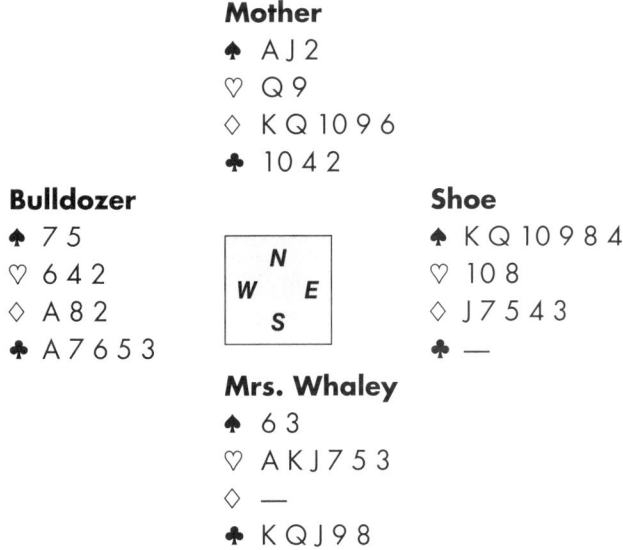

Mother
♠ A J 2
♡ Q 9
◊ K Q 10 9 6
♣ 10 4 2

Bulldozer
♠ 7 5
♡ 6 4 2
◊ A 8 2
♣ A 7 6 5 3

Shoe
♠ K Q 10 9 8 4
♡ 10 8
◊ J 7 5 4 3
♣ —

Mrs. Whaley
♠ 6 3
♡ A K J 7 5 3
◊ —
♣ K Q J 9 8

It did not turn out all that sweet, actually, unless you give style points for the beauty of the auction. After the club ruff, there was no way back to the ◊A, so Mrs. Whaley made exactly four. Mrs. Whaley's mother must have been related to the Shoe, too. Not only had she found the opening two club bid on the first hand, she now berated Mrs. Whaley for her failure to double four clubs. That contract, she observed acidly, was almost certainly going down more than the value of the game. Shoe reacted admirably, joining Mrs. Whaley's mother with an enthusiastic cry of "Yes, and how else was she to find out who had the clubs?" Then, he flashed a big wink at Mrs. Whaley, who announced, "Young man, you're crazy, but I like you." The system had died, but a remarkable friendship was born.

Eventually, it turns out to be the Shoe and the Bambino who love playing against Mrs. Whaley the most. On a day I remember particularly, Mrs. Whaley has her arm in a sling because her arthritis is bothering her. She is dealer, which is already a setback because it reduces the Shoe's odds of getting to open a weak two spades. Mrs. Whaley is sorting her hand, one card at a time, into a rack made for just such an arthritic moment. Her partner is the Wrinkle Lady from *There's Something about Mary*.

The sorting is obviously giving Mrs. Whaley a problem and is taking rather a long time. Mrs. Whaley eventually apologizes for taking so long, that her arthritis is bothering her today. The Bambino tells her not to worry, and playfully offers that Mrs. Whaley could open one heart, her partner could respond one spade and, by the time the auction came back around to her, she would know what to do. Mrs. Whaley lavishes an indulgent smile on the Bambino, and continues painstakingly to sort the hand. When she finally completes the task, her impish smile blossoms into a huge grin as she advises one and all, "As a matter of fact, I think I will open one heart." This goes pass, pass around to the Shoe, who has an awkward balancing problem holding, both vulnerable:

♠ Q 5   ♡ Q 6 3   ◇ A K J 10 8 7 5   ♣ Q

The Shoe takes an unusually long time, obviously lacking really solid excuses if balancing three notrump goes down in top tricks. Mrs. Whaley turns to him and asks archly: "Now I suppose *you're* going to bid one spade?" Shoe appears surprised he didn't think of it sooner. "One spade," he intones, without further delay. Bambino responds one notrump and the Shoe leaves him there on the theory that everyone will be in diamonds and if notrump makes three or more, it's a top board in any event. With seven running diamond tricks and a heart lead, the Bambino scrambles ten tricks for a very good result.

On the companion deal, it is no doubt the presence of Mrs. Whaley that prompts the Shoe to respond Blackwood to the Bambino's one diamond opening bid, holding:

♠ K   ♡ A K 3   ◇ Q J 10 9 6 2   ♣ A K 4

Naturally, there is a missing ace and now the Shoe has to guess whether his 20 HCP belong in six diamonds or six notrump. It's not a guess, actually, as the Shoe will be on play in six notrump: remember the Shoe's Second Rule of Bridge. Six notrump becomes the contract. Mrs. Whaley leads the queen of spades as dummy comes down with two small spades and the rest of the high-card points. The Wrinkle Lady wins the ace and the Shoe hesitates, obviously considering the play of a small club, but finally decides it would be dishonest to revoke on purpose, as well as not nice. He drops the ♠K.

The W. L. stares at him for a while, then announces: "Oh, you boys, you're always fooling around." Whereupon, the W. L. shifts to the two of hearts! Really. I swear. I saw it with my own eyes.

The Bambino had been present at the discussion of the weak two-bid debacle, and declared that whenever possible, hands must be opened two spades. The Shoe treated the Bambino's wish as his command, perhaps a little too much. Playing vulnerable with the Bambino against the non-vulnerable Mrs. Whaley, he picked up in first chair:

♠ 5 4   ♡ 7 4   ◇ Q J 4 3 2   ♣ Q J 7 2

He added up his points, arrived at 6 HCP, and opened the bidding two spades as mandated. Mrs. Whaley obliged with four hearts and when this came around to the Shoe after two passes, he should have known better, but needing to impress Mrs. Whaley, he carried on to four spades. Mrs. Whaley agonized over four spades but ultimately passed. Her partner produced an overly firm double and everyone had to pass. With a four-spade opening bid on his right, four spades doubled went down eight, -2300. The Bambino offered not one word of criticism, not even a raised eyebrow, when the Shoe felt compelled to observe that he must be the first person in history to take the vulnerable four-spade save against the non-vulnerable four spade game.

Other similar insanity followed, always with the Bambino as partner-in-crime. One of the greatest fixes of all time came from this weak two-spade bid from the Shoe as dealer, both vulnerable, Mrs. Whaley on his left:

♠ Q 9 5   ♡ Q 10 6   ◇ Q 9 2   ♣ Q 6 3 2

Mrs. Whaley surprisingly passed, as did the Bambino, and Mrs. Whaley's partner reopened with a double. The Shoe had nowhere to go and passed, and now Mrs. Whaley had to choose a bid:

♠ 7 4 3 2   ♡ A 7 3   ◇ A 7 5   ♣ 9 8 5

Pass was by no means obvious and after some deliberation she chose to bid three diamonds, hitting her partner's only four-card suit. The entire deal was:

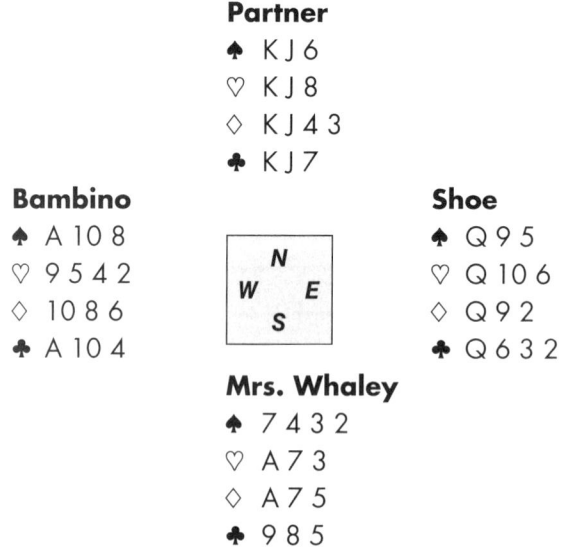

Partner
♠ K J 6
♡ K J 8
◇ K J 4 3
♣ K J 7

Bambino
♠ A 10 8
♡ 9 5 4 2
◇ 10 8 6
♣ A 10 4

Shoe
♠ Q 9 5
♡ Q 10 6
◇ Q 9 2
♣ Q 6 3 2

Mrs. Whaley
♠ 7 4 3 2
♡ A 7 3
◇ A 7 5
♣ 9 8 5

The Shoe was destined to score all four queens for a 200-point set. No one claims that things are always fair.

Sometimes things became fair in the other direction. The Shoe had once taken me aside and conspiratorially whispered: "Bungalow, Mrs. Whaley knows about taking saves." And indeed, she did, especially not vulnerable against vulnerable and even more especially in spades. Whenever their side had overcalled and raised spades, it became almost impossible to buy the contract. Maybe that was the best reason to open two spades: it took away the four spade save.

This observation led the Shoe to a sound general proposition at matchpoints, to the effect that when partner had raised your vulnerable opening bid and opponents, not vulnerable, had overcalled and also raised, you should always jump to game, especially if you didn't expect to make it. "Opponents cannot afford not to sacrifice," he opined "so you only need to get more than the value of your partscore."

As you might expect, the Shoe carried this philosophy to a bit of an extreme against Mrs. Whaley. It was the last round of a duplicate game at Bucky's, and Mrs. Whaley was playing with another of her favorite partners, Mr. Bailey. Mrs. Whaley was on the Shoe's right, for a change, with Mr. Bailey on the left. After two passes, the Shoe opened one vulnerable heart holding:

♠ 5 4   ♡ A Q 7 5 4   ◇ A K 9 4   ♣ A 3

Mr. Bailey overcalled one non-vulnerable spade and the Bambino raised to four hearts. Mrs. Whaley chimed in with four spades and the Shoe considered the prospects. It looked as though five hearts would make but five spades might not go down enough. The Shoe opted for a jump to six hearts. Maybe partner had the short spades. When this bid came around to Mrs. Whaley, she eyed the Shoe suspiciously but finally went for the bait and bid six spades. The Shoe doubled, perhaps a little smugly. He was not quite as pleased when the Bambino led a heart and the entire deal was:

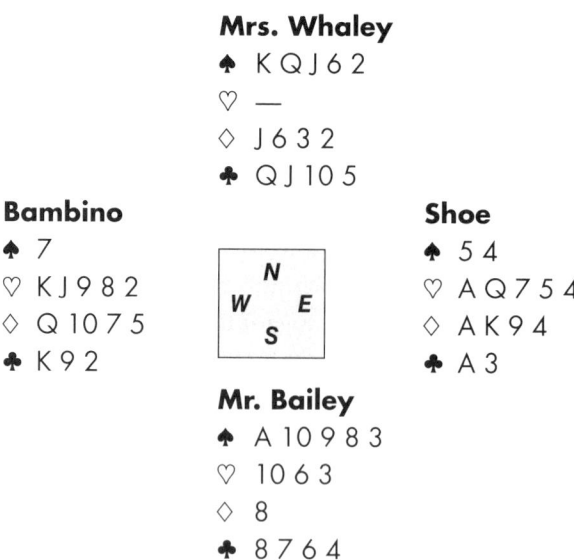

Mrs. Whaley
♠ K Q J 6 2
♡ —
◇ J 6 3 2
♣ Q J 10 5

Bambino
♠ 7
♡ K J 9 8 2
◇ Q 10 7 5
♣ K 9 2

Shoe
♠ 5 4
♡ A Q 7 5 4
◇ A K 9 4
♣ A 3

Mr. Bailey
♠ A 10 9 8 3
♡ 10 6 3
◇ 8
♣ 8 7 6 4

After dummy ruffed the opening heart lead, it was a simple matter to draw trumps and claim down two for -300. Even had they scored a club ruff, Bambino and Shoe could only get +500. What was worse, the vulnerable six hearts was going to make. When the Shoe looked at the score slip, every other pair in their direction had scored +680 in either four or five hearts.

By the time the Shoe finally got to play *with* Mrs. Whaley, she was 85 years old and playing Precision. Naturally, the hands they got suited the system. All night long, Mrs. Whaley was dealt one spade opening bids and the Shoe always had short spades with 11 or 12 high-card points; perfect for a forcing notrump response. Mrs. Whaley always rebid two spades and the Shoe rebid two notrump, always raised to three by Mrs. Whaley.

The opening lead would give the Shoe a trick and dummy would hit with 12 HCP and five spades. Shoe always made three notrump.

Finally, the Shoe had to ask Mrs. Whaley why she was raising to game on these cards. Mrs. Whaley explained patiently, much in the way that you would explain to a young child, that she had *extras*. Precision was a system where you could open on as few as 11 HCP, and she had twelve. She also had the fifth spade.

Not even the Shoe would argue with that logic: who could? And who could argue with winning by two full boards?

5

Three Minutes to Winning Bridge

Although the area is locally known simply as the Island, there are in fact four islands that make up the outer barrier that creates and protects Toronto's harbor. While three of these islands are operated solely as parks and recreation areas by the city, Algonquin Island actually includes homes, accessible for the inhabitants via a ferry service from the mainland. The residents own their houses, but lease the land they stand on from the city on a long-term basis. The City of Toronto has at various times attempted to remedy this situation, but the courts have always upheld the rights of the people who live in these homes. The Island is also host to various sailing clubs and marinas, including the prestigious Royal Canadian Yacht Club.

The Shoe's family lived on the Island, so the Shoe regularly induced the Albatross or the Hummingbird to play in local duplicate bridge games at the Algonquin Island Clubhouse. The best of these occasions were the "Smokers", held on Friday evening and offering the opportunity to play for a cash jackpot in a smoke-filled room full of inebriates, with shuffleboard, poker, euchre, darts and beer-fuelled debates going on all around you.

The Shoe never tires of telling the story of his most memorable Toronto Island outing. It was a Smoker with a 3½ table Howell that the Shoe had entered with the Hummingbird. They were heavily favored to win the money, a lofty $14 jackpot, good money in those days for an impoverished student. Unfortunately, with three rounds to go, they were dead average. With all the noise and with the intricacies of a 3½ table game, the game was running very late. Often, it took extra time to find people and get them to come back from the bar after their byes. Finally, the Bird had to leave to catch the last ferry back to Toronto. The third-last round was their turn to sit out, so the Shoe had twenty minutes to recruit a substitute for the final six hands. I have heard this story so often I can almost repeat it word for word:

"I scour all the other entertainments, but there is not a bridge player to be had. It takes a beer to pry Flashy away from the darts game. Flashy has at least played euchre at some point in his life, so he knows about taking tricks and about trumps. I have fifteen minutes to teach him how to play bridge. Alcohol always helps in this situation. I decide against a fifteen-minute lesson and opt instead to give the three-minute lesson and to repeat it five times. I really should copyright this, because it has never failed yet:

1. You take tricks just like in euchre, only there are no bowers;
2. Before you take tricks, you bid. To know what to bid, you add up your points: ace = 4, king = 3, queen = 2 and jack = 1;
3. The bidding starts with the dealer and proceeds clockwise. If you are bidding before your partner, or after your partner has passed, bid as follows:
    *   Less than 13 points = pass
    *   13+ points = bid one of your best suits and *never* bid again, *unless* you have:
    *   19+ points = bid again with next best suit.
4. If one of the opponents starts the bidding, just pass.
5. If partner starts the bidding, with 6 points bid your best suit and never bid again, *unless* you have 12 points, when you will bid your best suit and bid again.
6. Only lead when you personally won the last trick, or someone tells you to lead.
7. Always lead the first suit bid by partner; if partner has not bid a suit, lead fourth-best of your longest and strongest.

"The round is called and Flashy and I assume our seats. The first hand goes one spade on my right. I have a balanced nothing and I appear to be on lead, so I pass. This is a mistake, as dummy passes and Flashy is barred (see Rule 4: the opponents bid first). We defend weirdly but okay and hold it to two. On the two top, this is dead average as both other pairs played four spades: one made it and one went one down. We get a moral top, as we were the only pair that held it to eight tricks. This hand teaches me that I have to overcall more, especially as Rule 5 (respond in best suit) practically forbids a raise.

"On the second hand, my LHO opens one notrump. Flashy looks puzzled because I haven't told him about notrump. If he realizes that one notrump is a bid, then he's barred again! I'm beginning to dislike Rule 4. My hand is:

♠ J 4 2   ♡ 10   ◇ J 6 5 4 3   ♣ A Q 10 4

"Flashy and my RHO both pass, so I balance two diamonds. The notrump bidder continues with a smooth two hearts. Flash must pass (Rule 4), as does RHO, who is probably playing Rule 4 as well. It would probably have been better to balance two clubs because Rule 7 (lead the first suit bid by partner) is going to get Flashy off to a diamond lead. Hating my earlier bid, I rebalance three diamonds(!). The notrump bidder carries on smoothly to three hearts and everyone passes just as though nothing unusual had happened.

"Flashy has forgotten Rule 7 and leads the king of spades, which appears to signal an attempt to win a trick with his highest card. This is the whole deal:

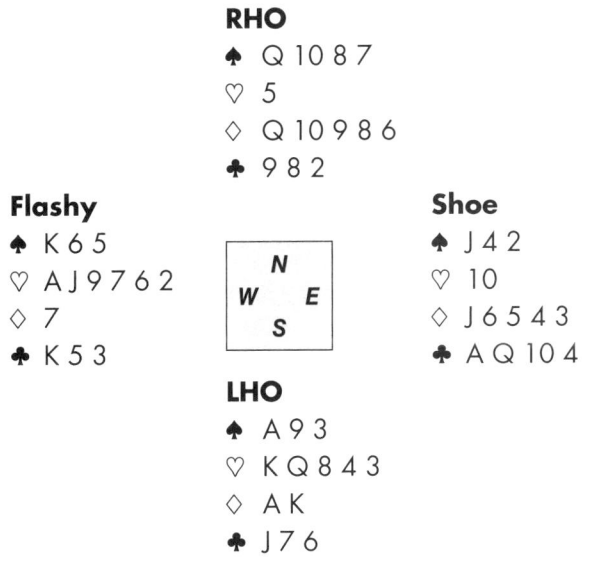

RHO
♠ Q 10 8 7
♡ 5
◇ Q 10 9 8 6
♣ 9 8 2

Flashy
♠ K 6 5
♡ A J 9 7 6 2
◇ 7
♣ K 5 3

Shoe
♠ J 4 2
♡ 10
◇ J 6 5 4 3
♣ A Q 10 4

LHO
♠ A 9 3
♡ K Q 8 4 3
◇ A K
♣ J 7 6

Flashy	RHO	Shoe	LHO
			1NT
pass	pass	2◇	2♡
pass	pass	3◇	3♡
all pass			

"It is obvious when dummy comes down that this is not the opponents' best spot. Dummy is berating declarer for opening notrump and then not once, but twice, failing to pass diamonds around to him so that he could make a double that could be heard all the way across Toronto harbor. I explain to Flashy about penalty doubles and how, even if they bid first, you can double if you have six cards in their suit. Flashy looks at the backs of his cards as though they are transparent. Later in the hand, we have to explain to Flash that the last suit bid becomes trumps, so that when he discarded a small heart on the king of diamonds, he actually won the trick. Three hearts is down four for -400 and since no one bid and made a game our way, that's both of the matchpoints.

"The third hand is a no-brainer for none of the obvious reasons. Flashy opens one diamond, his 'best' suit with 13 or more high-card points (Rule 3). I hold:

♠ A Q   ♡ 10 8 7 4   ◇ 3   ♣ K Q J 9 6 2

This is easy, because Flashy will not bid again unless he has 19 points (Rule 3). Sensitive exploratory auctions are out. We might miss a 4-4 heart fit, but I'm forced to bid the 'automatic' three notrump. No risk of missing a slam, because with 19 or more high-card points, he'll show his second best suit and we can reach six clubs, or maybe six notrump. Flashy passes. The opening lead is a spade, and he has:

♠ K 9 2   ♡ A 9 6 5 3   ◇ A K   ♣ 10 5 4

"It turns out we missed a 5-4 heart suit, so the definition of 'best' suit is going to need a little more work. There are eleven obvious tricks in notrump on any lead. The 3-1 heart split is overkill, as we get both matchpoints comparing to the +420 made by both other declarers in four hearts.

"We finish early and have time to work on a couple of beers each while we clarify the ranks of the suits. Then we move for the final round. The spot cards are kind of blurry and difficult to remember after all this time, but I hold something like:

♠ A 9 4 3 2   ♡ 8 3 2   ◇ A Q   ♣ Q 10 6

"I open one spade despite the tactical advantage of opening one club to let partner show his best suit (Rule 5) at the one-level. LHO doubles, Flashy passes (less than 6 HCP *guaranteed*, see Rule 5, he hasn't learned about doubles yet) and RHO takes a very long time to bid two notrump. LHO continues to three clubs and RHO bids an excessively firm three notrump, folds up his cards, puts them on the table and stares at his partner until he passes.

"I infer from the bidding that RHO has three or more spade stoppers and lead the unheard-of passive ♡2. The effect is magic, and it's not just the beer:

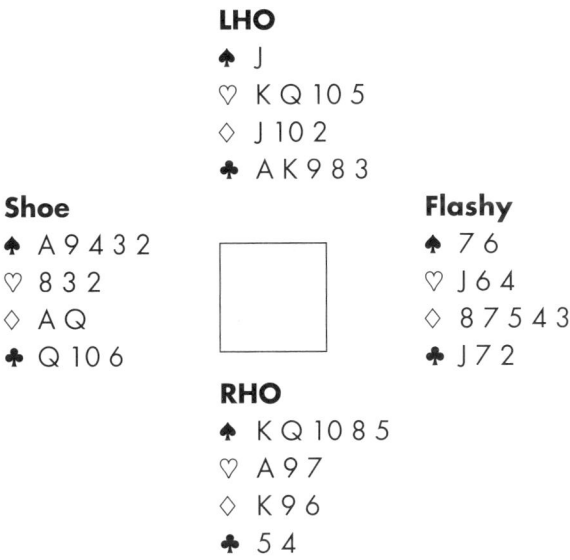

LHO
♠ J
♡ K Q 10 5
◇ J 10 2
♣ A K 9 8 3

Shoe
♠ A 9 4 3 2
♡ 8 3 2
◇ A Q
♣ Q 10 6

Flashy
♠ 7 6
♡ J 6 4
◇ 8 7 5 4 3
♣ J 7 2

RHO
♠ K Q 10 8 5
♡ A 9 7
◇ K 9 6
♣ 5 4

"Of course, RHO cannot resist the 'free' finesse against the jack of hearts. He only begins to wonder about hand entries when Flashy produces the jack. After a low spade to the jack holds, declarer plays on diamonds and the final result is three notrump, just in. Even the other guys at the Smoker can take ten tricks on this hand, so we score another perfect 'two'.

"On the second last hand, my LHO opens one heart. This bars Flashy from the auction (Rule 4). I suspect he probably has a few high cards, as I hold:

♠ 5 3 2   ♡ 9 6 4 3   ◇ 8 6 4 2   ♣ 9 3

The opponents hold a boring uncontested auction: 1♡ - 2♣ - 2♡ - 3♡ - 4♡. With Flashy on lead and holding all the cards on defense, I'm pretty sure our run of tops is over. I run for another couple of beers for Flashy and me. When I return, Flashy has led the four of clubs, and this is the whole deal:

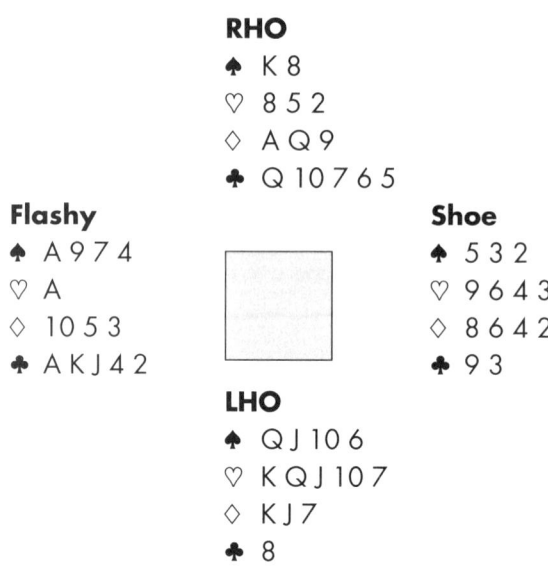

RHO
♠ K 8
♡ 8 5 2
♢ A Q 9
♣ Q 10 7 6 5

Flashy
♠ A 9 7 4
♡ A
♢ 10 5 3
♣ A K J 4 2

Shoe
♠ 5 3 2
♡ 9 6 4 3
♢ 8 6 4 2
♣ 9 3

LHO
♠ Q J 10 6
♡ K Q J 10 7
♢ K J 7
♣ 8

This is clearly Flashy's fourth highest card from his longest and strongest suit (Rule 7). All the best books tell us to consult our Rule of Eleven and declarer concludes that I have only one card higher than the four and further, that this must be the ace. I try to warn declarer that Flashy will lead fourth highest from *any* holding, so that if he led the *ten*, it would show exactly 100 honors. Declarer's ingrained assumptions triumph and he plays low. My hopes are fulfilled when I rise with the nine and find declarer with the eight. A club return taps declarer and he goes down one. Not surprisingly, the other defenders with Flashy's cards were unable to escape the endplay on themselves, and therefore were unable to tap declarer after winning the first trick with a high club.

"Our run of top boards was surviving to the last hand, but Flashy was not faring as well. The beer was taking over. Luckily, I was dealer and could hog the hand in notrump:

♠ 8 7 3   ♡ K 9 5   ♢ A K 5 2   ♣ A Q 10

Flashy had other problems. He had 7 points and was compelled to bid, holding:

♠ K 6 4 2   ♡ A 8 6 3   ◇ 8 6   ♣ 9 7 5

Apparently, someone had mentioned Stayman to him during the beer break, something where he bids two clubs and partner must choose a major. That sounded great on this hand, so he bid two clubs. When I responded two diamonds, Flashy was mystified. Wasn't I supposed to show a major? Flashy rebid three clubs, which ended the auction on this deal:

Shoe
♠ 8 7 3
♡ K 9 5
◇ A K 5 2
♣ A Q 10

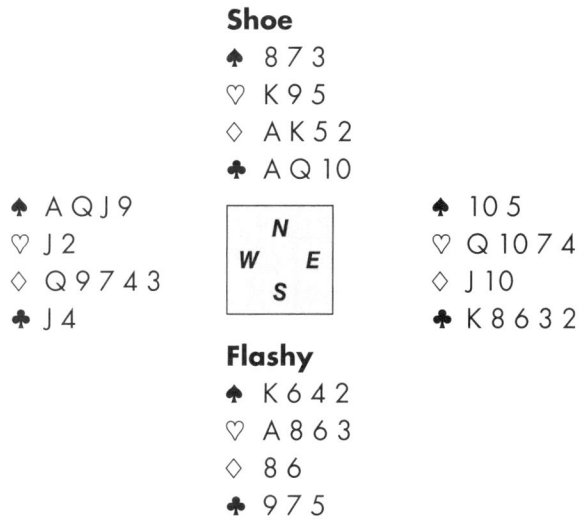

♠ A Q J 9
♡ J 2
◇ Q 9 7 4 3
♣ J 4

♠ 10 5
♡ Q 10 7 4
◇ J 10
♣ K 8 6 3 2

Flashy
♠ K 6 4 2
♡ A 8 6 3
◇ 8 6
♣ 9 7 5

"The opening lead was a small diamond. Flashy won dummy's king of diamonds and cashed the ace, then ruffed a small diamond as East discarded a spade. The ace and king of hearts were cashed and dummy's last diamond was ruffed as East discarded a second spade. A heart was led, ruffed by West, who next led the ace of spades as East showed out. A spade ruff was the third trick for the defense. East was trump tight and led back a small club to the nine, jack and queen. Unfortunately for East, he had to ruff the next round of spades and was then endplayed to lead into the ace-ten of clubs. Plus 110 is another top, as we apparently go one down in one notrump."

It's pretty clear to me that Flashy had indeed learned to play bridge in three minutes, though it was not entirely down to Shoe's rules. Flashy had considerable talent of his own. The boys end up taking 11 of 12 matchpoints on the six boards they play, enough to win the jackpot, which pays for the beer. Any scenario that pays for the beer is a good scenario, as far as the Shoe is concerned. At this point, he always turns to me and adds: "Flashy never played bridge again. His lifetime matchpoint percentage, 91.7%, has got to be the highest ever recorded. Let's drink to that."

6

A License to Steal

If there's anything I've learned from my years of watching the Shoe, it's that the problem of when to bid notrump has a short answer and a long answer. The short answer is "As often as possible." The long answer is a bit boring, from the Shoe's point of view, since it's not entirely frivolous. I shall recount the long answer as I saw it and heard it, just in case bridge ever becomes a university degree course.

The Shoe had been mightily impressed that night at the Metro Club when the Bambino told his story about the unusual use of the Unusual Notrump. Really, including notrump, there were five suits, and underusing notrump was like loading your six-shooter with only five bullets. Well, actually, it would have to be a five-shooter with four bullets, but who's counting? Plus, notrump scored more, plus they thought you had stuff to bid notrump, so they let you take saves in notrump undoubled, plus, no one could cuebid notrump, plus, no one could evaluate their short suit. The Shoe warmed up to the topic even more as he kibitzed the Victim playing rubber bridge. The Victim was vulnerable with a 30 partscore and picked up:

♠ 6 5   ♡ 9 8   ◇ A K Q J 9 8 7   ♣ 5 4

His RHO opened one club and the Victim overcalled one notrump. As he explained later, four diamonds seemed like a remote possibility, and where was the downside? The auction developed:

LHO	Partner	RHO	Victim
		1♣	1NT
2♠	2NT	all pass	

The whole deal was:

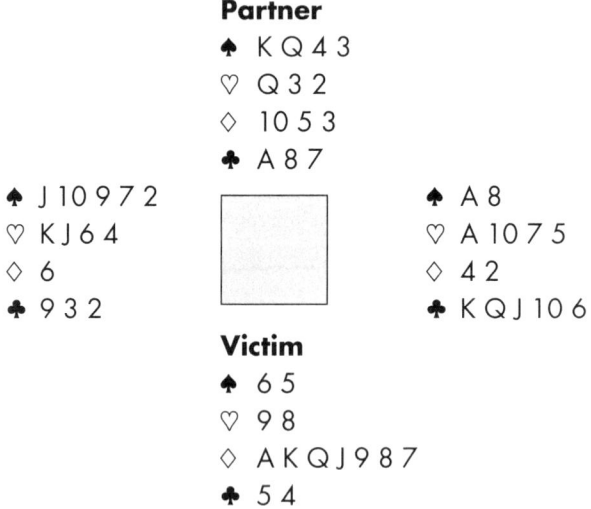

Partner
♠ K Q 4 3
♡ Q 3 2
◇ 10 5 3
♣ A 8 7

♠ J 10 9 7 2
♡ K J 6 4
◇ 6
♣ 9 3 2

♠ A 8
♡ A 10 7 5
◇ 4 2
♣ K Q J 10 6

Victim
♠ 6 5
♡ 9 8
◇ A K Q J 9 8 7
♣ 5 4

The only surprise was that RHO hadn't doubled, holding six sure tricks on a club lead. Two notrump was airtight and it was inescapable that four diamonds would go one down.

Early in his duplicate bridge career, the Shoe was playing the forcing diamond system with the Albatross, who opened one heart, showing a five-card major and at most 16 high-card points. RHO doubled. The Shoe took time to consider the options holding:

♠ 10 4   ♡ K 9 6 3 2   ◇ 8 7 6 5   ♣ 8 3

Bids of three or four hearts would certainly propel the opponents into their spade game, or worse, goad the Albatross into saving in five hearts, where four down looked like a real possibility. One spade was possible, but that psyche was showing up in every bridge book that had ever been written and in the absence of screens, which had not yet been invented, would permit his LHO the kind of resounding penalty double that would clear up all possible later misunderstandings about the spade suit. Besides, he was pretty sure he'd psyched a spade response against these opponents already.

The Shoe had not actually forgotten the list of the advantages of notrump, but two notrump was a limit raise in hearts and one notrump wasn't going to stop anyone. The Shoe decided to take a leaf out of the Bambino's book ("I didn't know what to do, so I passed"). Maybe they wouldn't force to game. No such luck, as LHO responded one spade and RHO cuebid two hearts.

The Shoe silently berated himself. How could it ever be right to choose pass over a bid, any bid? Was there a way to recover? Maybe a cuebid of two spades? At last, the Shoe hit on the bid of two notrump. This bid offered the possibility of a bidding misunderstanding by the opponents, such as a forcing three spades by LHO passed by RHO. It offered the additional bonus that declarer might finesse him for the Albatross' doubleton queen of spades.

LHO misinterpreted the Shoe's brief hesitation and, sensing that something was amiss, issued a firm double. The Albatross came to the rescue with a bid of three diamonds, doubled by RHO. The Shoe considered passing this bid, but was deterred by the possibility that the Albatross had thought two notrump was asking him to choose a minor (on which point the Albatross was close to the truth: this was *an* unusual notrump, just not *the* Unusual Notrump). The Shoe corrected to three hearts, not imagining that he had fooled anyone. However, the opponents were in a doubling mood. The Albatross went only one down, what with the double red-suit fit, while the opponents were touch and go for six spades.

Some time later, much the same auction occurred in the consolation round of a Regional tournament. The Shoe was playing with a partner who felt that bridge was a serious game that should be played with skill and respect. The Shoe agreed wholeheartedly and demonstrated that skill by hogging all seven of the first seven hands. Partner was getting pretty bent out of shape even though they looked to be three boards above average by then. The eighth board was coming up and Shoe's LHO opened one spade. Shoe's partner over-called a noticeably grumpy two hearts, followed by a raise to two spades by RHO. Shoe held, no one vulnerable:

♠ Q J 3   ♡ K 8 6 5 3 2   ◇ 6 2   ♣ 8 5

You didn't have to be Einstein to figure out that the opponents rated to make at least four spades. The Shoe tried an immediate bid of two notrump. Double ended the auction. Dummy had:

♠ 7 5   ♡ A Q J 10 7   ◇ A 10 3   ♣ J 7 6

True, the opponents could cash two spades and five or six clubs. Not surprisingly, they cleared the spades instead. They considered -490 to be a very unfortunate result, though not half so unfortunate as the Shoe's partner thought it was. He grew increasingly apopleptic as Shoe showed in to round after round of hearts, and the cash of the sixth heart from the closed hand was more than he could bear. Never mind that the Shoe had played his eighth hand in a row: how could he have suppressed six-card support for a two-level overcall? He loudly vowed never to play with the Shoe again. The Shoe turned to me with one of his famous equally loud asides, saying, "It's just as well, Bungalow. I hate playing with people who lack appreciation for works of art."

The Bambino shares a lot of the blame for encouraging further development of the notion of notrump as theft. Shoe believes that the Bambino first articulated the notion of the 'notrump save' on this hand:

♠ 9 4   ♡ A 6   ◇ Q 5   ♣ A Q 10 9 8 6 5

The Bambino opened one club and was faced with choosing a rebid on the auction:

Bambino	LHO	Partner	RHO
1♣	dbl	3♣	pass
?			

Three clubs was a preemptive raise, and the Bambino endorsed the rebid of three notrump — vulnerable or not, stoppers or not. The theory was that if partner held enough to set four of a major, three notrump might even make.

Sometimes, of course, notrump sorties can be very trying. You might go four down into your own partscore, or worse, into your game or slam in a suit. The Shoe and the Bambino were struggling along in a Swiss game at three wins and two losses, when they ran into an apparently good team that proclaimed itself to be from the *Bridge World* magazine. After five boards, the best result for the Shoe and the Bambino had been a bidding misunderstanding that led to the Shoe's double of five clubs, laydown for seven. On the sixth hand they were vulnerable against not, and needed a swing. With an opening bid of one diamond on his right, the Shoe picked up:

♠ 9 5   ♡ 10 6 2   ◇ A   ♣ A K Q J 10 9 8

Many players would consider the three notrump overcall 'automatic' on these cards, so the Shoe opted to overcall a more modest one notrump. LHO doubled promptly and firmly, and the Bambino ran out to two clubs, which he played as an all-purpose runout that gives the opponents the maximum opportunity to bid on rather than doubling for 1100.

The Shoe was demoralized by the scorecard and did not think of passing two clubs, which might even provide the opportunity to have the opponents double and then look vacant as he passed the Bambino's rescue redouble. Still elated with his clever one notrump underbid the round before, the Shoe continued to two notrump, waiting for LHO to double and make the safe diamond lead. LHO doubled, sure enough, but when he was on lead he declared (too late) that he sure hoped the Shoe did not have five hearts to the ten. A rather unsporting remark, as he then proceeded to rattle off his seven solid hearts, without a trick yet from his partner's opening bid. This had been the entire deal:

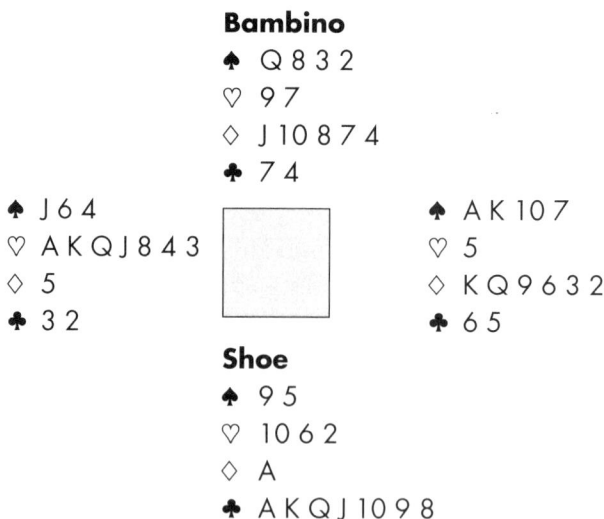

Bambino
- ♠ Q 8 3 2
- ♡ 9 7
- ◇ J 10 8 7 4
- ♣ 7 4

♠ J 6 4
♡ A K Q J 8 4 3
◇ 5
♣ 3 2

♠ A K 10 7
♡ 5
◇ K Q 9 6 3 2
♣ 6 5

Shoe
- ♠ 9 5
- ♡ 10 6 2
- ◇ A
- ♣ A K Q J 10 9 8

The Shoe swallowed his pride and kept all four spades in dummy on the run of the hearts. LHO felt in no danger and negligently continued with a low spade on which RHO did not have the courage to put the ten. Two more spade tricks made nine losers, down four for a not-so-brilliant -1100.

I am pleased to report that the Shoe did not cave in to this adversity, but politely asked the LHO what his teammates would bid on his cards. Suddenly, the opponents were panic-stricken, as apparently it was "Ron" in the Shoe's seat, and Ron would not only overcall three notrump, but would probably redouble. And so it almost turned out, as this was the hand that won the match for the Shoe's team. The overcall was indeed three notrump, but there was no redouble. A discouraged declarer pitched a spade from dummy on the run of the hearts, and an accurate shift by the Hummingbird to the ♠J collected the obvious seven heart tricks plus four spade tricks for +2000.

The Shoe idolized the Bambino's attitude to notrump, and adopted it root and branch. "Being in three notrump," the Shoe would pronounce, "means never having to say you're sorry." Once, he and the Bambino won a duplicate game by bidding every hand to three notrump. The Shoe claims he learned the preparatory bid from the Bambino, on a hand he calls "The Crime of the Century". The Shoe held:

♠ A 9 2　♡ 5 4　◇ 10 3　♣ Q 10 7 6 5 4

On this occasion, Bambino's RHO opened one heart and the Bambino overcalled two clubs. Next hand raised to two hearts and the Shoe considered some number of notrump but was deterred by his lack of a heart stopper and chose instead a raise to three clubs, at least keeping notrump in play. The Bambino converted to three notrump, vehemently doubled, then redoubled by the Shoe with his ace and six club tricks.

The play took some unusual turns. This was the whole deal:

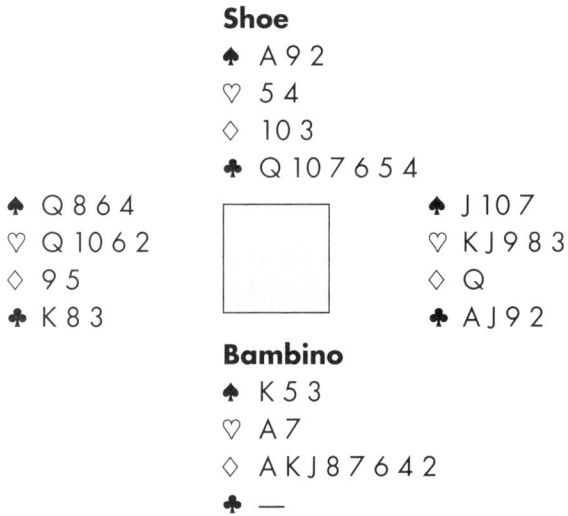

Shoe
♠ A 9 2
♡ 5 4
◇ 10 3
♣ Q 10 7 6 5 4

♠ Q 8 6 4   ♠ J 10 7
♡ Q 10 6 2   ♡ K J 9 8 3
◇ 9 5   ◇ Q
♣ K 8 3   ♣ A J 9 2

Bambino
♠ K 5 3
♡ A 7
◇ A K J 8 7 6 4 2
♣ —

After the automatic heart lead, the opponents had to come down to a four-card ending on the eight rounds of diamonds. This was a little discouraging for them, so no one managed to keep three spades. The Bambino took the first twelve tricks for three redoubled over-tricks, without the benefit of a single trick in clubs.

In the Shoe's world, it was decidedly more fun to steal than to bid to the right contract. It wasn't long before the Shoe began to pave the way for three notrump with bids that might not otherwise be in-tuitively obvious. He chose to open one club (natural) holding:

♠ A J 5   ♡ 10 6   ◇ A K Q 10 4 3 2   ♣ J

Of course, he wasn't going to be happy if partner passed, but over the expected one heart response, he would be none the worse for a three notrump rebid, maybe with a welcome marked spade lead, or a diamond lead. Even if partner responded one spade, there was always the 'reverse' into two diamonds to explore better contracts.

The Shoe quickly became convinced that notrump was the outstanding way to steal as declarer, as well as in the auction. People often were dealt the wrong hand to make the right lead, or they simply did not know how to defend. Sometimes, especially on the more balanced hands, it was even the best theoretical contract as well. The Shoe, for example, in the days when he played the gambling three notrump a little more constructively than is the vogue today, opened three notrump holding

♠ K 6   ♡ A K Q 10 8 6 2   ◇ 10 3   ♣ K 10

He received a heart lead! The whole deal was:

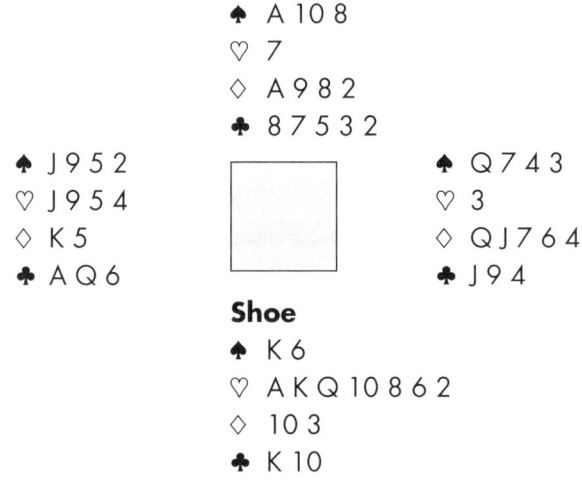

                    ♠ A 10 8
                    ♡ 7
                    ◇ A 9 8 2
                    ♣ 8 7 5 3 2
    ♠ J 9 5 2   ♠ Q 7 4 3
    ♡ J 9 5 4   ♡ 3
    ◇ K 5   ◇ Q J 7 6 4
    ♣ A Q 6   ♣ J 9 4
                    Shoe
                    ♠ K 6
                    ♡ A K Q 10 8 6 2
                    ◇ 10 3
                    ♣ K 10

Four hearts went down on this lie of the cards. With a spade lead instead, declarer can virtually assure three notrump by winning in dummy and finessing the ♡10 at Trick 2. Even taking away partner's spade ace, three notrump is better than 70% on a black-suit lead, while four hearts has less than a 20% chance.

If you need further convincing about balanced hands with solid majors, the Shoe will happily refer you to a hand played by Italy against Panama in the 1972 World Bridge Olympiad, at a time when the Italians had won umpteen world championships in a row. B. Jay Becker wrote up the hand and declared that Panama had been 'undeniably unlucky'. The Shoe disagreed. According to him, the Panama team had been undeniably outplayed. Garozzo opened one heart with:

♠ A 10 6   ♡ K Q J 10 7 2   ◇ A 3   ♣ J 7

LHO doubled and Forquet raised to three hearts, which RHO passed. Garozzo rebid three notrump. At the other table, on the same one heart-double-three hearts beginning, the player who held Garozzo's cards rebid four hearts. This was the whole deal:

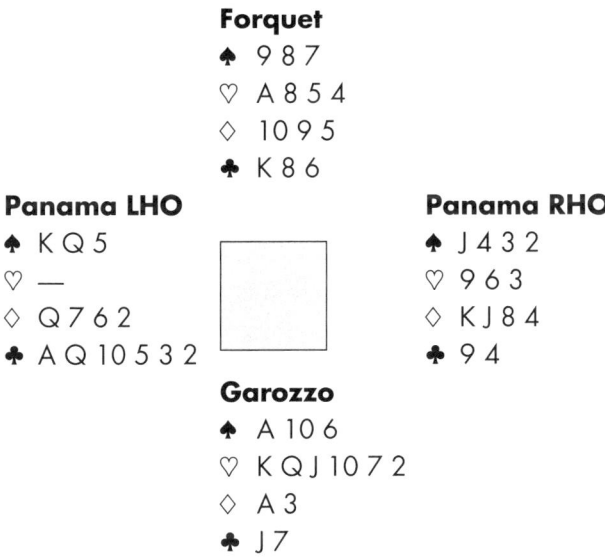

Forquet
♠ 9 8 7
♡ A 8 5 4
◇ 10 9 5
♣ K 8 6

Panama LHO
♠ K Q 5
♡ —
◇ Q 7 6 2
♣ A Q 10 5 3 2

Panama RHO
♠ J 4 3 2
♡ 9 6 3
◇ K J 8 4
♣ 9 4

Garozzo
♠ A 10 6
♡ K Q J 10 7 2
◇ A 3
♣ J 7

The analysis of 'unlucky' presumably refers to the fact that only nine tricks were available in either contract. Apparently, 'unlucky' does not consider which action is more likely to deter a four spade bid, or a bid of five of a minor, by opponents, and what the heart bidders were to do about defending such a contract, especially if the spade fit was 4-4, as seemed likely, not 4-3. 'Unlucky' does not factor in that dummy can convert three notrump to four hearts with a distributional hand, and that the opponents would probably not bid on, even if game would be odds-on for the opponents in dummy's short suit.

Three notrump rated to be the superior contract on all balanced dummies, even if the club king were exchanged for the diamond king, or for the club queen and the spade jack.

The Shoe expounded on and on, finally concluding that aspiring bridge players would do well to study the Italians, and that only a fool or a bridge columnist could write them off as 'lucky'.

7

The Old Guy Comes to Hart House

The Shoe lays claim to the world record for uninterrupted talking by a bridge player, a high bar to clear. I was there and can attest he went on for over an hour, which he says is 59.7 minutes longer than any of his marriages have lasted. "Are we still on the topic of talking?" I asked.

We were gathered at Fran's Restaurant, around the corner from the old Kate Buckman's Bridge Studio. Fran's was the regular hangout for post-game discussions. An old, comfortable place that was open 24 hours a day, Fran's offered an all-day breakfast and it had big, circular tables for large groups. It also had a plentiful supply of paper napkins and clean, white tablecloths, useful for writing down hands. Probably for slightly different reasons, the flagship location of Fran's on St. Clair was the haunt of another eccentric genius, pianist Glenn Gould.

On this occasion, we had Colonel Bulldozer, the Hummingbird, the Victim, the Bambino, the Snowman and the Owl and myself, 'Bungalow' Bill Miller, in attendance as Shoe's captive audience. Snowman had recently become the director at Bucky's and possessed a certain bridge-weirdness that delighted the Shoe. The Shoe apologized to me that I had missed the great event and began, "Bungalow should have been telling you about this extravaganza, but he was being unfaithful to me in some other duplicate game. You may find the whole story hard to believe. You may find it easier to believe that the Snowman bids normally. Even I had to start taking notes because I was afraid I'd think I dreamed the whole thing. I would invite the Old Guy to verify what I'm telling you, but he has already forgotten the hands. No, sorry, correction, he didn't actually see most of the hands to begin with."

"Actually," I chime in for one last interruption, "the Old Guy died a little while ago, so he is temporarily unavailable to attest." The Shoe is so set on his story that he steamrolls ahead, not about to be deterred by my trivial interruptions.

"I innocently show up at Hart House with Eric the Half Bee to play the Forcing Diamond system. As I'm no longer directing, I don't really know the schedule. It turns out that this is the day the Hart House Bridge Club decided to hold its annual Board-a-Match team of four championship.

"The only player available and looking for a game is the Old Guy. You probably remember the Old Guy from the old days at the Metro Bridge Club on College Street where, even in 1962, he looked like a remarkably well-preserved ninety-year-old. The Old Guy is explaining that his eyesight is fine, but sometimes when he calls for the three of clubs from the dummy, it turns out to be the four. As I recall, his hearing wasn't always perfect, either. He had a tendency to think aloud in rather firm tones. He could sometimes be heard several tables away, planning the play of the hand. In short, I love this guy. For the Board-a-Match teams, I draft the Old Guy, leaving only one spot to be filled.

"The only other available living bridge player is the director, Roy Hughes. He would have been, as they say, churlish to refuse. One of Roy's under-publicized talents is that he plays the Forcing Diamond system, so the Half Bee is dispatched to sit North-South with Roy while the Old Guy and I move off to play East-West.

"At the first table, the Old Guy opens with a bid of 'My game isn't as good as it used to be.' To which I slyly reply that it's as good as it ever was. I pick up, neither vulnerable:

♠ 4 3   ♡ A 9 6 2   ◇ K J 8 6 3   ♣ A 3

"I consider this to be a good start with the Old Guy, both because of the vulnerability and because it might turn out to be useful to hold enough high cards for added maneuverability. The good start evaporates as the Old Guy destroys me with an opening bid of three hearts, but by the time my RHO passes, I've recovered sufficiently to shoot three notrump 'on the way' to four hearts. My LHO reads my mind and doubles, just as though he knows what he is doing. The Old Guy sits for the double and so does my RHO, so I meekly run out to four hearts. No one finds a double of *that*.

"The play is instructive, and you may consider it a clear indicator of what is to come. This is the entire deal (rotated):

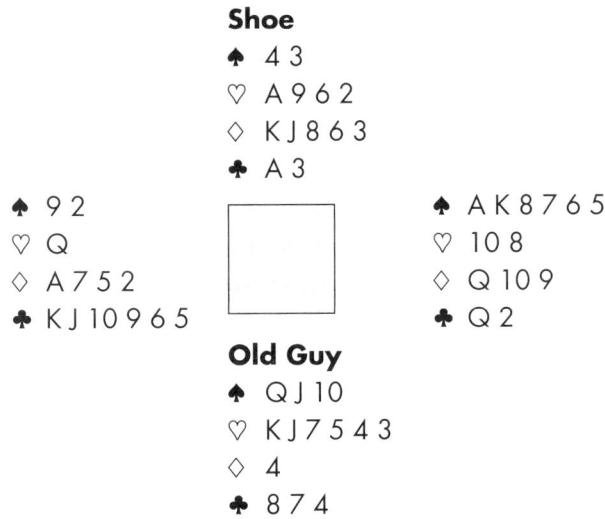

Shoe
♠ 4 3
♡ A 9 6 2
◇ K J 8 6 3
♣ A 3

♠ 9 2   ♠ A K 8 7 6 5
♡ Q   ♡ 10 8
◇ A 7 5 2   ◇ Q 10 9
♣ K J 10 9 6 5   ♣ Q 2

Old Guy
♠ Q J 10
♡ K J 7 5 4 3
◇ 4
♣ 8 7 4

"The opening lead is the *deuce* of spades from the doubleton, won by the king on the Old Guy's right. Not to be fooled by partner's cunning lead, the shift by the Old Guy's RHO is to the unerring queen of clubs. First missed opportunity for our side. That makes four top losers. The Old Guy wins in dummy and leads a heart to the king, trying to promote a loser if queen third is on his right: no punishment as hearts were 2-1. Opponents' first good chance out the window. Now, the Old Guy tries a low diamond and LHO misses the opponents' second good chance by ducking, apparently unable to count the obvious four top tricks on defense. The Old Guy misguesses, playing the jack from dummy. The unforced errors are now tied 2-2. RHO wins the queen and returns his last remaining club. Now, if LHO continues with the third round of clubs, the Old Guy will have to play carefully to avoid two down, as the ten of trumps is still outstanding.

"At this point, the Old Guy, without any apparent effort, hypnotizes the opponents. Instead of a third club, or even a spade for the fourth winner, LHO tries the ace of diamonds, ruffed by the Old Guy, who then crosses to the ace of hearts. Third missed opportunity for the opponents. With the favorable situation in the diamond spots, that suit is now good for three pitches, including the Old Guy's remaining two spades. The Old Guy, what with his eyesight and all, neglects to notice the diamond spots and ruffs one to set up the suit. Third missed chance for our side. The effort of setting up the two diamonds for discards apparently tires the Old Guy out, as he uses one to pitch a spade and one to pitch the club he could have trumped in dummy. Fourth and last chance. In tennis, four unforced errors would cost the game. Almost the same here, as the Old Guy concedes one down, the par spot. However, partners have no trouble converting this to a win by reaching three spades, making four.

"The play of this hand clarifies the task at hand and induces me to open one notrump (16-18) on the next hand, holding:

♠ Q 3   ♡ A 6   ◇ A 10 6 5 3   ♣ K Q 10 2

"A bit rash, especially vulnerable, but I feel it might be important to play the hand as often as possible. Maybe diamonds will run. The Old Guy corrects to two spades, which I assume in Old-Guy bridge shows some values, but not enough for game. I 'improve' back to two notrump and the Old Guy finds the miracle pass holding:

♠ A 9 6 5 2   ♡ J 9 8 7 5   ◇ —   ♣ 9 8 6

"I begin to have a sneaking hunch that the Old Guy understands me perfectly, perhaps from my previous life. The opening lead of the king of hearts does not hurt us, though my LHO appears to be in some degree of pain when he sees the dummy. I win and return my other heart, won by LHO with the queen while RHO discards a small club. The low spade shift is ducked to RHO's king, who returns the four of diamonds, covered smoothly by my five and LHO's seven. LHO shifts again, this time to a club to RHO's ace, and back comes the deuce of diamonds.

"I have a saying for this situation, of which the expurgated version is "Bid like a madman, play like a fox." I call for a time-out. It seems pretty obvious that LHO is 4-5-3-1 or 3-5-3-2. Why has he led every suit but diamonds? Probably he has something like Kxx or KJx, though it is barely possible that he has seen me bid notrump on diamond preempts before. If he had the diamond holding I pictured, the hand was not beyond hope, provided LHO refused to part with his hypothetical king of diamonds. In fact, even if it's queen third or jack third I have a winkle for one down if LHO does not unblock. You work it out.

"Any port in a storm. I rise with the ace of diamonds and no honor appears. Everyone shows in to the king of clubs, so the clubs are now good and LHO is 3-5-3-2. Spades are 3-3, not that I care. Disdaining the good clubs for fear of an unblock, I cash the queen of spades, followed by a diamond, which loses to LHO's hoped-for king as dummy discards a heart. On the earlier rounds of diamonds, I had discarded a heart and a spade from dummy, leaving a club, ace and one spade and the good jack of hearts. LHO is on lead with three hearts and a spade, into dummy, so I get a spade, a heart and two more clubs, just making. Spades had been 3-3 as expected. Making exactly two produces another win as partners defeat the insane contract of two spades by two tricks at the other table.

"That is more or less the end of the normal part of the game, as the evening now begins to take off into fantasy land. On the next round, I open a non-textbook bid of one spade holding:

♠ K 10 8 6   ♡ Q   ◇ A Q 10 3   ♣ 8 6 5 4

"The Old Guy responds two hearts, which leaves me with no option but two notrump, raised to three by the Old Guy. The opening lead is the four of hearts and the Old Guy, grinning from ear to ear, announces that he only had 6 points and he has taken a shot. The kibitzer and

I faint simultaneously, but I awake to find a rather acceptable dummy (hands rotated):

♠ A J 2
♡ A 10 9 8 7 2
◇ 5
♣ K 10 2

♠ K 10 8 6
♡ Q
◇ A Q 10 3
♣ 8 6 5 4

"I am still in shock after the Old Guy's playful comment, or perhaps it was the general atmosphere of the game, I don't know, but I let the opening lead ride, losing to the king. Even the merest kibitzer, even a kibitzer named 'Bungalow', knows that this is very unlikely to be right. If LHO has five hearts, as he probably does to have led dummy's suit, the only singleton with RHO where the play from dummy can make any difference is the king, in which case you must rise with the ace.

"RHO, who holds the singleton king of hearts and ♣AQJ over dummy's king, uses this undeserved golden opportunity to shift to the jack of clubs! I cannot afford to duck and proceed meekly to win and drive out the jack of hearts, losing in all two hearts and two clubs. Partners managed to set three notrump two tricks at the other table.

"It looks as though the gods are punishing me for my poor play on the previous hand, as I next pick up:

♠ 2   ♡ J 6 4 2   ◇ 9 8 6 5 3   ♣ 9 7 6

"Opponents bid their way unmolested to five clubs and the play is interesting. The Old Guy leads the jack of trumps, won by declarer, who takes an immediate spade finesse. This is the whole deal:

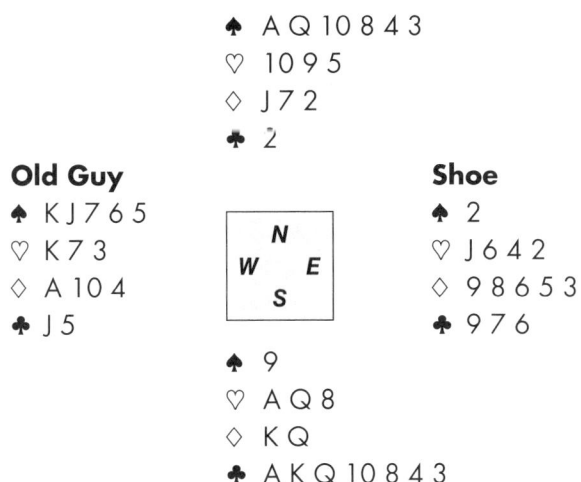

<pre>
                    ♠ A Q 10 8 4 3
                    ♡ 10 9 5
                    ◇ J 7 2
                    ♣ 2
   Old Guy   Shoe
   ♠ K J 7 6 5   ♠ 2
   ♡ K 7 3   N   ♡ J 6 4 2
   ◇ A 10 4   W   E   ◇ 9 8 6 5 3
   ♣ J 5   S   ♣ 9 7 6
                    ♠ 9
                    ♡ A Q 8
                    ◇ K Q
                    ♣ A K Q 10 8 4 3
</pre>

"I ruff the ace of spades that comes next, and I'm more than a little surprised to be overruffed. Trumps are drawn, and then the Old Guy follows up by ducking both rounds of diamonds. Then comes the eight of hearts, the Old Guy ducking again to dummy's ten and my jack. I return a diamond to break up the pseudo-squeeze and, although the Old Guy is severely tested to recall the spade situation so much later in the hand, especially as he is smarting at having his ace of diamonds ruffed out, a second heart trick eventually materializes, making five.

"It turns out that this deal was defense-proofed when Roy, at the other table, arrived in three notrump and received a low heart lead to dummy's ten and RHO's jack and won with the queen. Six of the seven rounds of clubs later, the position became:

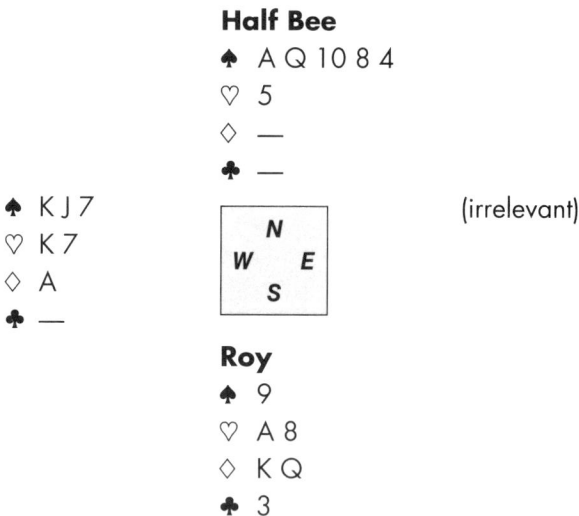

Half Bee
- ♠ A Q 10 8 4
- ♡ 5
- ◇ —
- ♣ —

♠ K J 7
♡ K 7
◇ A
♣ —

(irrelevant)

N
W   E
S

Roy
- ♠ 9
- ♡ A 8
- ◇ K Q
- ♣ 3

"On the last club, LHO could pitch whatever he wanted: Roy had the rest of the tricks! He chose a small heart and then the squeeze repeated on the cash of the ace and eight of hearts. Making seven! The Old Guy could have mailed in the defense to five clubs.

"However, the miracles might soon be over as on the next round, we face a pretty decent pair. I make a rather mangy three spade preempt on a six-card suit and my theory that the Old Guy knows me from a previous incarnation receives further vindication. The Old Guy jumps to five clubs and buys queen third from me. It costs him a trick trying to ruff two consecutive diamonds in dummy without returning to the closed hand in between: down two. No problem: partners doubled five clubs and set it two tricks on the lead of a trump.

"The Old Guy still looks visibly upset over the trick he had blown defending five clubs, as he opens a vulnerable four spades on the next hand, holding:

♠ A K J 10 5 3 2   ♡ J   ◇ 6 5   ♣ A K J

"My hand is:

♠ —   ♡ Q 9 5 3   ◇ A Q 9 3   ♣ Q 10 9 6 5

"so four spades ends the auction. Not to be outdone on the past lives psychic connection, I announce, as I table this fine hand, that with anyone but the Old Guy my life would be passing before my eyes. The Old Guy tells me not to worry. His LHO has a difficult choice of leads, as this is the whole layout (hands rotated):

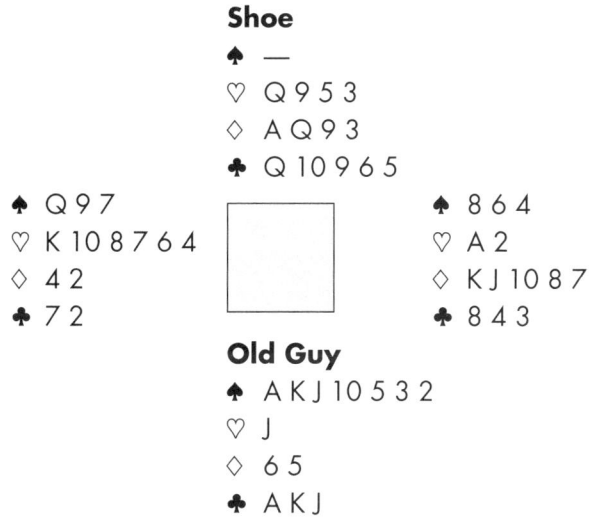

Shoe
♠ —
♡ Q 9 5 3
♢ A Q 9 3
♣ Q 10 9 6 5

♠ Q 9 7
♡ K 10 8 7 6 4
♢ 4 2
♣ 7 2

♠ 8 6 4
♡ A 2
♢ K J 10 8 7
♣ 8 4 3

Old Guy
♠ A K J 10 5 3 2
♡ J
♢ 6 5
♣ A K J

"LHO chooses the two of clubs. What is it with these leads of low cards from doubletons? I, of course, take a peek at all the hands. The Old Guy is not going to be fooled by the lead because he can't see exactly what spot card it is and anyway tends to forget what he thinks it is well before the end of the hand. He takes care to unblock, winning the ace, an astonishingly good play that suggests his foresight is better than his eyesight. Three rounds of spades clear the trumps. When LHO returns a diamond, I am foolishly thinking the Old Guy can claim with six spade tricks, five clubs and the ace of diamonds. The Old Guy takes the practice finesse in diamonds, losing to the king. Now RHO goes into an agonizing huddle. He probably saw his partner's club spot and is considering killing the dummy with the jack of diamonds back. The Old Guy graciously tables his hand, conceding a heart. At the other table, partners found the killing diamond lead to hold the hand to four. Standoff.

"Our momentum now seems to be seriously on the wane as I pick up:

♠ 10 7 4 2   ♡ A Q   ♢ K 10 6 4 3   ♣ J 3

"In third chair, after two passes, I produce the strategic one diamond opening bid, then immediately wish I had opened one spade. This wish is redoubled when the Old Guy responds one spade and everybody passes with both opponents giggling uncontrollably. I thought it was sinful that they should be so happy when I had so many spades, albeit few points. The opening heart lead produced another losing finesse for the Old Guy. No one could accuse him of winning by being merely lucky. The ensuing club shift ensured eight tricks as the whole hand was (rotated):

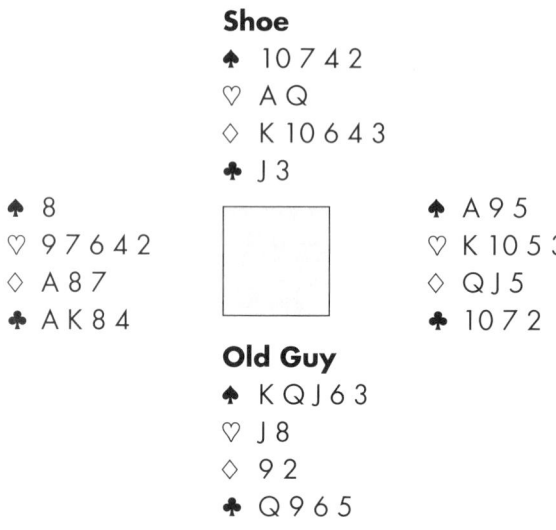

Shoe
♠ 10 7 4 2
♡ A Q
◇ K 10 6 4 3
♣ J 3

♠ 8
♡ 9 7 6 4 2
◇ A 8 7
♣ A K 8 4

♠ A 9 5
♡ K 10 5 3
◇ Q J 5
♣ 10 7 2

Old Guy
♠ K Q J 6 3
♡ J 8
◇ 9 2
♣ Q 9 6 5

"The opponents are still giggling as we depart. Mandatory drug testing is probably decades away. Partners missed the laydown heart game and scored plus 170, but we were understanding about it.

"A couple of hands later, I have this problem with neither vulnerable:

♠ A 4 2   ♡ Q J 9 5 2   ◇ A 4   ♣ K 9 2

"I solve it in my usual masterful way by opening one notrump (16-18). It worked with 15 points, why not 14? LHO saves me by overcalling two diamonds and the Old Guy contributes two spades, which I presume shows slightly more than if he had made the same bid without interference. RHO passes and I 'temporize' with a bid of three hearts, which goes *all pass!* How does the Old Guy know these things? The play was even more unusual than the auction, as this was the full deal (rotated):

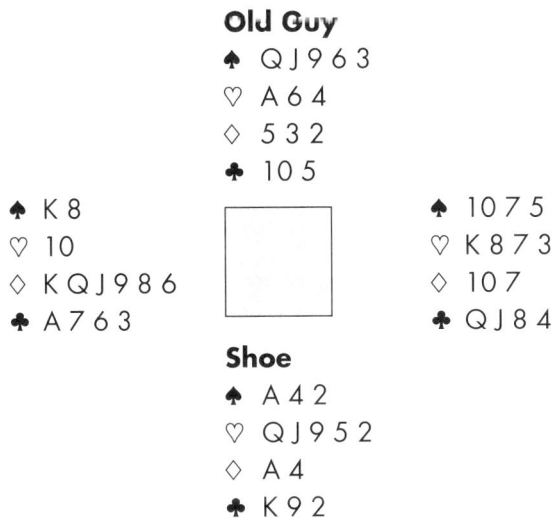

Old Guy
- ♠ Q J 9 6 3
- ♡ A 6 4
- ◇ 5 3 2
- ♣ 10 5

♠ K 8
♡ 10
◇ K Q J 9 8 6
♣ A 7 6 3

♠ 10 7 5
♡ K 8 7 3
◇ 10 7
♣ Q J 8 4

Shoe
- ♠ A 4 2
- ♡ Q J 9 5 2
- ◇ A 4
- ♣ K 9 2

"LHO produces the imaginative lead of the eight of spades which boomerangs when the queen holds in dummy. With nothing better to do, and to keep control of dummy entries and possible club ruffs, I lead a low heart to my queen, which holds as LHO contributes the ten. There do not seem to be any kings in this deck. Stuck in my hand, I decide to cash the ace of spades, dropping the king! I decide to believe the ten of hearts and lead the third round of spades over to dummy. The fourth spade is ruffed low by RHO, overruffed by me. Now a trump to the ace leaves RHO with the lone king. He squanders that trumping the fifth spade as I discard my losing diamond. I win the diamond return with my now bare ace and decide to play safe for the overtrick by leading a small club toward dummy's ten. It is not to be. LHO flies with the ace, forcing me to make five! Three out of three finesses offside, and I never 'lost' any.

"The Old Guy gets upset for the one and only time in the game, when he discovers I made five. He takes me to task. After all, hadn't he shown some values when he bid two spades? How could I not jump to game? I am left puzzling over which game I was supposed to bid.

"I can see you guys are getting bored, so I'll just order another pitcher of beer and provide the executive summary of the miracles from the middle of the game. You wouldn't believe them anyway. For example, I made a bad overcall and the Old Guy led my suit instead of cashing our two winners: four spades making seven. Meanwhile, partners bid and made the two-loser slam. I opened hearts, rebid diamonds and led a club against a spade contract. Declarer played me for fourteen or more cards by taking a safety play against my also having the ♠Q10xx, the only way to go down. I psyched another opening heart bid but this time the Old Guy decided to ignore me and led a club against two notrump. Down two for +200. With a heart lead it makes three. We had a Blackwood auction where I asked for aces after the Old Guy opened a strong two-bid in diamonds. The Old Guy, holding all four, responded five notrump. I correctly interpreted the response and, unable to ask for kings, blasted the grand slam in notrump. This had fifteen top tricks after the diamond finesse worked. I went down in a cold partscore when I mispulled a card. No problem: partners defended slam. Opponents took a phantom save and then got overboard in game. Declarer squeezed me out of the setting trick and then conceded one down. The Old Guy made a forcing raise of my opening psychic bid. Of course I had to bid game, but he only had 11 points; a ruff-sluff and a two-way finesse later, the contract came home.

"Sometimes despite his spotty memory, the Old Guy remembers stuff. I am sure he is remembering when I opened one notrump (but not the scant 14 points) where we reached three hearts making five. I am sure that he has this in mind, unless it really is a psychic connection from another life, when he raises my one notrump opening to two, holding:

♠ J 9   ♡ J 10 4 2   ◇ K 9 2   ♣ Q 8 7 2

"This is the Old Guy's version of going for the jugular, but whose? His telepathy comes through once again, as I just happen to hold a balanced 19 count consisting of:

♠ A K 4   ♡ K 9 8   ◇ A Q 10   ♣ K 9 6 4

"I smugly raise myself to game and the opponents lead a high spade spot to dummy's nine, which I win after it forces the queen. With the queen of hearts offside, nine tricks barely roll home. At the other table, they somehow stopped in partscore.

"As with all experienced players, the Old Guy saves the best for the very end. In this case, he appears to be basing himself on a theory he vaguely remembers from some textbook, omitting only inconsequential details of distribution and point count. My LHO opens one diamond and the Old Guy overcalls one spade. RHO passes and it's up to me, holding:

♠ Q   ♡ A 2   ◇ Q J 9 7 4 2   ♣ 8 6 5 4

"We are vulnerable, so I bid one notrump, only a little out of fright, to get the play from the right side. The Old Guy continues to two hearts and from fright greater than before, I try two notrump. The Old Guy has no problem raising to three. You shouldn't miss a vulnerable game, he has heard somewhere. A small diamond is led and the Old Guy observes, 'I sure hope you have something in that suit', as he tables this dummy:

♠ A K J 10   ♡ K Q J 10 9 4   ◇ —   ♣ J 9 2

"Although I can't figure out the bidding until later, the result is perfect. I win the opening lead and rattle off ten more top tricks in the majors, making five. The theoretical par is four hearts making about four. However, at almost all the other tables, including that of our partners, the bidding had gone one diamond, double, all pass. That either made or went one down, nowhere close to our magnificent score of plus +660.

"Pressed for an explanation of his bidding, the Old Guy reveals that he hadn't wanted to reverse into spades later in the auction with only 15 points. I congratulate him on his raise to game and tell him about the movie *Love Story* where they first articulated the proposition that 'Being in notrump means never having to say you're sorry.'

"We finally reach the last board and the roof has still not fallen in. I look up to verify this fact, and the roof is definitely still up there. The parting shot looks like a problem on my opening bid:

♠ —   ♡ —   ◇ K Q J 9 5 4   ♣ A Q 9 8 7 5 2

"My head is going round and round wondering what I will rebid if I open one diamond, one club, or pass. Having decided to open one club, I still can't decide whether to rebid four diamonds or two diamonds. The magic takes over, and an opening bid of two diamonds falls out of my mouth. We play that as a strong, forcing two-bid. At least I have a 'two-loser' hand. I really panic when the Old Guy makes a positive response of two spades, so I leap to five clubs. This forces the Old Guy into his first prolonged trance. I think he wants to ask for aces. He resolves all the issues with a leap to seven notrump, a mixed blessing because he's on play. The Old Guy's RHO expresses doubt about the contract with a firm double. At least he's not on lead. The Old Guy chooses to believe me, I can't see why, and issues an equally firm redouble. LHO tables the king of hearts (who could blame him) and this is the whole deal (rotated):

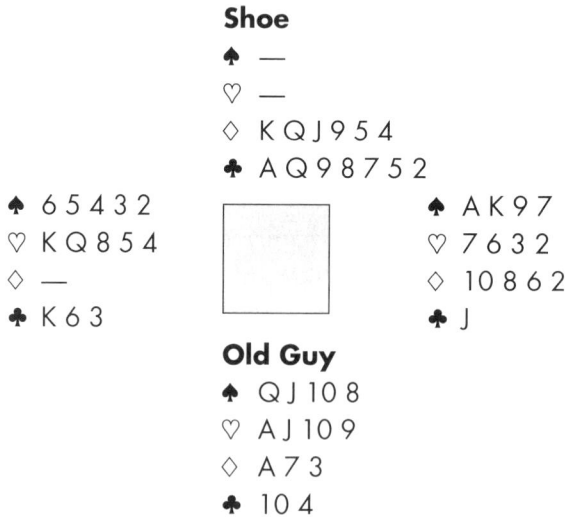

Shoe
♠ —
♡ —
◇ K Q J 9 5 4
♣ A Q 9 8 7 5 2

♠ 6 5 4 3 2
♡ K Q 8 5 4
◇ —
♣ K 6 3

♠ A K 9 7
♡ 7 6 3 2
◇ 10 8 6 2
♣ J

Old Guy
♠ Q J 10 8
♡ A J 10 9
◇ A 7 3
♣ 10 4

"The Old Guy makes short work of this one, winning the opening lead with the ace of hearts and playing the ten of clubs. When it's not covered, he assumes that LHO does not have the jack, and inserts the queen from dummy. That holds and the jack appears, so it's child's play to return to the ace of diamonds and take a finesse of the club nine.

"Because of the bad minor-suit divisions, there is no way to make more than six of a minor. Imagine partners' surprise when we win this board. They had defended six diamonds redoubled, just making. The rest of the scoring is almost as fortuitous, and we are all delighted with our landslide win, scoring 18½ on 22 boards."

There is a little pause as the spectators digest these atrocities. The Shoe also appears lost in thought. Finally, he emerges with: "Did you say the Old Guy died?" and I give him the "Yes". Shoe now fixes me with the stare that is meant to suggest it's my fault when he really knows it's his own. "Crap," he says, "this means I have to do a eulogy." Which, in turn, opens the door for a much shorter Shoe-diatribe that runs about like this:

"No wonder the Old Guy seemed to disappear from the bridge scene. I had a nice chat with him just recently, while he was kibitzing a chess game in the park. He was having trouble distinguishing the bishops from the pawns, but was otherwise enthusiastic, especially as the government was stupidly paying him enough money to house and feed him, *and* to permit him to spend three days a week at the racetrack.

"Unless it is for that sensational triumph at Hart House, the Old Guy will never be remembered for his bridge exploits. He never won a National or Regional championship. I doubt if he ever won a Sectional. He never made Life Master and, if you'll pardon the quasi-pun, the ACBL *Bulletin* probably never noted his passing.

"I would like, by way of praising the Old Guy, to mention his last appearance on my bridge scene. You may recall that I mentioned his tendency to think aloud. I am playing in the team qualifier for the Canadian Olympiad Team. My RHO is Eric Kokish. On an earlier occasion when I'd undoubtedly earned it, Eric had referred to me in my absence as an 'effer', as in 'I finally beat that effer, Shoe.' Be that as it may, I wasn't always as respectful to Eric as I should have been, and anyways, how was he to know I was on the other side of the door when he said it?

"It's the first quarter of the semifinals of the qualifier and we are all pretty tense. There is no cheerful banter. The Old Guy sits down between Eric and me to kibitz and it isn't long before Eric lands in a vulnerable four heart contract where he has a choice of safety plays and sweats blood trying to choose the right one. Finally, he picks the wrong one. Nothing matters, as all roads lead to making five. Eric looks immensely relieved until the Old Guy, gruffly but firmly, intones directly into Eric's ear and loud enough for all to hear, "You should have bid the slam." Eric flies from his chair and rises hugely in my estimation, as he sizes up the Old Guy from mid-air and lands again in his chair without saying a word, deferring to his obviously far greater experience. Eric and I shake our heads and smile ruefully at each other, probably for the first time.

"You should know that the stories about the Old Guy are all true. There were more stories in the same vein, and I wish I hadn't stopped taking notes. With his talent for miracles, I'm sure the Old Guy will surface again in the most unlikely of places. Perhaps it will be when I finally get to a world championship. I'll be so nervous I can hardly see as I pull the king of clubs from the dummy, only it turns out to be the seven of hearts. As I look up in surprise, there will be the Old Guy, beaming at me to win this one for him. Knowing his track record, the seven of hearts will be the perfect card."

8

Road Trip: The 1967 Summer Nationals

In Canada's centennial year, 1967, the Summer Nationals were held in Montreal, which is practically next door to Toronto, if you don't mind about 400 miles of driving. Canada still had miles, not kilometers, in those days. The Shoe and the Hummingbird were flushed with success in Kate Buckman's competition to win their entry fees to the Summer Nationals: the Bird won the Under-100 master point division while the Shoe had finished runner-up to the Owl in the Open. That gave them enough money to travel to Montreal in style: to wit, to hitchhike along the 401 and to stay six-to-a-room at the Drummond Street YMCA. Shoe insisted I come along, but I declined the hitchhiking opportunity and caught a ride with Abe Paul.

Abe was bragging about how he never got a speeding ticket until he got stopped twice on this trip, each one 25 mph over the limit. We arrived in Montreal telling our tale of woe about the tickets, only to have Harry Creed sneak up behind us and announce, "You think that's bad, I just got arrested for passing a cop that was chasing a speeder!" This, by the way, was the same Harry Creed who had long been banned from driving in New York State, where he had heard it was illegal to turn right on a red light. Accordingly, when he caught a red light on the way to a tournament in Rochester, he had given the matter some consideration and proceeded to turn left.

The Shoe and the Hummingbird arrived into this discussion and the Shoe began to hold forth about the time Harry was driving them home on the highway from Cleveland and let go of the wheel to jump into the back seat to try to strangle him. Those who were accustomed to the Shoe's so-called discussions were understanding of Harry's reaction, perhaps even wishing that Harry might have succeeded. The Shoe mentioned how Abe Greenspan had grabbed the wheel to prevent an accident, so it was unnecessary to invent a whole new interpretation of winning the post mortem.

A quaint story came from the hitchhike to Montreal. It seems Bird and Shoe caught a ride with a large red-necked gentleman behind the wheel of a good-sized American car of about 1959 vintage. It soon transpired that the driver was already pretty drunk, driving mainly just beside the road at 80 mph, while reaching down to continue to drain the last third of the forty-ounce bottle of rye that he had conveniently stored on the floor right next to the gas pedal. If that was not enough, he regaled them with the story about how his wife and sixteen-year old son were conspiring to keep the no-good boy in school, when any fool knew that once you reached sixteen you were meant to go out and earn your keep. This, you might not recall, was when the Shoe was finishing his sixth year in university, the Bird only his fifth. They kept tactfully quiet about their wasted lives, but at the next available exit, they broke all existing land speed records for time of departure from a stopped vehicle. They felt much safer on their next ride, a guy with a truckload of onions who had been driving for the past sixty hours.

They should have been overawed, what with it being their first Nationals and with all those famous bridge players in attendance. In the Men's Pairs, they played the last two boards of the opening round against Mr. Fishbein and Mr. Solomon. The tam-o-shanter made it obvious that Mr. Fishbein really was Harry Fishbein, inventor of the (now forgotten) convention that bore his name: double of preempts for penalty and next step for takeout. Some such convention is more than ever necessary in the present-day era of irresponsible pre-empts. Mr. Solomon, the shiny, bald-headed one, made sure that it was not lost on anyone that he was the current president of the World Bridge Federation. When the Shoe did not appear to react to the news, he added a fatherly "You need a haircut", obviously aimed at the Shoe, with his usual shoulder-length hair. Shoe smiled sweetly and replied, "That's easy for you to say." He then turned to me and stage-whispered something along the lines of: "The authority of the follically challenged at bridge, as at the barber shop, is vastly over-rated."

On the first hand, not vulnerable against vulnerable, the Hum-mingbird opened with a weak two-bid in diamonds. Even from be-hind the Shoe, it was obvious that he was no longer contemplating punishments for Mr. Solomon, and had frozen a little as he held:

♠ J 10 3   ♡ K Q 4 2   ◇ Q 9 7 6 4 3   ♣ —

Mr. Solomon on Shoe's right contributed a double and the Shoe re-covered in time to ask if that was Fishbein. "No", snarled Fishbein. Skip bid announcements had not yet been invented, so the Shoe leaped without further fanfare to six diamonds. "Double", intoned Mr. Fishbein and the Shoe could not resist asking, before he passed it out, whether *that* was Fishbein. A fistfight did not break out and it turned out that they weren't even playing Fishbein. Six diamonds doubled became the final contract. On a heart lead, that was lay-down for seven, as this was the entire deal:

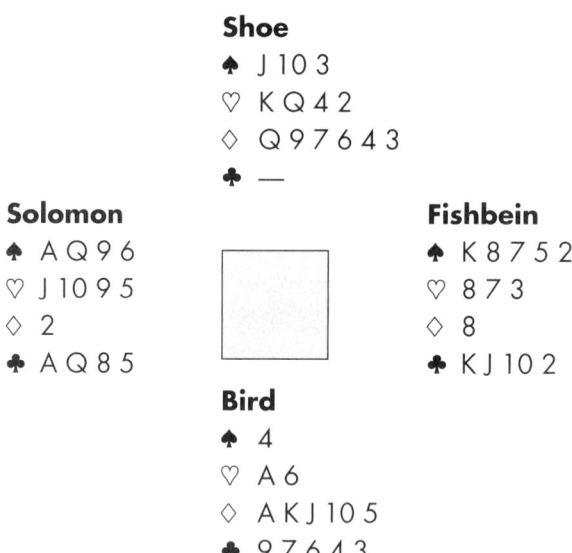

Shoe
♠ J 10 3
♡ K Q 4 2
◇ Q 9 7 6 4 3
♣ —

Solomon
♠ A Q 9 6
♡ J 10 9 5
◇ 2
♣ A Q 8 5

Fishbein
♠ K 8 7 5 2
♡ 8 7 3
◇ 8
♣ K J 10 2

Bird
♠ 4
♡ A 6
◇ A K J 10 5
♣ 9 7 6 4 3

The second board gave the Shoe fresh opportunities to focus on Mr. Solomon. He held:

♠ K Q J 3   ♡ K 10 8   ◇ A 9 2   ♣ Q 10 2

Mr. Fishbein opened one spade on the Shoe's left, the Bird passed and Mr. Solomon bid two diamonds. This is where the Shoe's inexperience showed, as he took maybe three minutes to pass. It was probably unique in his experience to pass holding an opening one notrump bid. Mr. Fishbein bid two spades, the Bird, to no one's surprise, passed again, and Mr. Solomon tried two notrump. The Shoe passed relatively smoothly, taking no more than a minute and a half this time. Now Mr. Fishbein bid three clubs and Mr. Solomon ended the auction with an authoritative three notrump. The Shoe muttered something along the lines of having underestimated Kojak, and showed considerable additional discomfort about the opening lead, before he selected the boring ♠K. This was the deal:

Fishbein
♠ A 10 8 7 4 2
♡ Q 7 6
◇ —
♣ A K 4 3

Shoe
♠ K Q J 3
♡ K 10 8
◇ A 9 2
♣ Q 10 2

Bird
♠ 9 6 5
♡ 9 5 4 2
◇ J 8 7
♣ 8 6 5

Solomon
♠ —
♡ A J 3
◇ K Q 10 6 5 4 3
♣ J 9 7

The first trick was ducked, as the Hummingbird played low and Mr. Solomon pitched a low club. The Shoe took another couple of minutes to continue a small spade, as Mr. Solomon guessed to play the eight from dummy, won by the Bird with the nine. The Bird wasted this valuable entry to shift to the ◇7, but Mr. Solomon guessed wrong again, playing the king. The Shoe won and shifted back to spades. Eight tricks were now inevitable for declarer.

One down seemed like another good result for the bad guys, but Mr. Solomon couldn't let it rest, remarking that there was nothing he could have done to make the hand. The Shoe immediately volunteered, "Not unless you were at the table." He continued to expand on this theme, noting that with all the problems he had displayed on defense, perhaps Mr. Solomon could have placed him with most of the missing points. "Notrump", he philosophized to me, "is not for children." Mr. Fishbein finally joined the fray by remarking that the Shoe was not a very nice person to play bridge with, in reply to which the Shoe apologized and granted him that perhaps he was right.

The Hummingbird won his one-hundredth master point somewhere amid all this excitement, and that qualified him and the Shoe to enter the Golder Masters Pairs. The Bird kicked serious butt in this event while the Shoe was mainly just kicking himself over things that he might have done better. Even down the home stretch, it looked like they might still have been in contention when the Shoe fumbled the ball one final fatal time. This was his hand:

♠ A K Q   ♡ Q 3 2   ◇ A K J 7 6 4 3   ♣ —

He was vulnerable against not, and after two passes, decided to open the plebeian one diamond. Next hand passed and the Bird responded one spade. The passed hand on the right intervened with an overcall of one notrump, showing what you'd expect: some sort of weak takeout into clubs and hearts. The Shoe looked perplexed and I wondered what could be wrong with a double. The Shoe later explained that double just postponed the problem, so at the table he leaped to four spades. In those days, who worried about ruffing with the high trumps?

Now came five hearts by LHO, pass, pass to the Shoe. It was not the Shoe's finest moment for inference. Unfortunately, he was probably remembering missed opportunities from earlier in the game, so he did not pause to consider the Bird's likely hand which had to contain short hearts (no double), not super-long spades (no five spade bid), so probable diamond tolerance with ruffs in the short hand. Dazzled by the unfavorable vulnerability and the fact that it was matchpoints, the Shoe bid the insanely optimistic five spades. That was no big success, as the opponents doubled and set it 1100. The Bird tactfully refrained from mentioning that six diamonds was cold. After the game, the Shoe took this hand to every expert he could find, seeking opinions as to what should be bid over the one notrump overcall. The experts were almost unanimous in recommending a cuebid of two notrump. What else could it show?

Later in the same session, the Bird and the Shoe came up against Eric Kokish and Joey Silver, who in those days were intercollegiate bridge stars but still little more than promising rookies in the real world. More masterminding could be anticipated from the Shoe. His first hand, both vulnerable, was:

♠ 5 3 2   ♡ J 9 8 7   ◇ A K 7 6 3   ♣ 7

Eric, Shoe's RHO, opened one spade, Shoe passed and Joey bid two clubs, which the Bird doubled. A vulnerable double in this position had to show a pretty good hand: after all, it was into a forcing auction, and two notrump was available for two-suited preempts. If the Hummingbird did not hold a black ace, he rated to have all the missing top hearts and diamonds. That, in turn, meant that at least one opponent was bidding light and on distribution. How many defensive tricks could there be? Not many. How many hearts could make? Probably at least four, depending on how many spades the Bird held. The Shoe seemed to have regained some of his ability to reason, now that the game appeared lost.

Eric rebid two spades and the Shoe, having realized that he could make four hearts but maybe not five, while the opponents probably could make four spades, 'temporized' with a bid of three hearts. This went pass, pass, back to Eric, who bid three spades. Shoe, looking as vacuous as his beady eyes allowed, volunteered the vulnerable four hearts in the direct chair. All the best books on matchpoints tell you that you must double to obtain the magic 200 number, and somebody did. The Bird had the expected:

♠ 6 ♡ A K Q 10 5 ◇ Q J 10 8 ♣ 9 3 2

so there was no miracle available for the defense — four hearts doubled made five. The Shoe could not resist asking whether they really thought he had bid this way in the hot seat, just to give them the magic two hundred number. That question appeared to influence the outcome on the second board, where the Shoe had, at favorable vulnerability:

♠ J 4 2 ♡ K Q 5 2 ◇ 7 4 ♣ A K 8 5

The Hummingbird opened one notrump (15-17) and Eric overcalled three spades. The Shoe later explained the lunacy that followed by noting there were only 10-12 missing high-card points, or at most 13 or 14 if the Bird felt it was his turn to make a move. After the remark about the two hundred number, Shoe could not envision Eric with anything less than seven or eight solid spades, possibly with diamonds on the side. If they made three spades doubled, the taunting would never end but, on the other hand, if spades were solid, they were splitting and three notrump was three or four down. The Shoe decided to place the Bird with a doubleton spade and heart tolerance and bid the admittedly ridiculous four hearts! I think he was making up for missing the same inference on the six diamond hand.

The opponents were obviously sufficiently rankled to continue bidding. Joey contributed five diamonds, doubled by the Bird and corrected back to five spades by Eric, doubled by the Shoe and corrected back to six diamonds by Joey, doubled by the Bird, all pass. That went for 1700 into the non-vulnerable game, as the whole deal was:

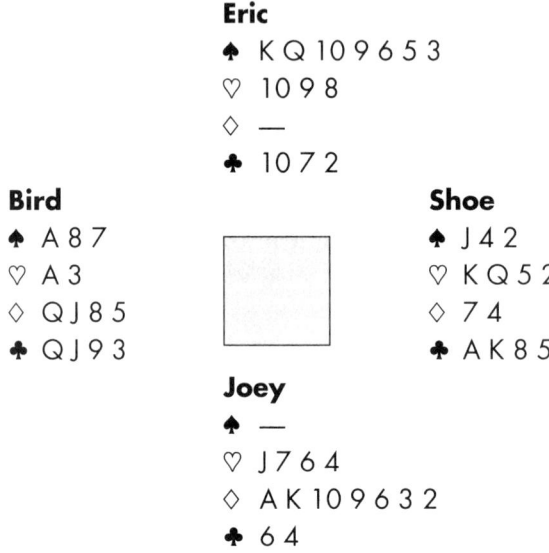

Eric
♠ K Q 10 9 6 5 3
♡ 10 9 8
♢ —
♣ 10 7 2

Bird
♠ A 8 7
♡ A 3
♢ Q J 8 5
♣ Q J 9 3

Shoe
♠ J 4 2
♡ K Q 5 2
♢ 7 4
♣ A K 8 5

Joey
♠ —
♡ J 7 6 4
♢ A K 10 9 6 3 2
♣ 6 4

So much for Joey's 'short hearts' inference for partner's hand.

On the last round, it was pretty obvious that despite the late recovery, the Shoe had thrown away so much that only a couple of top boards could put them in contention. The opponents looked about right, the kind of little old man and little old lady that you think only exists in bridge books. On the first hand, they defended against the Shoe's two spades making when they happened to be on for six clubs. Now came this hand for the Shoe:

♠ 4 ♡ 6 5 ♢ K Q 10 8 4 2 ♣ 6 5 4 2

The little old man, the Shoe's LHO, opened one club and the Bird overcalled one notrump, which the little old lady passed. The Shoe began to ruminate, but I had not kibitzed him all these years for nothing: he was obviously going to bid three notrump. He was probably looking for something to say if it didn't make. Like a good robot, the Shoe eventually raised to three notrump. I was placed so I could see the opener's hand, which was:

♠ K 7   ♡ Q J 7 5 3   ◇ A 9 3   ♣ A 10 8

Really, that was the one club opener. The opening lead was the ♣9, which went to RHO's ace and the Bird's jack. The Shoe pretended he was Colonel Bulldozer and took a peek into both opponents' hands. He got a look on his face that could only have said "Aaaaaaagh!" This was the whole deal:

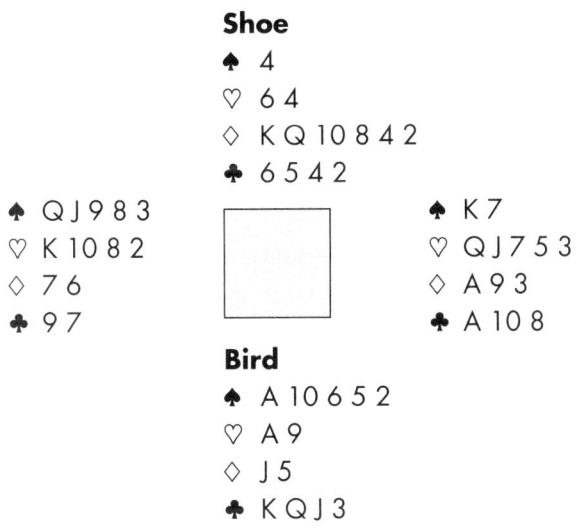

Shoe
♠ 4
♡ 6 4
◇ K Q 10 8 4 2
♣ 6 5 4 2

♠ Q J 9 8 3
♡ K 10 8 2
◇ 7 6
♣ 9 7

♠ K 7
♡ Q J 7 5 3
◇ A 9 3
♣ A 10 8

Bird
♠ A 10 6 5 2
♡ A 9
◇ J 5
♣ K Q J 3

RHO made the 'clever' shift to the ♡J, won by the Bird with the ace, deuce from LHO. RHO ducked the first round of diamonds and won the second. He then led a low heart, which LHO had to overtake, having squandered the deuce. Fearing setting up a heart trick for the Bird because of the queen that her partner had so carefully hidden, she shifted to a spade. The Shoe turned and whispered to me, not audible a table away, for a change: "What a stupid defense, all for the same zero for our side."

The Bird continued, as he had all game, to appear singularly cheerful. He won the ♠A and continued by cashing the two high clubs. Next, the Hummingbird reached into his hand and allowed the ♣3 to flutter to the table. Dummy still had the ♣6 and was now high! Making four.

So it transpired that the Hummingbird had succeeded in putting their names up in lights after all. Smaller lights than might have been, thanks to the efforts of the Shoe, as they placed fifth overall. What disappointment there might have been was mitigated by the observation that they had beaten Joey and Eric by half a matchpoint. Coincidentally, half a matchpoint was all they had dropped in their head-to-head round, as some other lunatic had also collected 1700 on the second board.

There were lots of players with available rides, so the Shoe and the Bird did not have to hitchhike back. Just as well, perhaps, as I couldn't picture them explaining the two notrump cuebid to the onion truck driver.

9

The Shoe Finds Love

The Shoe had been sailing along beating up the bad players and learning from other talented rookies. It never really dawned on him to do anything to good players except to attempt to drive them crazy. It took a long while for him to realize he could actually beat good players by outplaying them.

Squeezes were a similar story. Early on, executing squeezes consisted simply of rattling off winners and waiting for the opponents to make a mistake. Still a great system today, claims the Shoe. He quotes one of the Bambino's hands from Kate's in support of his theory:

Dummy
♠ 6 2
♡ K J 10 7 4 2
♢ 5
♣ A 6 5 3

Bambino
♠ Q 9 7 4
♡ A Q 8 5 3
♢ A 10 2
♣ Q

The Bambino's own words tell this story much better than I ever could. His tone is one of perfect normalcy. He never even considers accounting for the potential matchpoint disaster that five hearts was cold.

"I opened the proceedings with one notrump and partner[2] raised to three notrump. He knows how well I play these contracts. The king of diamonds was led and I took the ace for want of anything better to do. Now what? I decided to run the hearts, crossing back and forth between my hand and the dummy so that each defender would have to discard first in turn. East was the first to feel the pinch. It turned out he had four clubs to the J1098 and he was religiously determined to guard them. He eventually pitched all his diamonds and kept ace and one spade.

"It came down to a six-card ending on the run of the hearts and West, uncertain about the diamond position, kept his three winners and had to guard the king of clubs. When I came off dummy with a spade, East rose with the ace, crashing his partner's now bare king. With the forced black-suit exit from East, I now had three spades for eleven tricks.

"Both defenders admitted that this was the first time they had felt the pressure of a simultaneous double pseudo-squeeze."

Everything changed when someone, probably the Victim, showed up at Kate's with a copy of Clyde E. Love's book on squeezes. The Shoe hated everything the book represented: counting, concentration and the complete absence of hilarity. He was forced to admit, however, that if he wanted to get better and to beat good players, it might well be useful to learn how to squeeze tricks out of them legitimately.

The first step was to absorb the idea of 'rectifying the count': simple squeezes only operated if you were trying for one extra trick and there were no free cards to discard. For this to work, you had to have lost all the tricks you could afford and one opponent had to be responsible for the outstanding guard in two suits. In other words, if you had eleven tricks in a slam needing twelve, you had to have lost a trick for the squeeze to operate. Losing the right number of tricks was called 'rectifying the count'.

Sometimes the opponents couldn't help but rectify the count for you, as on this deal where I was watching the Shoe play an undramatic partscore hand in three diamonds. The auction had been:

---

2. The anonymous word 'partner' spares my blushes. I can only say in mitigation that we were all very young. — Ed.

West	Half Bee	East	Shoe
		pass	1◊
1♡	2♣	pass	2◊
pass	3◊	all pass	

The Shoe had been lucky to avoid three notrump, as West had an entry to the hearts. This was the deal:

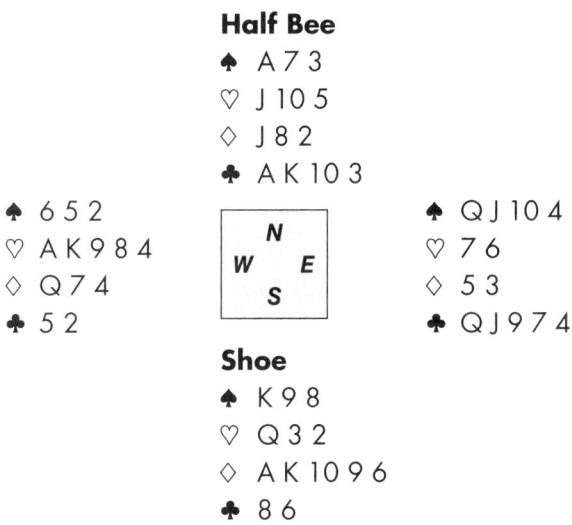

Half Bee
♠ A 7 3
♡ J 10 5
◊ J 8 2
♣ A K 10 3

♠ 6 5 2
♡ A K 9 8 4
◊ Q 7 4
♣ 5 2

♠ Q J 10 4
♡ 7 6
◊ 5 3
♣ Q J 9 7 4

Shoe
♠ K 9 8
♡ Q 3 2
◊ A K 10 9 6
♣ 8 6

West began with two high hearts and a third heart, trumped by East. East returned the ♣Q, won in dummy. Three rounds of diamonds put West in with the queen and rectified the count. East had to keep three clubs, so he discarded a club and a spade. The club return was won in dummy and a club was trumped, but the jack did not fall. This was the ending:

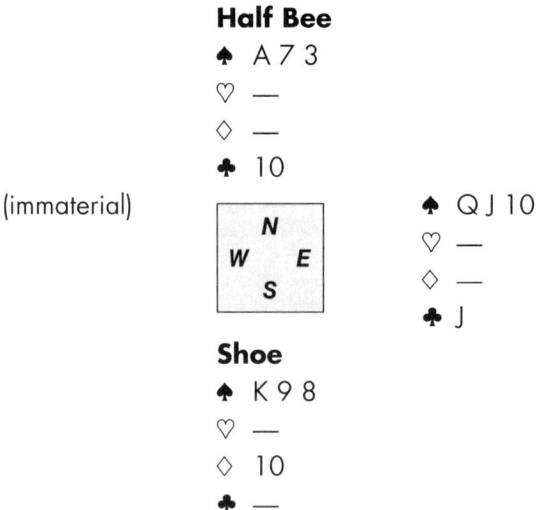

Half Bee
- ♠ A 7 3
- ♡ —
- ◇ —
- ♣ 10

(immaterial)

```
    N
W       E
    S
```

♠ Q J 10
♡ —
◇ —
♣ J

Shoe
- ♠ K 9 8
- ♡ —
- ◇ 10
- ♣ —

On the cash of the last trump, Shoe discarded a small spade from dummy. East had to keep the ♣J to cover dummy's ten, so he discarded a spade, hoping his partner had the nine. Since the Shoe had the ♠9, all three of his spades were high. The same kind of ending happens if East returns a spade after the heart ruff and West continues spades after he wins his trump queen. Then after the Shoe cashes the last trump, he has the ♠9 and two small clubs. Dummy has ♣AK10. East has to come to three cards, so he can't keep the high spade unless he gives up the club stopper.

All the elements were there for the simple squeeze on East: Shoe had lost four tricks and had eight winners. There were accessible threats in both black suits and only East could guard against them. The Shoe could reach all his threats and did not have to discard any threats before East.

Here's another simple squeeze from a slam hand:

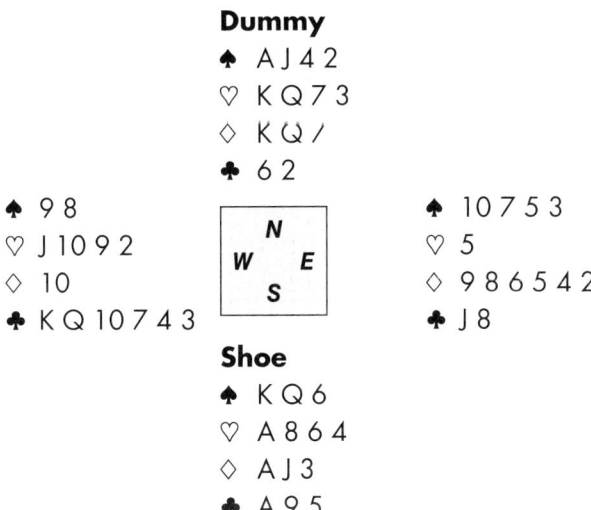

Dummy
♠ A J 4 2
♡ K Q 7 3
◇ K Q 7
♣ 6 2

♠ 9 8
♡ J 10 9 2
◇ 10
♣ K Q 10 7 4 3

♠ 10 7 5 3
♡ 5
◇ 9 8 6 5 4 2
♣ J 8

Shoe
♠ K Q 6
♡ A 8 6 4
◇ A J 3
♣ A 9 5

The Shoe arrives in six notrump after a club preempt by West, and receives the lead of the ♣K. He is happy to discover that he has twelve tricks if the hearts behave. Just in case they fail to break, he ducks the opening lead to rectify the count. Whatever West continues, Shoe wins and cashes the ♣A, leaving West solely responsible for the clubs. Now if West has the four hearts (unlikely, it's true), there will be a squeeze. Shoe runs his winners. With the lead in dummy and one spade yet to be cashed, this is the position:

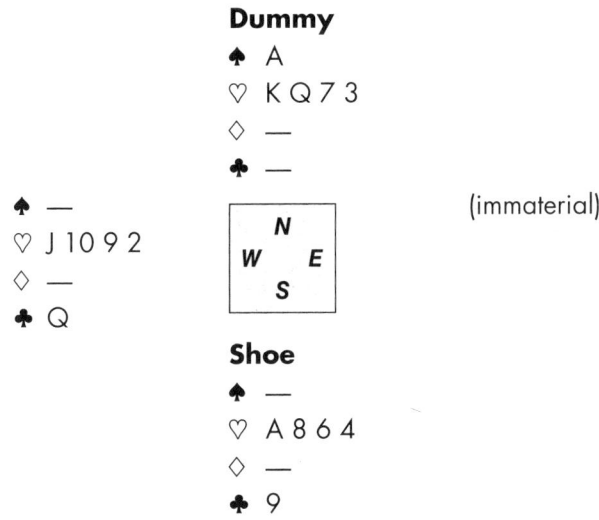

Dummy
♠ A
♡ K Q 7 3
◇ —
♣ —

♠ —
♡ J 10 9 2
◇ —
♣ Q

(immaterial)

Shoe
♠ —
♡ A 8 6 4
◇ —
♣ 9

On the cash of the last spade from dummy, discarding a small heart from the closed hand, West must discard either the master club or one of his four hearts, both with the same effect of giving Shoe the twelfth trick. I have the nerve to point out to the Shoe that this was not such a difficult hand.

The Shoe admonishes me: "Bungalow, watch what happens if you don't rectify the count." If you win the first club trick, this becomes the end position:

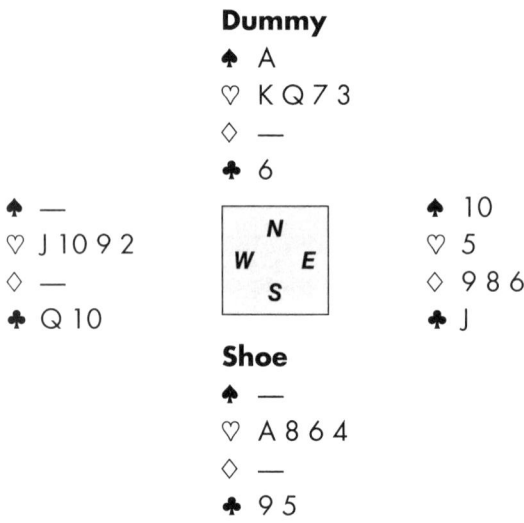

Dummy
♠ A
♡ K Q 7 3
◇ —
♣ 6

♠ —
♡ J 10 9 2
◇ —
♣ Q 10

♠ 10
♡ 5
◇ 9 8 6
♣ J

Shoe
♠ —
♡ A 8 6 4
◇ —
♣ 9 5

"On the spade ace I again pitch a small heart and my fate is now entirely up to West. If West is up to the pitch of the queen of clubs, as he should be, you can split the clubs 1-1, but East will be in to cash three diamonds. Alternately, you can try the hearts and go one down. Of course, Bungalow, now that you are an expert on squeezes, you would know that had LHO led a suit other than clubs, you would have won and responded by ducking a club in both hands, to rectify the count. Right?"

The Shoe is keeping it simple for me, but after the game we are joined by the usual crowd at Fran's Restaurant: the Hummingbird, Colonel Bulldozer, the Owl and the Snowman. The Owl had finally got to visit Israel, but having returned, has reassumed his role as principal terrorizer of older ladies at Kate's. The Shoe impresses on everyone that their bridge game should be aiming for something a little more glorious and legitimate.

As usual, he is drawing hands on the tablecloth, in pencil of course, so that he can't be accused of out-and-out vandalism. The squeeze seminar kicks off with something still simple, but complicated enough to be interesting. The Shoe starts to describe handling this deal in three notrump, playing matchpoints:

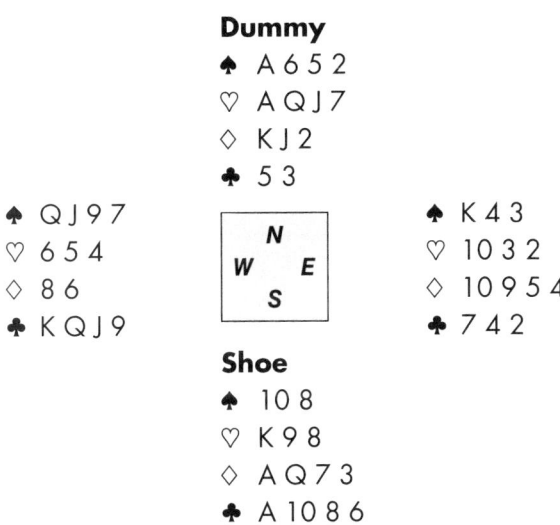

Dummy
♠ A 6 5 2
♡ A Q J 7
◇ K J 2
♣ 5 3

♠ Q J 9 7   ♠ K 4 3
♡ 6 5 4   ♡ 10 3 2
◇ 8 6   ◇ 10 9 5 4
♣ K Q J 9   ♣ 7 4 2

Shoe
♠ 10 8
♡ K 9 8
◇ A Q 7 3
♣ A 10 8 6

"Okay, this is Squeezes 101, or maybe just Matchpoints 101 against bad opponents. West leads the king of clubs and you can see that you have ten top tricks with little chance for trick number eleven. East plays the deuce of clubs and you duck in the closed hand. This gives you two chances: on a second high club, you will duck again and hope that a third round of clubs will make your club ten into the eleventh trick. The other chance is that LHO will do something foolish and that you can wind up gaining a trick by way of a squeeze.

"On this hand, 'something foolish' constitutes a shift to a low spade, the seven to be exact, which is what happened at the table. You consult your trusty Rule of Eleven to discover that RHO, East, has only one spade higher than the seven, so you duck in dummy to force him to use it up. Now you have rectified the count for a squeeze on West, provided he started with ♠QJ9 and ♣KQJ, or any five-card club suit. All you have to do is to win the ace of whatever black suit East returns and run your red tricks, making sure you end up in the hand whose black ace has been *removed* (so that the threat card whose entry has been removed remains accessible). West has the high card in that suit and the only guard in the other suit, a simple squeeze that is called a Vienna Coup. For example, on a club back, you win the ace and run red tricks ending in the closed hand. With one diamond to cash, the ending becomes:

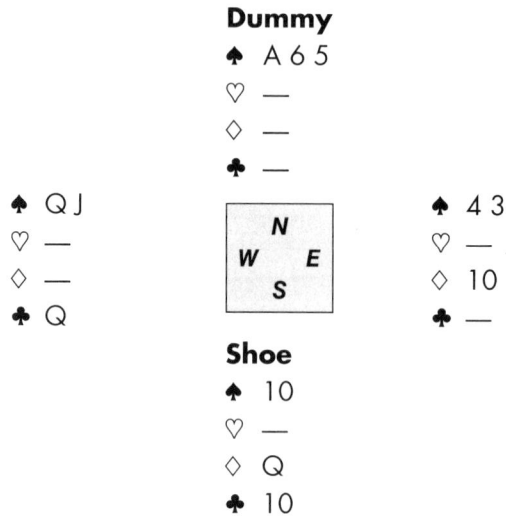

Dummy
♠ A 6 5
♡ —
♢ —
♣ —

♠ Q J
♡ —
♢ —
♣ Q

♠ 4 3
♡ —
♢ 10
♣ —

Shoe
♠ 10
♡ —
♢ Q
♣ 10

"Whichever black card West pitches on the queen of diamonds, declarer will make two tricks in the black suits: if it's a spade, the last two spades in dummy are high, and if it's a club, declarer scores the ten of clubs and then the ace of spades. This was probably hard to picture until the Rule of Eleven alerted you to the possibility that your six of spades in dummy was actually high."

The people who were waiting for the punch line are disappointed, but there are a few admiring murmurs nevertheless. The Shoe goes on to explain that he has a personal theory that the name 'Vienna Coup' arose because Vienna was the first place where you could get high but never have any fun with it. Now the people waiting for the punch line are regretting that they got what they wished for.

"Of course if you are defending, you will try to foil rectifying the count." Another deal is pencilled onto the table cloth:

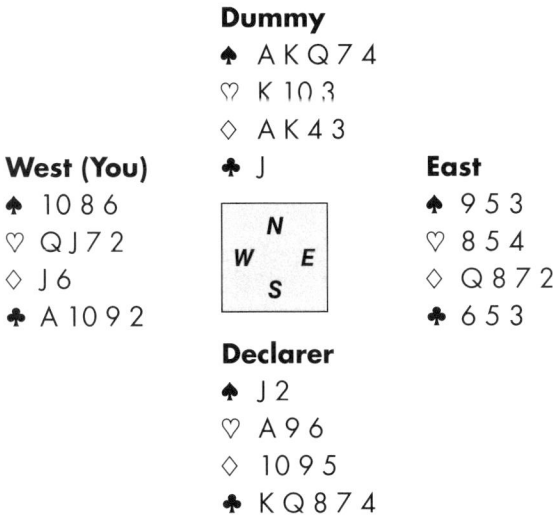

Dummy
♠ A K Q 7 4
♡ K 10 3
◇ A K 4 3
♣ J

West (You)
♠ 10 8 6
♡ Q J 7 2
◇ J 6
♣ A 10 9 2

East
♠ 9 5 3
♡ 8 5 4
◇ Q 8 7 2
♣ 6 5 3

Declarer
♠ J 2
♡ A 9 6
◇ 10 9 5
♣ K Q 8 7 4

"Your nasty, aggressive opponents have reached six notrump redoubled, so you'd better be setting this. Declarer wins your opening spade lead in dummy and tables the jack of clubs, which you duck. Now comes a spade to the jack and the king of clubs. You'd better be ducking this, or you've rectified the count for a heart-club squeeze against yourself. Once you duck, declarer can no longer cash the tricks in a way that lets him make it. His best ending is:

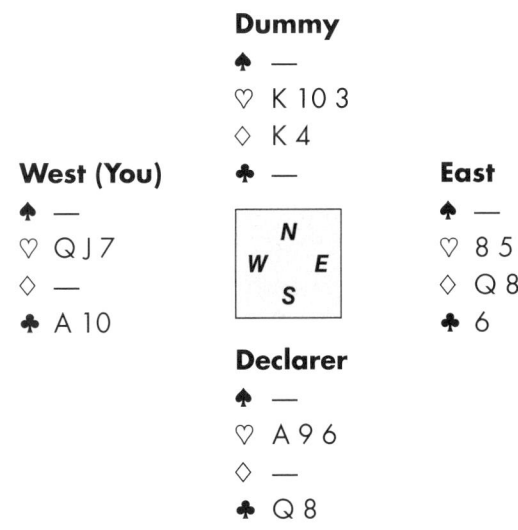

Dummy
♠ —
♡ K 10 3
◇ K 4
♣ —

West (You)
♠ —
♡ Q J 7
◇ —
♣ A 10

East
♠ —
♡ 8 5
◇ Q 8
♣ 6

Declarer
♠ —
♡ A 9 6
◇ —
♣ Q 8

"Now on the final diamond cash from dummy, you can spare the ten of clubs when declarer pitches a heart. He's in the wrong hand to drive out your club ace. He now needs two hand entries, one to drive out the club ace and one to get back to cash the good club, and he only has one.

"Naturally, that was not how it happened in real life. I was actually the nasty overbidding declarer, with the Hummingbird, light years ahead of the curve when it comes to squeezes, on my left and the Victim, world's greatest poker player, on my right. Everything developed as expected, so there was going to be no squeeze and I was all set to go one down when, on the last spade, the Victim threw the six of clubs!

"Now the ending was:

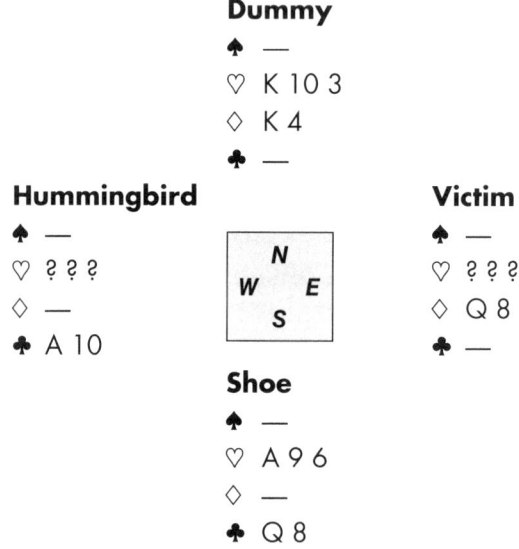

Dummy
♠ —
♡ K 10 3
♢ K 4
♣ —

Hummingbird
♠ —
♡ ? ? ?
♢ —
♣ A 10

Victim
♠ —
♡ ? ? ?
♢ Q 8
♣ —

Shoe
♠ —
♡ A 9 6
♢ —
♣ Q 8

"Could the squeeze be on again?? I could now play king and a diamond and if the Bird was to be trusted for his squeeze-avoidance technique and hold the queen and jack of hearts, execute a suicide squeeze by playing king and a diamond, pitching a heart and a club from my hand. In the three-card ending, the Bird would have to keep four cards: the ace of clubs and three hearts to the queen-jack. They could no longer cash the ace of clubs if I played two rounds of diamonds.

"However, I was supposed to be a good player now, so I forced myself to reconsider. Was it not an insult to the Victim's intelligence to assume he had reinstated the squeeze by pitching his club? What was the Victim doing?

"I was forced to reject the possibility of split heart honors, as the Victim would know to keep Qx or Jx of hearts and a club over to the ace, so two rounds of diamonds would not work for me. To have kept three hearts, the Victim *must* have held ♡QJx. I had been playing the wrong squeeze all along! This was to be a strip squeeze on the Victim.

"Accordingly, I played king and a diamond and pitched both my clubs while the Bird threw a heart and the ten of clubs. The Victim led the jack of hearts, just as good players do when they are endplayed into breaking the heart suit. This was the ending, with the jack of hearts led:

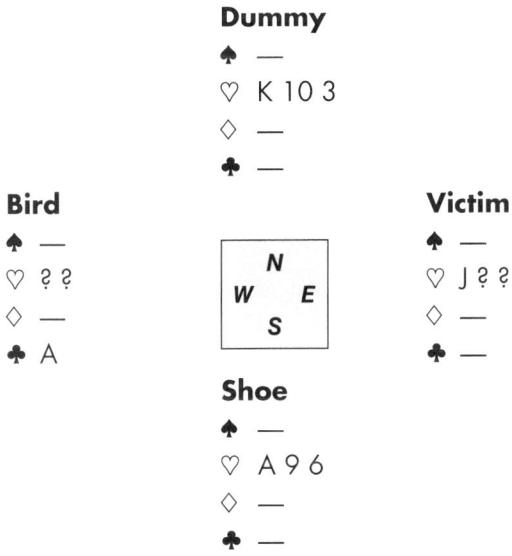

Dummy
♠ —
♡ K 10 3
♢ —
♣ —

Bird
♠ —
♡ ? ?
♢ —
♣ A

Victim
♠ —
♡ J ? ?
♢ —
♣ —

Shoe
♠ —
♡ A 9 6
♢ —
♣ —

"My flawless analysis allowed me to let the heart ride to dummy and finesse the nine on the way back, claiming. Then, the Bird won the queen of hearts and cashed the club ace for two down. After the hand, the Victim cheerfully announced he'd never have tried that play against Mrs. Whaley, who would have just played for split honors, but with a squeeze-obsessed Shoe, he just had to try it. Did I mention that the Victim is the best poker player in the world? Even at bridge.

"Of course, squeezes will not work if you have to pitch your threat card before the person you are squeezing. At least, they're not supposed to. I was playing in a National Individual, where strange happenings are commonplace, bemoaning my low score. The only good thing that had happened was that they were throwing a cocktail party between sessions. The Victim walked over and bet me that I hadn't been fixed as badly as he had.

"Apparently, the Victim had been sitting there minding his own business, defending game after game and gleaning whatever matchpoints the opponents might chance to throw his way before his partner had a chance to throw them back. The opponents reached three notrump and he was happy to be dealt a hand that looked as though most of the defensive decisions would be his:

♠ Q 10 5 2   ♡ Q 10 8 4   ◇ 7 2   ♣ A K 6

"As is often the case with players who cannot decide which of two equal suits to lead, he led neither. The neutral diamond lead turned out to be a very good one as the whole deal was:

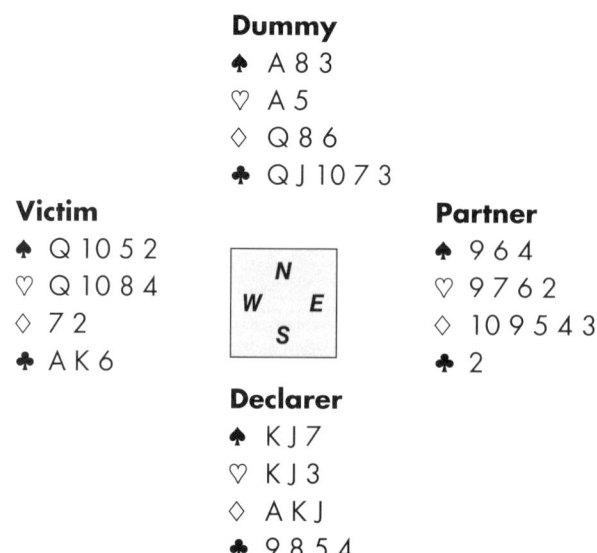

Dummy
♠ A 8 3
♡ A 5
◇ Q 8 6
♣ Q J 10 7 3

Victim
♠ Q 10 5 2
♡ Q 10 8 4
◇ 7 2
♣ A K 6

Partner
♠ 9 6 4
♡ 9 7 6 2
◇ 10 9 5 4 3
♣ 2

Declarer
♠ K J 7
♡ K J 3
◇ A K J
♣ 9 8 5 4

"Obviously, on a major-suit lead, declarer has eleven top tricks after she drives out the ace and king of clubs. Even with this great lead, declarer has a good chance of pseudo-squeezing the Victim's partner, who must keep all three spades to the nine.

"The play proceeded carefully, with declarer, a sweet elderly lady, winning the diamond king in the closed hands and leading clubs. The Victim worked out that with declarer's 16-18 notrump, there was no room for partner to have as much as a jack, so he cashed the two high clubs and exited safely in a minor, making certain that he did not give back the trick he had saved on opening lead. Declarer became increasingly suspicious that the major-suit queens were offside, given the curious defense. She watched the pitches on the club suit like a hawk, facing all the cards again as the fifth club was due to be led from dummy. Then it was on to the cash of the major-suit aces and finally, the diamond queen, declarer playing the jack.

"It was now a three-card ending and the Victim had to pitch from queen-ten in each major. Since declarer was marked with both major-suit kings and both major-suit jacks, he had expected to see a jack that would help his decision. While he pondered this miserable problem, declarer suddenly discovered that she still had four cards remaining! Somehow, she had managed not to discard on the fifth club trick. The director was called and he was not impressed with the morality of the situation. He ruled that the hand must be completed as it was. Thus, this became the position, with the Victim still to discard:

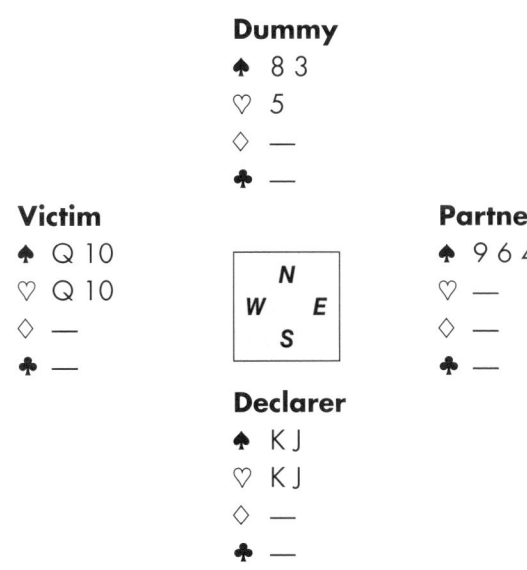

Dummy
♠ 8 3
♡ 5
♢ —
♣ —

Victim
♠ Q 10
♡ Q 10
♢ —
♣ —

Partner
♠ 9 6 4
♡ —
♢ —
♣ —

Declarer
♠ K J
♡ K J
♢ —
♣ —

"After the Victim discarded the ten of spades, declarer could cash both major-suit kings to decide which jack was good. So declarer came to eleven tricks like everyone else, on a hand where there was never a squeeze because declarer would have had to discard her threat card before the Victim had to choose. She saw how disappointed the Victim looked and consoled him with, 'Never mind that I had two chances at it. It made no difference. After you discarded the ten of spades, I would have guessed it anyhow.' The Victim assured her firmly that he was a masochist and that she should stop spoiling his fun."

The squeezes could be more complicated, of course. The Shoe continues his dissertation, a fairly interesting one, actually, by drawing out this deal:

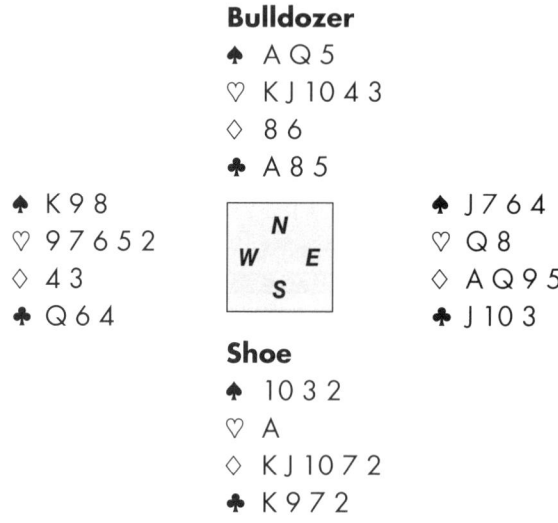

Bulldozer
♠ A Q 5
♡ K J 10 4 3
♢ 8 6
♣ A 8 5

♠ K 9 8
♡ 9 7 6 5 2
♢ 4 3
♣ Q 6 4

♠ J 7 6 4
♡ Q 8
♢ A Q 9 5
♣ J 10 3

Shoe
♠ 10 3 2
♡ A
♢ K J 10 7 2
♣ K 9 7 2

"It is best not to ask how I got to be declarer without a spade stopper," he said. "Bulldozer is very polite about letting me play notrump. He thinks that I hypnotize the opponents and this hand did nothing to change that impression. My own theory is much simpler: they don't know how to defend notrump.

"The opening heart lead went around to my singleton ace, with East gratuitously contributing the queen. For want of something better to do, I led a club to the eight, which won the trick! East probably thought I'd called the ace. I've made the same mistake myself. Now I tried the eight of diamonds from dummy, covered by the nine and won in my hand with the jack. A club over to the ace and another diamond down successfully won the ten after East ducked again after some hesitation. Since East hadn't opened the bidding and had already showed up with the queen of hearts, the ace-queen of diamonds and a mystery honor in clubs, he couldn't have the king of spades. I took that successful finesse.

"Then I cashed dummy's three high hearts, pitching my king of diamonds and my ten of spades. East parted with the jack of clubs and queen of diamonds. So here I was, on a hand where nine tricks would be tough, having taken the first nine tricks and looking for a squeeze in the four-card ending:

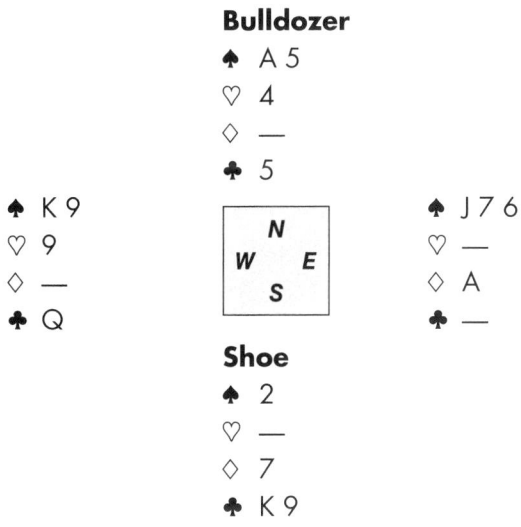

Bulldozer
♠ A 5
♡ 4
◇ —
♣ 5

♠ K 9   ♠ J 7 6
♡ 9   ♡ —
◇ —   ◇ A
♣ Q   ♣ —

Shoe
♠ 2
♡ —
◇ 7
♣ K 9

"On the club to the king, East could spare a spade. On the cash of the nine of clubs, West finally came into the play. He had to keep his nine of hearts to beat dummy's four, so the spade pitch brought him down to one spade. I pitched dummy's now-superfluous four of hearts, and East had a similar problem as he had to keep the ace of diamonds to cover my seven. With the spades now dividing 1-1, dummy's ace and five of spades took the last two tricks. Making seven was the surprise result.

"There *is* such a thing as a simple double squeeze," intones the Shoe. He is forced to buy a round of beer to stop the audience from mutinying. "Imagine that you miss your 4-4 heart fit because East opened one heart, a five-card major. Instead you arrive in the equally disastrous three notrump as South:

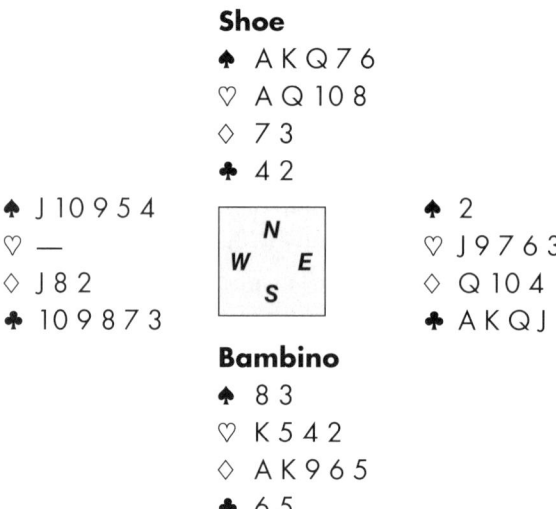

Shoe
- ♠ A K Q 7 6
- ♡ A Q 10 8
- ◇ 7 3
- ♣ 4 2

West:
- ♠ J 10 9 5 4
- ♡ —
- ◇ J 8 2
- ♣ 10 9 8 7 3

East:
- ♠ 2
- ♡ J 9 7 6 3
- ◇ Q 10 4
- ♣ A K Q J

Bambino
- ♠ 8 3
- ♡ K 5 4 2
- ◇ A K 9 6 5
- ♣ 6 5

"The ten of clubs is led. Fortunately, the clubs block, so East can only cash four of them. As you are by now well aware, that rectifies the count, as the Bambino has eight winners. He pitches a low spade and a low heart from the dummy, and two small diamonds from his hand. East exits with the two of spades, taken in dummy.

"Bambino comes to the king of hearts and then returns to the ace of hearts in dummy, producing this ending:

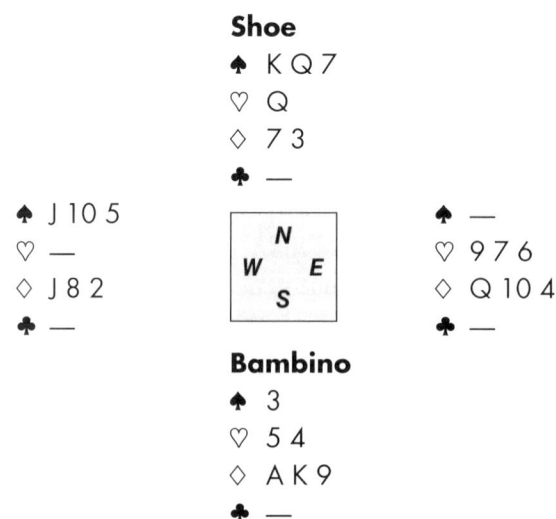

Shoe
- ♠ K Q 7
- ♡ Q
- ◇ 7 3
- ♣ —

West:
- ♠ J 10 5
- ♡ —
- ◇ J 8 2
- ♣ —

East:
- ♠ —
- ♡ 9 7 6
- ◇ Q 10 4
- ♣ —

Bambino
- ♠ 3
- ♡ 5 4
- ◇ A K 9
- ♣ —

"When the queen of hearts is cashed, West must keep all three spades to guard against that suit in dummy, so he is forced to come down to a doubleton diamond. Now, cashing the king and queen of spades does the same thing to East: he has to keep a heart above Bambino's five, and therefore has to let go a diamond in the three-card ending. Now Bambino can finally pitch the five of hearts: its job is done. The remaining diamonds split 2-2 and three notrump makes. Sound the applause.

"Okay, one last double squeeze before the beer runs out. It's a little tougher, to show you it's not a mystery. I arrived in my normal contract of three notrump, where I received the lead of the ◇4 on this layout:

Dummy
♠ K Q J 7
♡ 5 4
◇ A J 8 6 3
♣ Q 6

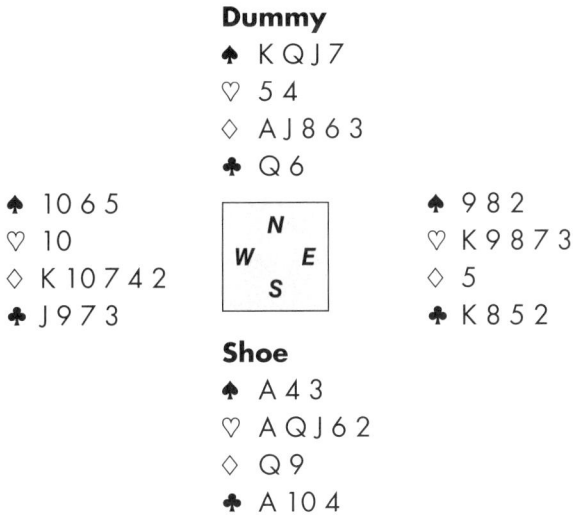

♠ 10 6 5
♡ 10
◇ K 10 7 4 2
♣ J 9 7 3

♠ 9 8 2
♡ K 9 8 7 3
◇ 5
♣ K 8 5 2

Shoe
♠ A 4 3
♡ A Q J 6 2
◇ Q 9
♣ A 10 4

"I won the five with the queen, preserving dummy entries. Next came the nine of diamonds to the jack, East showing out with a high club. The heart finessse succeeded and it was back to dummy with a high spade for a second successful heart finesse, West pitching a low club. There were now eleven top tricks, three in each red suit, four spades and a club. The stage was set for a squeeze, except I had yet to lose a trick. You remember all about rectifying the count by now. Out I go with the two of hearts, discarding a diamond from dummy and won perforce by East with the three. Ironic, to lose twelve tricks at notrump and to win your only trick with a three. I won the spade return in the closed hand with the ace. Take it away, Bungalow."

That was a rude awakening for me. As I recall, the Shoe claimed, stating that the clubs were going to be 1-1. That announcement produced howls of outrage from both opponents. West insisted that he had two clubs remaining while East topped that as he had three. The Shoe was a little embarrassed by the misunderstanding and diagrammed the four-card ending after he cashes the ♡A pitching dummy's ♣Q, then comes to dummy with a spade:

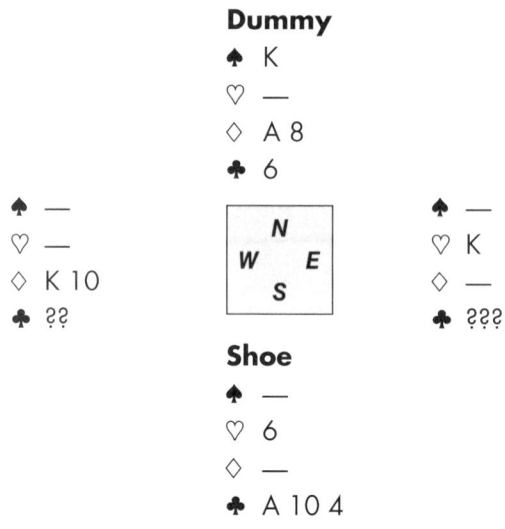

Dummy
♠ K
♡ —
◇ A 8
♣ 6

♠ —
♡ —
◇ K 10
♣ ??

♠ —
♡ K
◇ —
♣ ???

Shoe
♠ —
♡ 6
◇ —
♣ A 10 4

On the cash of the last spade, East must keep a heart, so discards a club, coming down to two. Declarer pitches the ♣10. West must keep two diamonds to guard against the ace-eight in dummy, so comes down to one club. Now, when dummy cashes the diamond ace, East must still keep a high heart to guard against declarer's six of hearts, so comes down to a singleton club. Declarer finally pitches the ♡6, and makes the last two tricks with clubs breaking 1-1.

The opponents were suspicious that they had been conned into revealing their club holdings to the Shoe: no amount of explaining could console them. So, the moral of the story is: if you become this good at squeezing, please resist the urge to do it in public.

10

The Kibitzer Sees Most of the Game

People often ask me why I kibitz the Shoe. Almost as often, they include their own answer with words like 'lunatic'. I prefer to think of it as imagination. Also, the Shoe always stokes my ego machine, introducing me to bridge players as the inventor of the Winning Butterfly and holding me responsible if said butterfly fails to make an appearance.

On a good day with the Shoe, things start with the impossible and get better from there. You will often see him land in a perfectly ridiculous three notrump and hypnotize the opponents. This deal is typical:

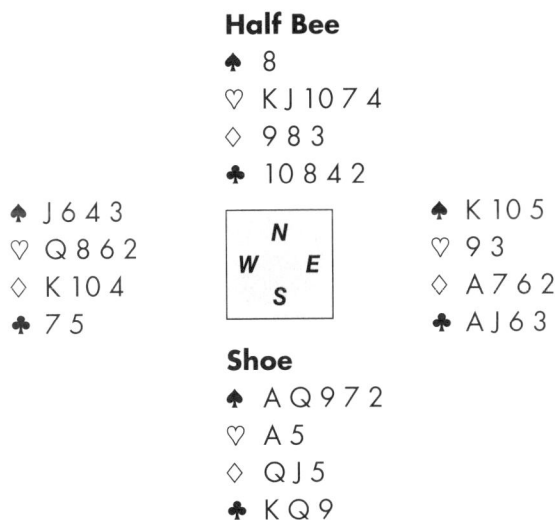

Half Bee
- ♠ 8
- ♡ K J 10 7 4
- ◇ 9 8 3
- ♣ 10 8 4 2

West:
- ♠ J 6 4 3
- ♡ Q 8 6 2
- ◇ K 10 4
- ♣ 7 5

East:
- ♠ K 10 5
- ♡ 9 3
- ◇ A 7 6 2
- ♣ A J 6 3

Shoe
- ♠ A Q 9 7 2
- ♡ A 5
- ◇ Q J 5
- ♣ K Q 9

LHO led the ♡2 and Shoe thanked the Half Bee politely, usually a sign that he's going down. Shoe had no choice but to win the ♡A to unblock the suit. Then he successfully finessed the ♡J in the dummy.

Hearts were not about to run, but I was puzzled to see him abandon the ♡K in dummy. That's why I'm Bungalow Bill, humble kibitzer, and he's the Shoe. Next came the ♣10, trying to induce a cover with the jack. RHO obliged. The ♣Q and ♣K won the next two tricks. The ♣9 was also ducked with LHO discarding a spade. Getting out for one down was beginning to look like a possibility, but were the opponents ever going to win a trick? Shoe tried the ♢Q and that, too, held the trick.

The Shoe did not look puzzled for more than an instant and continued with the ♢J. Maybe this would also win? LHO spoiled that possibility by winning the king to shift to the last remaining suit, spades. Shoe won RHO's king with the ace. Now the exit with a low diamond went to LHO's ten. RHO was determined never to win a trick, declining to overtake. This was the four-card ending:

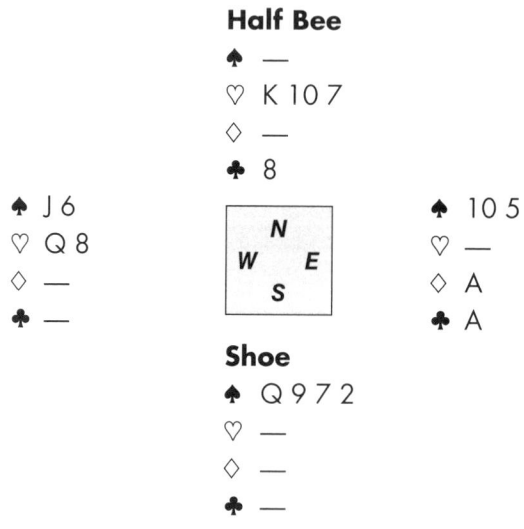

Half Bee
♠ —
♡ K 10 7
♢ —
♣ 8

♠ J 6
♡ Q 8
♢ —
♣ —

♠ 10 5
♡ —
♢ A
♣ A

Shoe
♠ Q 9 7 2
♡ —
♢ —
♣ —

LHO led the ♠J, the club went from dummy and Shoe ducked! Mystery solved: suddenly, I realized why the Shoe had abandoned the heart suit. LHO now had to yield either three tricks to dummy's hearts or three tricks to the Shoe's spades. A low spade from the jack was no better at Trick 10, as Shoe would win RHO's ten and exit a spade to LHO for the heart endplay. Making ten tricks had the Shoe observing (aloud, of course) that it was a pity LHO didn't have the ♠10 and RHO the jack. Then the ♠10 at Trick 10 might have been overtaken by RHO, which would have permitted the Shoe to make five.

Here was another unlikely result from the finals of some Regional knockout that the Shoe was winning with the Bambino. The layout was:

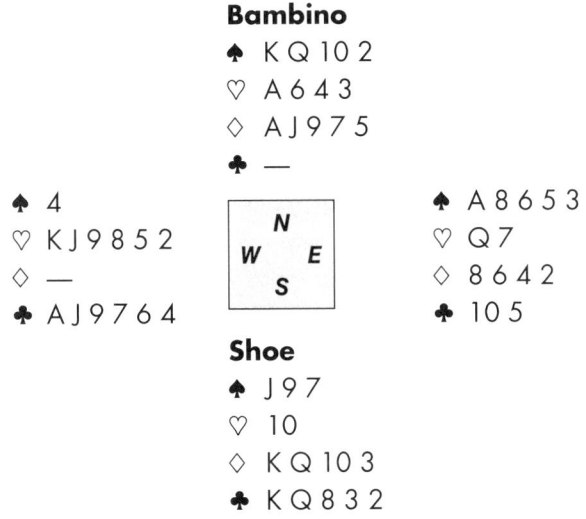

Bambino
- ♠ K Q 10 2
- ♡ A 6 4 3
- ◇ A J 9 7 5
- ♣ —

Shoe
- ♠ J 9 7
- ♡ 10
- ◇ K Q 10 3
- ♣ K Q 8 3 2

West:
- ♠ 4
- ♡ K J 9 8 5 2
- ◇ —
- ♣ A J 9 7 6 4

East:
- ♠ A 8 6 5 3
- ♡ Q 7
- ◇ 8 6 4 2
- ♣ 10 5

No one was vulnerable, and at the other table the result had been a mundane four diamonds doubled making five for minus 610. The result was only mundane because five diamonds was always making and four spades might even make, so the loss against par was about 3 IMPs. At the Shoe's table, however, the auction went:

LHO	Bambino	RHO	Shoe
1♡	dbl	pass	2♡
3♣	4♣	pass	4◇
pass	4♡	pass	4♠
pass	5◇	pass	6◇
all pass			

The opening lead of the ♡8 went to the ace and the Shoe immediately ruffed a heart. Then he tried the ◇K and LHO showed out, so he continued with the ♣K, covered with the ace, and trumped in dummy. Next came a low spade, won by the ace on the right. On the club return, Shoe won the queen, pitching a heart. Then it was a simple matter to travel to dummy on spades, trump the last remaining heart, draw trumps and claim. Making six was +920, win 7 IMPs.

Sometimes, the enjoyable plays can be so insignificant that you hardly even notice them. Playing with the Albatross, who is well known for paying close attention, albeit sometimes to the detriment of the score, the Shoe picked up:

♠ Q 9 6 2   ♡ Q 10 3   ◇ A 8 2   ♣ 10 6 2

The auction proceeded:

Shoe	LHO	Albatross	RHO
	1◇	pass	1♡
pass	2◇	pass	2♠
pass	3♣	dbl	3NT
all pass			

The Shoe obediently began with the ♣2, which showed either a singleton or three or more. Shoe would have led a high card from the same holding had partner not doubled. Dummy appeared with:

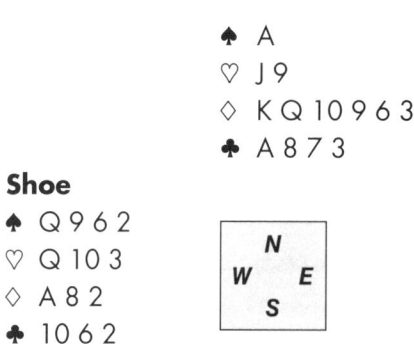

Dummy played low to the first trick and the Albatross won the queen as declarer contributed the five. The Albatross returned the ♠8 to dummy's singleton ace. The ♠8 probably showed four spades headed by no more than the ten or jack. Shoe contributed the deuce of spades, discouraging. Declarer led a heart to the king and then a diamond to the ten and the Albatross's jack. The Albatross went into a considerable study and finally placed the ♣K on the table. That killed the dummy and declarer was held to seven tricks.

The Shoe seemed inordinately proud of this result and, sure enough, most pairs had made three notrump. I asked the Shoe what had happened and he pointed out that the ♠2 had been the important play on the hand. Any encouraging spade would get an over-imaginative partner like the Albatross to picture declarer with something like

♠ Q 9 4 2   ♡ A K Q 10   ◇ 5   ♣ J 10 8 5

Now a high club return would give declarer the contract. You have to help the Albatross picture that declarer bid three notrump on ♣J5 and that your lead was from three clubs, not a singleton. If partner returns a spade, declarer would jump up with the king and make the hand by continuing diamonds. This was the entire deal:

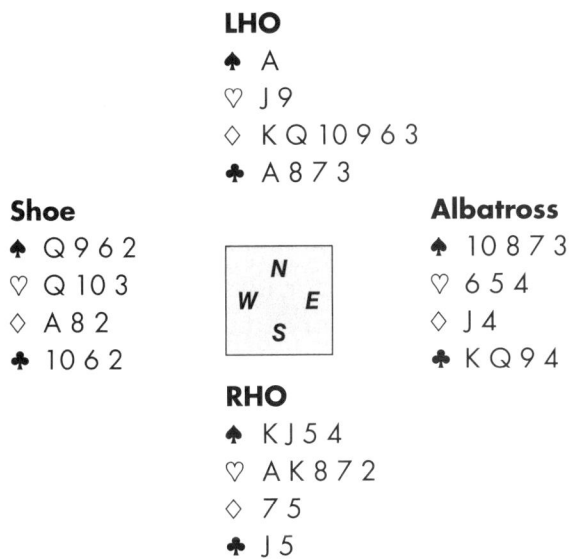

LHO
♠ A
♡ J 9
◇ K Q 10 9 6 3
♣ A 8 7 3

Shoe
♠ Q 9 6 2
♡ Q 10 3
◇ A 8 2
♣ 10 6 2

Albatross
♠ 10 8 7 3
♡ 6 5 4
◇ J 4
♣ K Q 9 4

RHO
♠ K J 5 4
♡ A K 8 7 2
◇ 7 5
♣ J 5

Sometimes, there is the sheer joy of watching a play that might never have occurred to you. Here's a simple example from a team game: Shoe and the Bambino reached three notrump on an auction that began with two notrump from the Shoe. It was a single dummy problem on the lead of a spade.

Bambino
♠ A 6 3
♡ K 10 8 5 3
◇ 10 4
♣ 7 4 2

Shoe
♠ K Q 8
♡ Q 9
◇ A K 5 3
♣ A K 6 5

After a brief study, the Shoe won the opening lead in hand, led the ♡9 and floated it! That lost to the jack and ten tricks were easy after the ♡Q was overtaken to drive out the ace. The Shoe was quick to point out that only two heart tricks were required to ensure the contract. The play of the ♡9, counter-intuitive though it appeared, had been the only play to guarantee two heart tricks even if the nine were allowed to win, given there was only one dummy entry.

Maybe my favorite hand that I kibitzed was simpler. The problem was to see it. It was in some nondescript Swiss tournament where the Shoe and the Hummingbird were well on the way to losing. The Shoe picked up:

♠ A K Q 4   ♡ A J 9   ◇ A 4 3   ♣ A 8 7

Just to illustrate how things had gone so far, on this hand the other team's pair had opened the 22 HCP hand with one notrump (16-18 HCP). They had no trouble raking in seven tricks opposite partner's ♡Q. The Shoe, on the other hand, opened two clubs and rebid two notrump over a negative two diamond response. The Bird bid the second negative (pass) and the auction died at an uninspiring two notrump. LHO led the ♠2 and this was the deal:

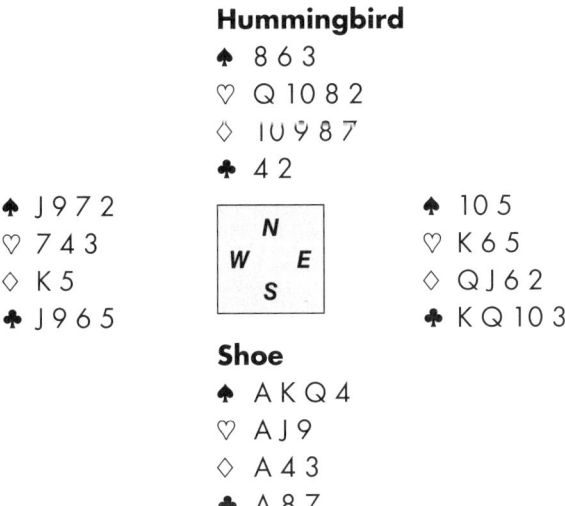

Hummingbird
♠ 8 6 3
♡ Q 10 8 2
◊ 10 9 8 7
♣ 4 2

♠ J 9 7 2
♡ 7 4 3
◊ K 5
♣ J 9 6 5

♠ 10 5
♡ K 6 5
◊ Q J 6 2
♣ K Q 10 3

Shoe
♠ A K Q 4
♡ A J 9
◊ A 4 3
♣ A 8 7

The Shoe refused to be as depressed as the prospects seemed to be. He needed three heart tricks, but the opponents could duck the heart suit out of existence. He studied for more than his usual thirty seconds, then turned to me and said "It's on a finesse." I couldn't see what he was talking about.

He then played the ♡J and overtook it with dummy's queen! RHO was helpless. In the actual event, he ducked and Shoe finessed the ♡9 on the way back to score eight tricks. It was delightful to see Shoe's partners' surprise when it turned out they had won an IMP on this board. A small reward on the scoresheet, but for me, this was a winner of the coveted Bungalow Bill Miller Seal of Approval.

Another partscore hand was a close second. The Shoe had gotten mightily annoyed with some play or other that the Half Bee had or had not made, so on the next hand, he opened three diamonds holding:

♠ Q 9 8   ♡ 6   ◊ K 3 2   ♣ A K J 8 6 2

His LHO overcalled a smooth three hearts, and when this was passed to him, the Shoe had not calmed down enough to pass it out. Instead he balanced with three spades, which went all pass.

This was the entire deal, on the lead of the ♡A:

Half Bee
♠ K 10 6 4
♡ J 9 3 2
◇ 9 6 5 4
♣ 10

♠ A 5
♡ A K Q 10 4
◇ J 8 7
♣ Q 9 5

```
      N
  W       E
      S
```

♠ J 7 3 2
♡ 8 7 5
◇ A Q 10
♣ 7 4 3

Shoe
♠ Q 9 8
♡ 6
◇ K 3 2
♣ A K J 8 6 2

It is obvious that the Shoe had lost it once too often. The prospects were not good, as it looked as though the opponents made about +90 in notrump, or an assortment of minuses if they bid on, while the Shoe made two or three clubs. Any minus was a near bottom, so how was he going to make the hand? I could see the ◇A was onside. LHO held most of the rest of the cards. The Shoe trumped the second round of hearts and smoothly tried the ♣6 toward the ten!

LHO found the "automatic" duck so the ten won — Trick #2. Next came a diamond from dummy, won by RHO with the ace. The crafty ◇10 was returned, won by the king, Trick #3. Two high clubs got rid of the remaining diamonds in dummy (Tricks #4 and #5). Now, a low diamond ruff survived in dummy and was followed by a heart ruff (Tricks #6 and #7) as everyone showed in. This was the ending:

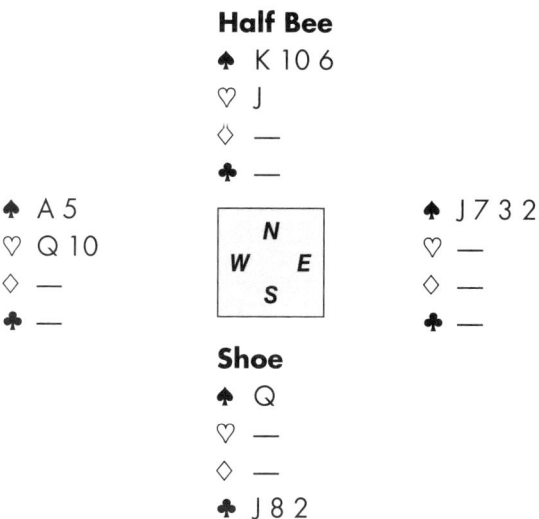

Half Bee
♠ K 10 6
♡ J
♢ —
♣ —

♠ A 5　　　　　　　　　　　♠ J 7 3 2
♡ Q 10　　　　　　　　　　 ♡ —
♢ —　　　　　　　　　　　　♢ —
♣ —　　　　　　　　　　　　♣ —

Shoe
♠ Q
♡ —
♢ —
♣ J 8 2

This turned out to be an interesting hand. Neither opponent had yet showed out, so LHO had two spades and two hearts remaining. RHO had four spades. Too bad Shoe was trumping good clubs, so when RHO overruffed, he had an obligatory trump return that ensured three losers.

However, Shoe suddenly became sharply focused, as he seemed to be performing some detailed numerical calculation, possibly adding up the federal budget deficit. There was a display of impatience by the opponents, which the Shoe greeted with a big smile. Finally, Shoe triumphantly led another good club and trumped with the *king* of spades (Trick #8). After a heart ruff back to the closed hand, nine tricks were in, and they had another top board, as at the other tables, pairs their way had made two clubs or had gone one down in three.

Shoe did not have time to notice the score, as he was busy explaining the hand to LHO: "You see, you had to have at least one high spade or I can't make the hand. What I didn't know was whether you had the ace of spades or the jack, I just knew you had to have at least one of them. So, if I trump the club with the ten of spades and your partner has the jack, he overtrumps and returns a spade to your ace. Then you get to cash the queen of hearts and I go down. However, if I trump with the king of spades, even if your partner overtrumps and returns a spade, I win the queen and still have the ten of spades in the dummy."

Just like the Hideous Hog before him, Shoe grabs a cocktail napkin and draws out:

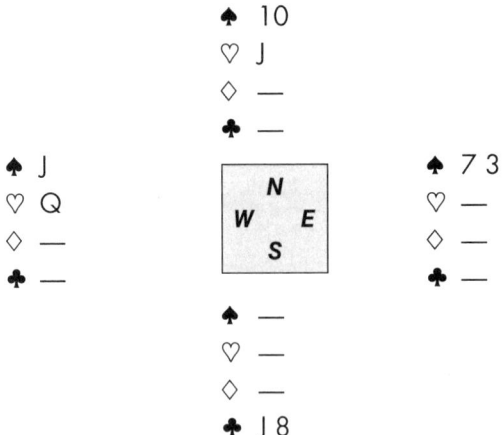

```
              ♠ 10
              ♡ J
              ◇ —
              ♣ —
   ♠ J                      ♠ 7 3
   ♡ Q          N           ♡ —
   ◇ —      W       E       ◇ —
   ♣ —          S           ♣ —
              ♠ —
              ♡ —
              ◇ —
              ♣ J 8
```

"Now when I lead another club, if you trump with the jack, I throw away the heart, but if you don't, I trump it. Either way, I make the ten of spades *en passant*."

Of course, there were bigger rewards on more spectacular hands. One that stands out for me was the squeeze without a name. Maybe it actually was a double guard squeeze, since that's what the Shoe called it. It was the Shoe and the Bambino again, and a competitive auction had the Shoe blasting six spades doubled after RHO opened diamonds and LHO raised preemptively, something like:

Bambino
♠ 8
♡ J 10 7 4
◇ Q 9 8
♣ A Q 10 9 8

♠ 9 6 4
♡ 9 8
◇ J 10 6 5 2
♣ J 4 3

```
      N
  W       E
      S
```

♠ 10 3
♡ A 5 3
◇ A K 7 4 3
♣ K 6 5

Shoe
♠ A K Q J 7 5 2
♡ K Q 6 2
◇ —
♣ 7 2

LHO	Bambino	RHO	Shoe
		1◇	1♠
3◇	dbl	pass	6♠
pass	pass	dbl	all pass

The final bid was ridiculously optimistic, but dinner had been a pitcher of beer. Six hearts pretty much would have needed only a heart split and no club lead.

On the opening lead of the ♡9 to the ace, Shoe dropped the queen. A heart was returned and not ruffed, won in the closed hand with the king, unblocking the jack for show. Six hearts would now have been cold and the Shoe spent some time working out all the angles, but he could find no way to blame the Bambino for missing the heart fit.

Reluctantly, he concentrated on the hand. He did not believe the club finesse would work. Three rounds of spades drew trumps, and Shoe now travelled to dummy on the ♡10 and led a low diamond. RHO rose with the king and the Shoe rose visibly in his chair. All that was needed now was for RHO *not* to have the ◇10 (as well as the jack, which he had just denied). An avalanche of spades produced this ending:

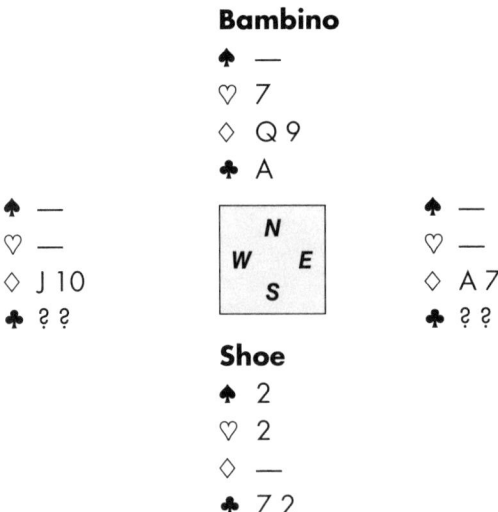

Bambino
♠ —
♡ 7
♢ Q 9
♣ A

♠ —
♡ —
♢ J 10
♣ ? ?

N
W   E
S

♠ —
♡ —
♢ A 7
♣ ? ?

Shoe
♠ 2
♡ 2
♢ —
♣ 7 2

On the play of the ♡2 to dummy's seven, both opponents were caught having to guard the same suit, diamonds. What a squeeze! With the lead in dummy, LHO could not spare the ♢10 else the ruffing finesse started by leading the ♢Q would squash the jack, so LHO came to a singleton club. RHO could not spare a diamond, else the lead of the nine from dummy would have him fanning the air with the ace as the Shoe trumped, so RHO also had to keep two diamonds and therefore only one club. The Shoe now cashed the ♣A, pitching the seven, and with the remaining clubs breaking 1-1, was able to claim the last two tricks with the two black deuces.

In addition to all the other benefits, kibitzing offers many chances to watch the stars in action. One year in the Spingold, the Shoe drew the defending champions for his first-round match. Spingold matches lasted all day in those days, and the Shoe's team trailed by 86 IMPs at the half. They decided to pair the Bambino with the Shoe to create a few swings. Swings do happen when those two are at the table.

The most interesting hand wasn't particularly large or outrageous, but it set the tone for pickups that came later. Bambino and Shoe were seated against Peter Weichsel and Alan Sontag, who were playing Precision. The auction proceeded:

West	North	East	South
Weichsel	*Bambino*	*Sontag*	*Shoe*
		1♣ (16+)	dbl
pass	1♡	1♠	pass
pass	2♣	pass	2NT (!)
all pass			

This was the deal:

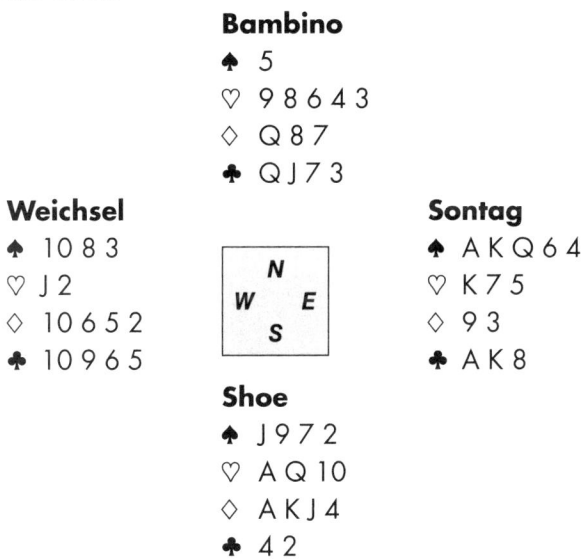

Bambino
♠ 5
♡ 9 8 6 4 3
◇ Q 8 7
♣ Q J 7 3

Weichsel
♠ 10 8 3
♡ J 2
◇ 10 6 5 2
♣ 10 9 6 5

Sontag
♠ A K Q 6 4
♡ K 7 5
◇ 9 3
♣ A K 8

Shoe
♠ J 9 7 2
♡ A Q 10
◇ A K J 4
♣ 4 2

The opening lead was a small spade and the Shoe wasn't threatening anyone down 80 IMPs, so Sontag didn't even bother to falsecard in spades, winning the queen. Then he returned a small spade, and it became relatively easy for the Shoe to rise with the jack. After all, Weichsel had been silent over Shoe's double and had not raised spades later, holding three.

Weichsel and Sontag appeared to become unsettled once the ♠J held, though I suspected that the Shoe didn't see any obvious road to eight tricks. Attacking clubs was out of the question, as the opponents had two club winners and four spade winners. The Shoe crossed to dummy on the ◇Q and finessed the ♡Q. Then magic things began to happen. Weichsel couldn't signal with the ♡J to show his doubleton: that signal would subject partner to a later endplay in hearts, so he played the deuce.

The Shoe ran his high diamonds to exert pressure on Sontag, who had to find two discards. The first was easy: the ♣8, but then he fell from grace. Basing his decision on the auction and partner's play of the deuce of hearts, he discarded a small heart. The Shoe had pseudo-squeezed a world-class expert! Sontag should, of course, have taken the trouble to work out that if Shoe really had a doubleton heart, he could spare one of his good spades, then win any lead and get out with a heart to set up six tricks for their side.

This should not have been a big deal; after all, two hearts always makes for the Bambino and the Shoe. But an avalanche of swings began from this harmless snowball. It got so bad that on the last board, the Bambino opened one vulnerable spade and was so mistrusted that the opponents ended up in six spades doubled down two. The match was actually winnable at one point, but there were two big adverse swings at the other table. Avoiding either one wins the match. As it was, the boys gained back some self-respect but still lost by 23 IMPs.

11

Looking for Mr. Goodbridge

Despite his discovery of squeeze play, in the Shoe's eyes, nothing was quite as boring as attempting to beat good players by outplaying them rather than by driving them crazy. He hated the idea of building partnership confidence by bidding what he had in his hand. There was so much more scope for adventure if you had license to bid everybody's hands, as he did playing with Mrs. Whaley or the Old Guy or even, heaven forbid, with me. Shoe didn't care for fanatically counting and planning ahead, preferring to rattle off the tricks and play for an error. He treasured his partnerships with the best-playing lunatics of his era: the Bambino, Colonel Bulldozer, the Victim and the Hummingbird.

The Shoe considered the notion of being consistently good to be a synonym for being consistently boring. However, that changed drastically when the Shoe chanced to be paired with the legendary Shorty Sheardown at the Canadian National Regional Knockout Teams. Aside from founding the Hart House Bridge Club, Shorty had probably been Canada's best bridge player for more years than the Shoe had been alive. In addition, Shorty had qualifications with which the Shoe was utterly unfamiliar: Shorty was a classics scholar and a perfect gentleman.

Shoe claims he is thinking of none of these things as he sits down to start the event against a very capable married couple from Nova Scotia. The Shoe claims to be trying to figure out how to use the information that Shorty is known never to underlead a king against suit contracts. I get the honor of kibitzing Shorty after I am introduced as Bungalow Bill Miller, inventor of the Winning Butterfly. Shorty welcomes me with a genuine smile. He has absolutely no discussion about system or carding with the Shoe and picks up his first hand:

♠ 4 2   ♡ 8 6 4 2   ◇ A Q 3   ♣ K 6 5 2

The opponents bid smoothly to four vulnerable spades on an uncontested auction:

LHO	RHO
1♠	2♣
3♣	3♠
4♠	

Shorty is on lead and without any hesitation whatsoever, leads the ♣2. So much for the advance scouting report about underleading kings! This was the whole deal:

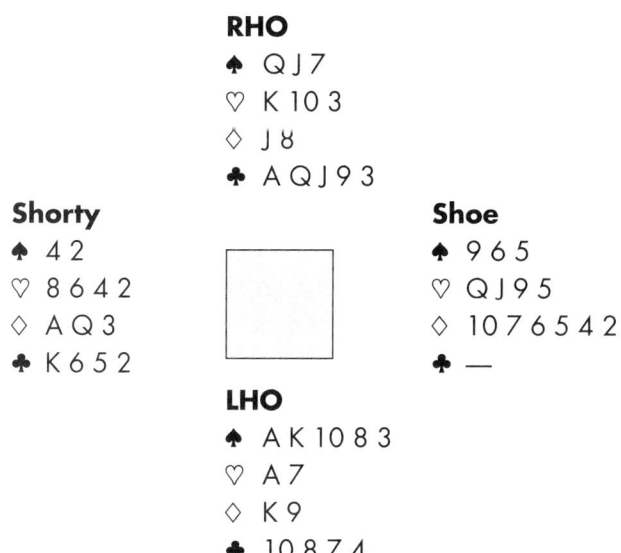

RHO
- ♠ Q J 7
- ♡ K 10 3
- ◇ J 8
- ♣ A Q J 9 3

Shorty
- ♠ 4 2
- ♡ 8 6 4 2
- ◇ A Q 3
- ♣ K 6 5 2

Shoe
- ♠ 9 6 5
- ♡ Q J 9 5
- ◇ 10 7 6 5 4 2
- ♣ —

LHO
- ♠ A K 10 8 3
- ♡ A 7
- ◇ K 9
- ♣ 10 8 7 4

Declarer decides against the club finesse and Shoe ruffs the ace. The rest of the hand is automatic: diamond back, king, ace. Club king, club ruff, diamond back to the queen, club ruff. Down three, +300.

These opponents are playing a nondescript club opening bid and the next auction goes one club-pass-pass to the Shoe, who holds:

♠ A K 10 3 2   ♡ Q 10 7 5   ◇ Q 4 2   ♣ 5

Shoe balances with double, pass by opener, pass by Shorty, rescue redouble by responder, pass by the Shoe. Opener removes to one diamond, which is doubled by Shorty, then everyone passes. This is a lot of bidding to reach one diamond doubled. Shorty leads the ♠7 on this deal:

Responder
♠ 9 8 6
♡ 8 6 3 2
♢ K 8 3
♣ 10 9 3

Shorty		**Shoe**
♠ 7 4		♠ A K 10 3 2
♡ 9 4		♡ Q 10 7 5
♢ A 7 6		♢ Q 4 2
♣ A 8 7 6 4 2		♣ 5

Opener
♠ Q J 5
♡ A K J
♢ J 10 9 5
♣ K Q J

The defense takes under a minute: Shoe wins the ♠K and returns his singleton club. Shorty wins the club and returns his highest club, the eight, for Shoe to ruff. Shoe plays ace and a spade for Shorty to ruff. Shorty returns his next highest club, the seven, which Shoe again ruffs. The seven is easy to interpret, and Shoe returns the fourth round of spades, his lowest spade remaining, the three, for a ruff and discard. Shorty trumps with the ace and plays the fourth round of clubs for another ruff and discard: this one allows Shoe to score his now-singleton ♢Q *en passant*. That's the first eight tricks, down two, for +500.

At this point, another kibitzer shows up to watch the famous Shorty in action. He's a polite kibitzer who asks permission to kibitz. The unfortunate gentleman who played the first two hands pleasantly informs the would-be kibitzer that the match is already over. Normally, the Shoe loves to explain stuff, but when he played with Shorty, things suddenly needed no explanation. The Shoe realized that Shorty was not approaching the game in the same way that the Fran's coterie did: he simply played good bridge.

Eventually, playing serious bridge had the advantage of introducing the Shoe to real squeezes, not just the illusions he and the Bambino performed against matchpoint players. In the short term, however, it led to study groups that turned into lectures from the Shoe on 'good bridge', beginning with his favorite subject, bidding notrump. As usual, he held forth at Fran's Restaurant to all who were willing to listen and to a few who weren't. Objections were drowned in pitchers of beer.

"Bungalow will take notes," he began. "It is clear that the tendency of most players is to play too many hands in suit contracts. Statistics from World Championships bear this out: where the choice of contracts was between three notrump and four of a major, three notrump succeeded twice as often as the major-suit game.

"We're not going to waste time on hands where you and your grandma would correctly land in a suit contract, but there are a few areas of avoiding notrump that you may not have considered and my conscience would bother me not to mention them." The Shoe has to quell the interruptions as a side discussion breaks out about the Shoe's conscience. As a compromise, the Shoe promises just to show them a couple of hands where notrump is wrong and to buy all the beer until he's done with the hands.

"The first category is abuse of the West Coast cuebid, which everyone here at Fran's knows is a request for a partial stopper that incorporates the wish to reach three notrump into a scientific effort to get there from the right side." The Shoe wrote out the following:

♠ A K 5   ♡ A 9 4   ◇ 4 3 2   ♣ K J 5 3

"Partner opens a spade and RHO overcalls two diamonds. Now, it is true that I have a very nice 15 HCP and enough to force to game, so I yield to the temptation to cuebid. Actually, I've never encountered a temptation to which I couldn't yield. When partner rebids three notrump, I recognize the error of my ways. Too late to say how sorry I am, I have to pass, not knowing whether partner has a full stopper or a partial stopper. I should have preferred a bid of three clubs. Then I can afford to pass if partner bids three notrump and reach four spades if that's the right spot. Against three notrump, RHO leads the ace of diamonds and this was the deal:

Shoe
♠ A K 5
♡ A 9 4
◇ 4 3 2
♣ K J 5 3

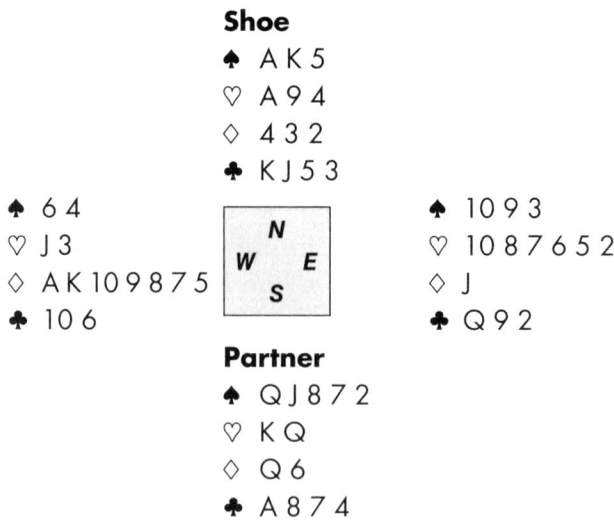

♠ 6 4
♡ J 3
◇ A K 10 9 8 7 5
♣ 10 6

♠ 10 9 3
♡ 10 8 7 6 5 2
◇ J
♣ Q 9 2

Partner
♠ Q J 8 7 2
♡ K Q
◇ Q 6
♣ A 8 7 4

"The hand was misdefense-proof for three down. Of course, the diamond overcaller might have started a low diamond from his entryless hand, but here we are trying for 'good' bridge."

Shoe ordered another pitcher and drew out:

♠ J 10 9 7 6 5 3   ♡ A   ◇ 6 5   ♣ 8 7 6

"Partner opens one diamond and rebids three clubs over your one spade response. You're going to rebid spades (four, if that's weaker in your system) but if you rebid three and partner continues to three notrump, you are always going to convert to four spades, as your hand will be entryless after the opening lead.

"On two-suiters you must resist the temptation to bid notrump if you have a loser in one of the key suits, unless you have at least slow double stoppers in both the side suits. Look at this deal from the 1969 playoff against the Aces to determine the Bermuda Bowl team:

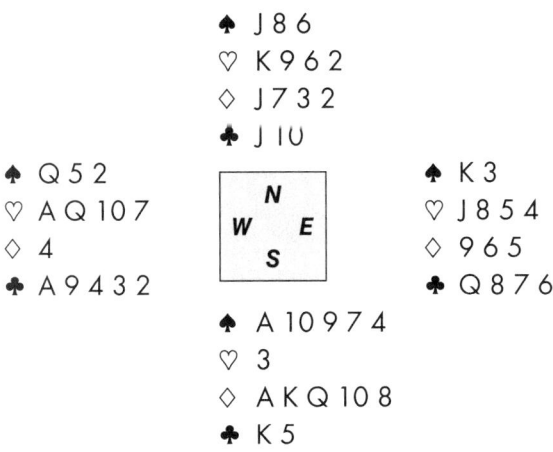

♠ J 8 6
♥ K 9 6 2
♦ J 7 3 2
♣ J 10

♠ Q 5 2
♥ A Q 10 7
♦ 4
♣ A 9 4 3 2

♠ K 3
♥ J 8 5 4
♦ 9 6 5
♣ Q 8 7 6

♠ A 10 9 7 4
♥ 3
♦ A K Q 10 8
♣ K 5

"Both Wests, the eventual defenders, opened one club and subsequently raised hearts. The Walsh team reached three notrump North-South while the Aces' Lawrence and Hamman bid and made the easy four spades.

"Three notrump received a heart lead, which on the best of days guaranteed one down. After the heart lead was won in dummy, the spade was lost to West and three hearts were cashed, ending with East. Now on the low club shift, declarer had read too many books about how much it paid at IMPs to make the contract, so played RHO to have left his senses and LHO to have psyched the opening bid, and rose with the king. That led to five down instead of one down, but only cost an additional 3 IMPs.

"Okay, one more and we'll get to the important part, actually bidding notrump. Suppose you have:

♠ A Q 8   ♥ 5 4   ♦ A 9 7 6 4   ♣ Q 10 9

"Partner opens the bidding one club and the opponents do not interfere. You are playing some kind of execrable natural system, such as those preferred by everybody here. Over your response of one diamond, partner jumps to two hearts. You make a temporizing bid of two spades and partner rebids two notrump, forcing. Assuming you played your spade bid as nothing in particular, but encouraging, it should be clear that partner has 2-4-2-5 or 3-4-1-5 with the king of spades. That, in turn, lets you know that all partner's pointed suit losers are covered by the ace of diamonds and the ace-queen of spades.

"Mrs. Four-Notrump would know what to do. If Roman Keycard Blackwood shows there's a missing ace, you subside in six clubs to protect against a diamond lead. This is where some ace-asking gadget like four diamonds comes in handy: you won't have to go *back* to six clubs if partner has two aces and two kings. Here, whatever type of Blackwood you prefer discloses ace-king of clubs and ace-king of hearts. Now if you're desperate, you can bid the laydown seven clubs or let partner bid it. It'll be odds-on even without the jack of clubs. Even six clubs will almost certainly be better than six notrump. The whole deal is:

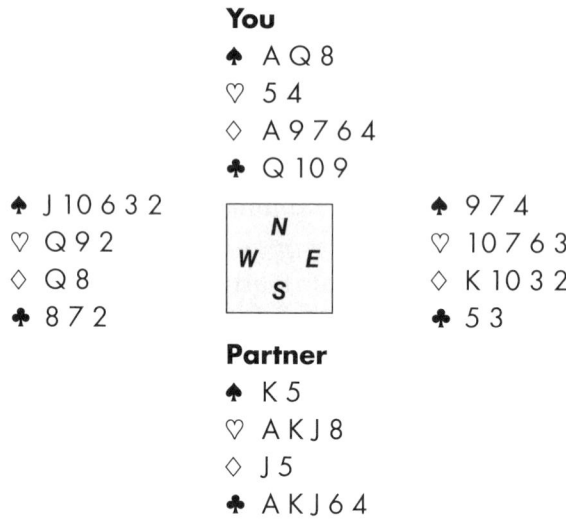

You
♠ A Q 8
♡ 5 4
◇ A 9 7 6 4
♣ Q 10 9

♠ J 10 6 3 2
♡ Q 9 2
◇ Q 8
♣ 8 7 2

♠ 9 7 4
♡ 10 7 6 3
◇ K 10 3 2
♣ 5 3

Partner
♠ K 5
♡ A K J 8
◇ J 5
♣ A K J 6 4

"Okay, now you have to buy your own beer because I'm hitting the much more interesting subject of *how* to bid notrump rather than *whether* to bid notrump. As you all know, this consideration violates my Second Rule of Bridge that notrump always plays better from my hand. I am assuming that good bridge is what we're after, and good bridge requires a good partner. The presumption that you play one or two tricks better than partner is no longer workable. It may still be true, but it is not a hypothesis on the road to becoming 'good'.

"Look at this example. I hold (both vulnerable):

♠ 9 7 6 ♡ A 9 4 ◇ Q J 9 7 3 ♣ K 4

"I am playing one of my rare outings with Bungalow, who opens with one club, and rebids one heart over my one diamond response. At this point a one spade bid (natural, not fourth suit) stands out for at least four good reasons:

1. If Bungalow can bid notrump, he has a real stopper and the hand will be safer played from partner's side;
2. Inhibiting a spade lead will probably help our side;
3. One notrump is an underbid, a heart raise is a shot, and a forcing bid is an overbid;
4. If Bungalow shows a two-suiter, I can safely support hearts.

"None of these advantages come home on the actual hand, but there is still another factor: the confusion caused for the opponents. Bungalow rebids one notrump, which I pass. LHO doesn't like the auction and balances with a double. This comes around to me and being greedy, as is my wont, I try the effect of a redouble. That, in turn is passed around to my RHO, who is going to have to lead holding:

♠ Q 8 5 4   ♡ J 6 5   ◇ K 6 5 2   ♣ 10 3

"The auction to date has been :

Shoe	LHO	Bungalow	RHO
		1♣	pass
1◇	pass	1♡	pass
1♠	pass	1NT	pass
pass	dbl	pass	pass
redbl	pass	pass	?

"RHO's problem is to decide whether partner is showing a trap pass of diamonds or merely making a reopening bid. True, RHO had been content to pass the double, but the redouble has given him a chance to rethink the entire proposition. Even if it was a trap pass of diamonds, could the defense run enough diamonds and side winners before the entire club suit was run against them? Plagued by thoughts like this, and perhaps by the tempo of my redouble, RHO runs to two diamonds, which I do not double because I don't know whether we can set two spades.

"We augment this imaginative auction with a flashy defense, as this is the deal:

LHO
- ♠ A 10 3
- ♡ K 8 2
- ◇ A 10 8
- ♣ J 9 7 5

Shoe
- ♠ 9 7 6
- ♡ A 9 4
- ◇ Q J 9 7 3
- ♣ K 4

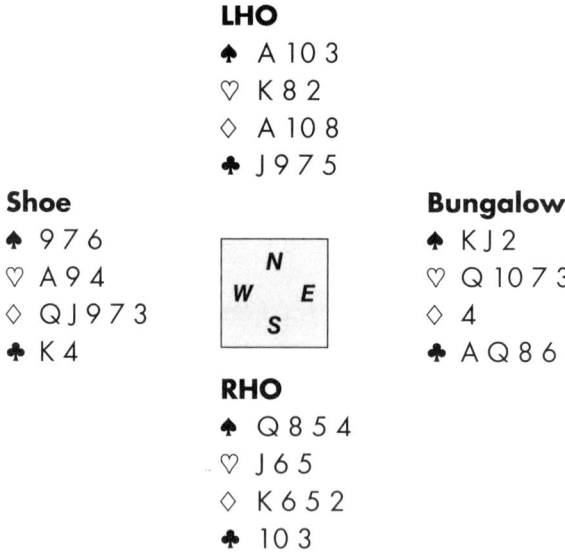

Bungalow
- ♠ K J 2
- ♡ Q 10 7 3
- ◇ 4
- ♣ A Q 8 6 2

RHO
- ♠ Q 8 5 4
- ♡ J 6 5
- ◇ K 6 5 2
- ♣ 10 3

"I lead the king of clubs, followed by a low heart. Declarer misconstrues the opening lead and plays low from dummy on the heart, losing to Bungalow's queen. Bungalow now cashes the ace of clubs and continues with the deuce. Declarer is still misconstruing the opening lead and has no real discard to make, so he ruffs low and I overruff. I return the spade nine which runs to Bungalow's king. He cashes the club queen as the demoralized declarer discards something. Now a heart to my ace means we have already taken the first seven tricks and I have two trump tricks yet to come, so that's four down for +400. The opponents are still arguing today whether or not Bungalow would have made one notrump redoubled.

"We've already done using the West Coast cuebid on the wrong hand. Here it is on the right hand:

♠ A 8 2 ♡ K J 4 ◇ A 6 3 ♣ J 9 8 3

"If partner opens one heart and RHO overcalls two diamonds, you should cuebid three diamonds.

"Here it is as fourth-suit forcing on the right hand:

♠ A 5 3 ♡ A 6 5 2 ◇ A 7 4 3 ♣ J 5

"If partner opens one club and rebids one spade over your red-suit response, you should make a forcing bid in your other red suit. Your hand cannot profit by being led to. With good holdings such as QJxx, Q10xx, AQ or AJx in the opposing suit you will bid notrump immediately.

"You have probably never seen this auction in your bridge career, but I've been blessed twice with the opportunity to use it." And, with that, the Shoe demolished another tablecloth as he wrote out:

Partner	RHO	You	LHO
1♣	pass	1◇	pass
1♡	pass	1♠	pass
2♠	pass	3♣	pass
3◇	pass	3♡	pass
3♠	pass	3NT	all pass

"What meaning can you attach to this auction?" asks the Shoe, and the usual discussion ensues, not entirely complimentary and somewhat over-focused on the mental health of the Shoe and anyone who would play with him.

"You are right in a way," admits the Shoe. "The first time we had this auction, the Bambino and I had left our hands in the duplicate board and were playing 'no-peek' in the game where we had decided to play every contract in three notrump. The opponents, a pair of dear little old ladies, followed the auction with great concentration and growing alarm. We played the hand for whatever it was supposed to make and, as we scored it up, one of the ladies remarked how all the fun had gone out of the game now that the young players had begun to play these fancy conventions. Duly reprimanded, we took our hands out of the boards for the second deal, and bid almost naturally to three notrump.

"The second time we had this auction, it represented real bridge. I was playing with the Victim who, as you all know, is a bright guy on his dull days and mistakenly expects the same from me. The Victim opened one club and I held:

♠ A 9 6 ♡ 9 6 3 ◇ K Q 6 3 2 ♣ A Q

"Of course we're getting to three notrump, but the hand was too good to make an early move, so I responded one diamond. The Victim continued with one heart and I had a problem. If you've been paying attention, you will know that I opted to bid one spade. The Victim raised to two spades holding:

♠ K 8 5 2 ♡ K Q 8 4 ◇ A ♣ 9 7 5 4

So, now you already have the rest of the auction in front of you, but look how much sense it makes in the quest to play 'good' bridge. I now had a pretty good picture of the Victim's hand: he had to be either 4-4-1-4 or 4-4-0-5. I still wanted the Victim's hand led up to, so I bid the 'impossible' three clubs. I was safe in all suits as long as the Victim's clubs were headed by as little as the jack. The Victim, who could see clearly that the weakness on the hand centered on the club suit, countered with a raise to three diamonds, a suit in which he was known to hold at most one card. Three diamonds also put him in the position of having bid all four suits below three notrump.

"I still could not picture the problem from his side, so I bid three hearts. The Victim now had to weigh the possibility that my hand had a heart void, but he ruled this out because I wouldn't be doing all this with a heart void and a real spade fit. His three spade bid made one last attempt to get to three notrump from my side, while also leaving open the possibility that I had indulged in a string of self-cuebids on a spade auction. I resigned myself to bidding three notrump which, after five transfer bids, turned out to be played from the right side.

"Maybe it was only because we ran out of bidding space."

12

The Stuff that Dreams Are Made Of...

The Shoe was once again holding forth over a pitcher of beer at Fran's Restaurant while the usual late-night players enjoyed a 2:00 a.m. breakfast. We didn't quite know where he was heading, but he had the floor and he was not about to surrender it.

"The Canadian qualifying event of 1975 had taken its toll, and after a long and grueling series of matches, experience had won out once again. You will recall that the team of four that finally won would acquire the right to accompany Eric Murray and Sami Kehela to the 1976 World Olympiad in Italy. My all-Toronto team swept to the win, with the Old Guy playing with Mrs. A.A. Whaley and (Bungalow) Bill Miller playing with me."

Now, instead of wondering where this was heading, I am wondering if the Shoe has started on some substance stronger than alcohol, as I am sure the Old Guy and I were kibitzing when the Shoe completed a miracle win in the semifinals, only to lose the finals to a worse team.

The Shoe continued to his puzzled audience, "I had been added because the eventual winners had been unable to find a fourth and my team had deemed me expendable on account of an unavoidable hangover. I was delighted to seize the opportunity, because after all the times Bungalow had carried me to victory, I owed him an actual game in an important event. Also, I was lifetime undefeated playing with the Old Guy. Sure enough, we won. We were on our way to Italy.

"In the Olympiad, with Murray and Kehela anchoring, we had surprisingly little difficulty reaching the final against the Aces, representing the United States. Some opponents commented that the Old Guy had been incredibly lucky, or words to that effect. Bungalow, who is a much better player than people expect since he usually elects to kibitz me, played beautifully as my partner.

"Toward the end of the third quarter, our team trailed by a dozen IMPs despite the fact that the Aces had failed to make any of four slams, all of which had been missed by our pairs and all of which had gone down on a bad lie of the cards. There was another standoff on one of the last boards, when the Old Guy and Mrs. Whaley defended a quiet two spades for minus 110 while Murray and Kehela set six hearts one trick for +100.

"Disaster struck on an early board of the final quarter. Murray and Kehela bid a vulnerable seven notrump, which could be made via a squeeze, but there was a choice of squeezes. Kehela pondered a very long time about the solution to this problem, which rated to be crucial in the outcome of the match. He was oblivious to his cigar, which became shorter and shorter until the burns actually happened to his lips. He had to be rushed to hospital. For some inexplicable reason, Murray was eager to accompany him.

"There was no choice but to bring in Bungalow and me as emergency replacements. After another long delay, I selected the wrong squeeze and ended up down two. In the other room, six notrump was bid and made, and we trailed by 29 IMPs. The rest of the quarter was a wildly swinging melee and with three boards to go, the deficit was up to 35 IMPs.

"On the face of it, our results on the final three boards were not promising. On the first, I had made one notrump doubled with an overtrick, which rated to be a moderate gain. On the next board, the Aces had taken the completely obvious save in seven spades, -200, against the cold seven diamonds. This was clearly their optimum result. On the final board, Bungalow had found a strong defense to set a vulnerable three notrump. This might be a pickup of 12 IMPs.

"On the antepenultimate hand, Mrs. Whaley was in first chair holding:

♠ A 8 3   ♡ A Q 9 2   ◇ A 6 5   ♣ A K 8

"You could see she was a little piqued because the Old Guy had refused to learn a club system. With an air of long suffering, she opened the bidding one heart. The next two hands passed and RHO balanced with a double. Mrs. Whaley toyed with the idea of a redouble, but her table presence told her that if she passed, LHO might just be foolish enough to pass, and she did not want to give RHO a chance to run out. Sure enough, everybody passed. The Old Guy appeared to have fallen asleep. This was the entire deal: I will draw it conveniently for you on the tablecloth.

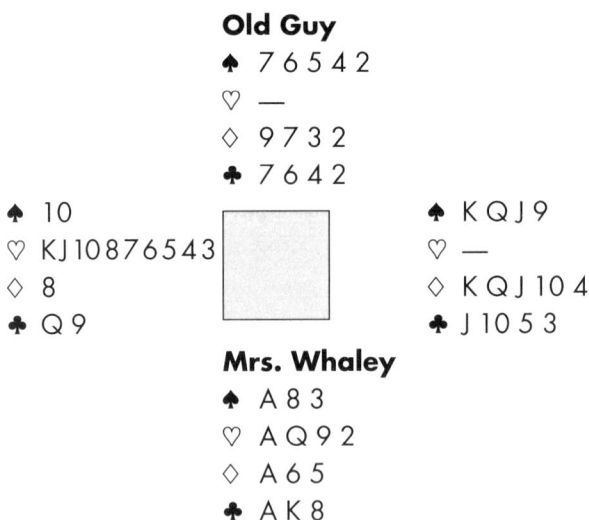

Old Guy
♠ 7 6 5 4 2
♡ —
◇ 9 7 3 2
♣ 7 6 4 2

♠ 10
♡ K J 10 8 7 6 5 4 3
◇ 8
♣ Q 9

♠ K Q J 9
♡ —
◇ K Q J 10 4
♣ J 10 5 3

Mrs. Whaley
♠ A 8 3
♡ A Q 9 2
◇ A 6 5
♣ A K 8

"Mrs. Whaley knew that this auction portended a bad split in the trump suit, so she won the opening lead of the ten of spades with the ace and cashed her other winners, the ace of diamonds and the two top clubs. LHO decided he needed to go to the washroom. When he returned, Mrs. Whaley led a loser. LHO made the inevitable ruff and led the jack of hearts. In the excitement, Mrs. Whaley mistook it for the king and won the ace to lead another loser, again ruffed by LHO. The ten of hearts went to Mrs. Whaley's queen and the lead of a third loser forced LHO to ruff once more.

"Mrs. Whaley was shocked to see the king of hearts led a second time and there was a lot of finger wagging as Mrs. Whaley told LHO it was naughty to take the king of hearts back out of the pile and to play it again, especially at this stage of a World Championship. LHO politely assured Mrs. Whaley that the previous king of hearts had been the jack and showed it to her from the tricks pile. Mrs. Whaley was flustered, but not so flustered as to throw away the nine of hearts. That was one heart doubled making, +160.

"She wondered aloud whether she could have made an overtrick had she not wasted the ace of hearts on the jack. The Old Guy did not hear her, as he was having a sneaky feeling that the standard of play in these big championships was not all it was cracked up to be. He wondered in a rather loud whisper if he hadn't just seen the opponents trump three of Mrs. Whaley's losers only to get endplayed in the trump suit each time? In any event, one heart doubled making opposite one notrump doubled making two was a pickup of 10 IMPs and the Aces' lead was down to 25 IMPs.

"The Old Guy was exhausted after such a long event. He didn't really have time to pursue his investigation into the defense as it was necessary to wake himself up for the final two boards. He had picked up a thirteen-card spade suit! 'Skip bid', he announced, 'seven spades', adding with a chuckle, 'Even I know how to bid this hand, I could play it in my sleep.'

"'Probably just as well', chimed both opponents in unison. The Old Guy never did notice that the eight of spades was a club.

"His LHO with the spade void could scarcely be blamed for diagnosing the thirteen-card suit, especially as the Old Guy had accidentally counted them, very quietly and under his breath, of course. LHO held:

$$\spadesuit — \quad \heartsuit A K Q J \quad \diamondsuit A K Q J 10 7 5 2 \quad \clubsuit A$$

"Naturally, he bid seven non-vulnerable notrump. The Old Guy doubled in outrage.

"Mrs. Whaley dutifully led her eight of spades. It was really too late in the game and somehow it seemed only fair that if these boys had the gall to bid seven notrump without a stopper in her partner's thirteen-card suit, Mrs. Whaley should have one to lead. He cashed from the top down, so that when he reached the eight, the Aces were able to claim six down, -1100 in the old math, which, together with our +200, was a pickup of 16 IMPs, so that we trailed by only nine.

"On the final hand, each side rolled into the vulnerable three notrump. The hand looked identical to one in Sheinwold's *Fourth Book of Bridge Puzzles*, where you just had to duck a couple of tricks in the club suit and wait for partner's congratulations when you made your game. This is exactly what declarer tried against us. If I recall rightly, the Victim had commented one time that the analysis wasn't as simple as the book made out. The entire layout was:

Dummy
- ♠ J 10
- ♡ 7 6 5 2
- ◇ A K Q 10
- ♣ A 4 3

Bungalow
- ♠ 8 7 6 5 3
- ♡ A 9 8
- ◇ 8 7 3
- ♣ K Q

Shoe
- ♠ Q 4 2
- ♡ Q J 10
- ◇ 9 6 5 2
- ♣ J 9 8

Declarer
- ♠ A K 9
- ♡ K 4 3
- ◇ J 4
- ♣ 10 7 6 5 2

"At our table, Bungalow led a spade and to a point, the play proceeded swiftly and relentlessly. Dummy's card was covered by the queen and won by declarer with the king. A club was ducked, a spade returned, again won in the closed hand. A further club was ducked and Bungalow paused to consider the situation. Declarer had five clubs and three spades. He was going to great lengths to keep the Shoe off lead, so his hearts were probably headed by the king. A doubleton diamond was definitely a possibility, with the jack providing an entry. If declarer had a doubleton diamond, how could he untangle the minors if Bungalow played a diamond now?

"Bungalow returned a diamond and he could almost feel the Winning Butterfly lighting on his shoulder, as declarer went into a long, unhappy hesitation. Finally, he won in dummy and cashed the ace of clubs and the rest of the diamonds. Next came a heart toward the closed hand, and when the ace was offside, he had to lose three heart tricks for down one. With defenses like that, you can see why our team exceeded expectations.

"At the other table, the Old Guy pushed into three notrump, painfully aware he had dropped six tricks on defense on the hand before. He was wide awake now, although I feel constrained to add that being wide awake was not always an advantage for the Old Guy. After a high spade lead and the same sequence of spade plays at Trick 1, the Old Guy played safely by immediately attacking diamonds, which could not possibly contain a loser. As luck would have it, the Old Guy, who had played so consistently throughout the tournament, had the three of hearts in with his diamonds, so that the actual play at Trick 2 was in fact the three of hearts, won by RHO with the ten.

"RHO paused to analyze his chances. Declarer was going to win a spade return in dummy and play a heart. If he had the ace, hearts were breaking for ten tricks. If the heart was the king, it would lose to the ace, but the fourth heart would still set up for the ninth trick before partner could gain entry to the long spades. The best chance was to find partner with as little as K10x of clubs, plus the ace of hearts. Accordingly, RHO shifted to the nine of clubs.

"The Old Guy won the queen of clubs with the ace and cashed the diamonds as he had originally intended. On the fourth diamond, LHO was caught in a progressive whatsit. If he pitched a high club, a club lead from dummy would set up declarer's club and the most they could cash would be two more hearts. He didn't want to come down to a singleton heart ace and, with partner disdaining the spade return, it seemed obvious to pitch a spade. This was now the situation:

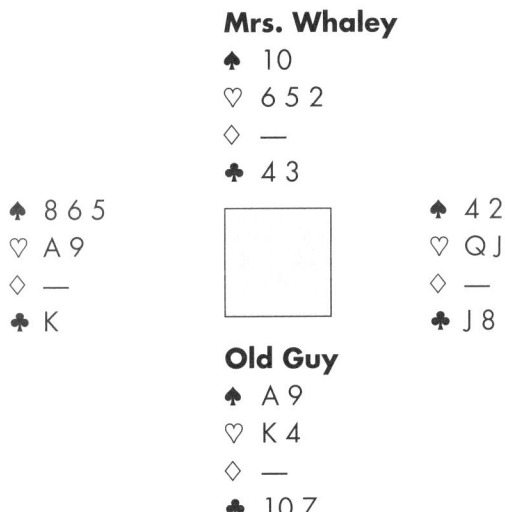

Mrs. Whaley
♠ 10
♡ 6 5 2
♢ —
♣ 4 3

♠ 8 6 5   ♠ 4 2
♡ A 9   ♡ Q J
♢ —   ♢ —
♣ K   ♣ J 8

Old Guy
♠ A 9
♡ K 4
♢ —
♣ 10 7

"The Old Guy, who could still, if the occasion demanded it, remember back as far as Trick 1, cashed the two high spades and exited with his club loser. LHO could cash a spade but was then endplayed in hearts.

"The endplay was barely completed in the bedlam that erupted. We had won by 3 IMPs! The kibitzers risked causing serious injury to the Old Guy and Mrs. Whaley by hoisting them on their shoulders and carrying them to the presentation ceremony. Of course, Murray and Kehela were voted the outstanding pair of the competition. They modestly announced their intention to share the award with all their teammates, showing once again that success would never be more important to them than the spirit in which they played the game.

"So", continued the Shoe, "I dreamed this when I fell asleep in the Victim's car as he was droning on and on about that Sheinwold *Bridge Puzzles* hand and finding the crucial diamond shift after the second club duck. We all know what the Moo Cow did to me in the real qualifier, so I'm not fooling anybody, but I can dream, can't I? How do you like my story?"

"It has a certain *je ne sais quoi*," contributed the Victim.

13

The System

As we have seen, the Shoe had been developing his card play, learning how to win tricks legitimately rather than by a bizarre blend of falsecards and flim-flam. He had even begun to reduce his psychics to fewer than one a round. All this in the cause of playing 'good' bridge. The component of partnership confidence had to wait until Bozo arrived (so-called because he was intelligent, go figure, but also known as 'Putz' to his friends). He brought the System.

The System was tough on the opponents, reasonably easy to play and fabulous for IMPs. For the Shoe, it had the drawback that if you misdescribed your hand, you could never recover. Every bid meant something, but without the encyclopedic notes and inferences required if you were seriously playing Standard American.

The System was the brainchild of a number of Canadian players who were trying to emulate the success of Blue Team Club. The Shoe immediately loved the System, especially because he had authored a similar attempt with the Forcing Diamond back in the days of Hart House. This was it in outline:

1♣:	17+ HCP unbalanced or 18+ balanced, asks for controls
	1◇ negative
	1♡ 6+ HCP, 2 or fewer controls
	1♠ 3
	1NT 4
	2♣ 5
	2◇ 6
	2NT 7+
	Suit jumps were long suits with a weak hand
1 of a suit:	11-16 HCP, new suit rebid = Canapé style, second suit is 5 cards or longer, at least as long as the first
1NT:	14-17 HCP balanced
2♣:	Precision
2◇:	Multi
2M:	Roman — 5+ major, 4+ clubs
2NT:	any preempt you like

The Shoe had always favored systems where you knew right away what was forcing, and whether you had enough controls for slam. Here there were immediately obvious forcing and non-forcing auctions that eliminated all the touchy jump rebids necessary in Standard American.

The System added the bonus that bidding the four-card suit before a possible five-card suit meant that the opponents did not always have such a good takeout double. The beauty of ruining the takeout double had long ago been impressed on the Shoe by the Hummingbird and the Victim. Indeed, there turned out to be some spectacular results on misfits where the opponents' overcall beat the Shoe to the canapé suit.

Another weird outcome of this style of bidding that appealed strongly to the Shoe was that opening bids, if they did not show a canapé, would be a weak notrump or a one-suiter. In competition, partner would assume you had a weak notrump, so you were almost forced to bid again to show a canapé or a very good suit, even at high levels with nothing extra. This amounted to a license to bid too much: no more worrying if it showed extras.

Of course, there were other things that attracted the Shoe to bridge with Bozo, such as the auction that went:

Shoe	LHO	Bozo	RHO
1♠	dbl	1NT	dbl
1♠	dbl	1NT	DIRECTOR!

The Shoe, never one to miss out on a good argument, opined that LHO had condoned the one spade bid, so there was no reason to call the director as Putz's one notrump bid was sufficient. The director agreed with the Shoe, except for the part about the need to call the director. Bozo opined that the Shoe was being disrespectful to call him Putz and the Shoe promised to call him Mr. Putz in future. The final contract became one notrump doubled, cold for -500 but in actual fact at the table, just making for +180. The Shoe decided that there was another reason to like playing with Bozo: notrump did not play worse from Bozo's side. Perhaps he deserved to be called Mr. Putz. Despite the Shoe's feeble efforts at rebellion, serious play was destined to be part of the unavoidable future.

The System also made defense tougher for the opponents. Forcing raises or game raises in a major often included a hidden five-card or longer suit with declarer. That created more possibilities than ever for the ridiculous misdefense or the impossible squeeze. I was kibitzing the Shoe, in accordance with my official status, and watched an early outing for the System in a Regional Swiss game. Team Bozo vaulted swiftly to two wins and then met a famous team of experts in the third match. At Shoe's table, they were being gradually ground into the dust to an accompaniment of a never-ending stream of gratuitous advice. The Shoe hates to receive advice, especially when he's losing.

Somewhere around the fifth board, this was the Shoe's hand, both vulnerable:

♠ A Q 10 9 7 5 4 2   ♡ A K 10 9   ◇ 6   ♣ —

In accordance with the System, the Shoe opened one heart, preparing for an almighty canapé into about four spades. LHO passed and Bozo raised to four hearts, which showed a weak five-card raise to game. A stronger five-card raise would have splintered, while anything resembling a forcing raise would have gone through the 'modified' Jacoby two notrump. The Shoe felt obliged to advance to six hearts. After some thought, LHO led the unfortunate small spade, and the whole deal was:

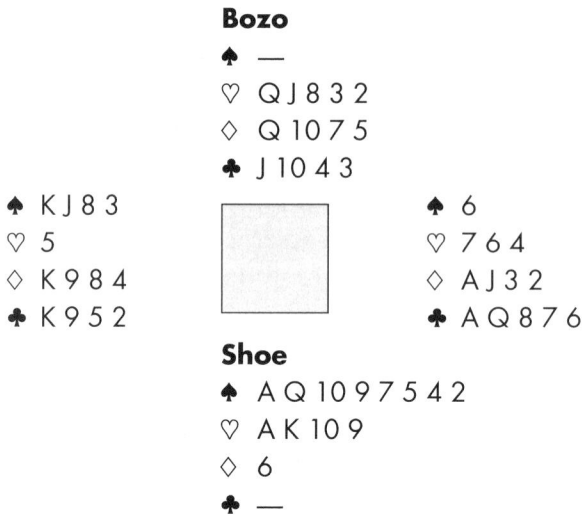

Bozo
♠ —
♡ Q J 8 3 2
♢ Q 10 7 5
♣ J 10 4 3

♠ K J 8 3
♡ 5
♢ K 9 8 4
♣ K 9 5 2

♠ 6
♡ 7 6 4
♢ A J 3 2
♣ A Q 8 7 6

Shoe
♠ A Q 10 9 7 5 4 2
♡ A K 10 9
♢ 6
♣ —

Making six was a 13 IMP pickup for team Bozo, who won, appropriately, 13-12. During the comparison, the Shoe complains about all the advice he was getting from the rude bastards at their table, and is advised that a rude bastard is standing behind him waiting to verify the score. The rude bastard has enough verve and aplomb to advise the Shoe: "I am *not* rude."

Playing with John Carruthers and John Guoba, Bozo and the Shoe took the System all the way to the finals of the 1975 Canadian Team Championship. In the semifinals, they had been all but eliminated by Team Kokish. Down 31 IMPs, the System produced a dozen hands that you never write famous stories about: partscores where the Shoe and Bozo stopped in something they could make, or beat the opponents a trick. Unfortunately, they missed two vulnerable diamond slams, one on power where the opponents had preempted clubs, and the other with a singleton heart opposite three small.

The two Johns proved what perfect teammates they were. They'd been struggling through a flat match and on Board 8 of the 16 board final quarter, John Guoba, by all reports for the first and only time of his entire career, psyched an opening Precision two club bid on a king. John Carruthers responded a forcing natural two spades on a king and the auction died in three clubs two down, -100. On the next hand, opponents were duly rattled and blasted three notrump after an inverted diamond raise. That lost the first five heart tricks, +100 for Team Bozo. So the two missed slams at +620 each converted to wins of 11 IMPs and 12 IMPs respectively.

Some say the final total was win by five, others that it was win by nine, but either way, John Guoba emerged with the still-famous whoop of "Make them pay!" which could be heard plainly in the other room, where it was immediately attributed to the Shoe. His fragile truce with Team Kokish was in jeopardy.

I was unable to attend the final and the Shoe blamed me for the absence of the Winning Butterfly. The sad story went like this: Team Bozo managed to avoid six slams, all under 50%. That was without counting the unfortunate hand where Bozo had made a lead-directing double of a club cuebid when his LHO held the ace queen, allowing LHO to count twelve tricks with the known winning club finesse. The worst was a grand slam that needed a trump pickup, a finesse and a squeeze that required RHO to hold five of five missing cards. Sad to say, all six slams made and opponents bid them all, so Team Bozo lost by something like 30 IMPs and it was back to the drawing board.

Of interest was one last misfortune suffered by Bozo and the Shoe in those team finals. Everybody loved to interfere with the forcing club, so Bozo and the Shoe developed a system of step responses over interference. The primary objective was to have a penalty double available, both to punish unwise interference and to help pick up the mandatory psychic bids that occurred from time to time. This strategy had proved very effective.

In the Canadian Team Championship finals, even that was not to be. Maybe it's true that I should have been kibitzing the Shoe when he picked up, at unfavorable vulnerability:

♠ 8 6 5 2 ♡ A 6 3 ◇ Q 10 6 5 4 ♣ 4

Bozo opened one club (forcing, asks controls) and Shoe's RHO over-called one heart (natural). Shoe bid one spade, which denied a penalty double and showed six or more HCP with two or fewer controls. The bid did not promise spades. This was the whole deal:

Bozo
♠ A 4
♡ —
◇ A K 9 7 3
♣ A Q J 10 3 2

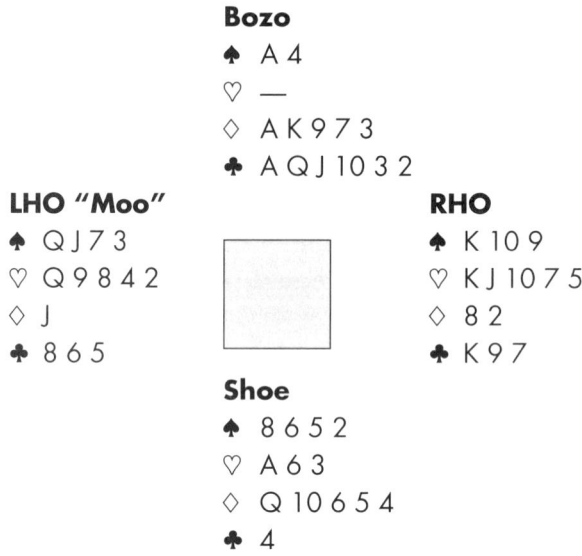

LHO "Moo"
♠ Q J 7 3
♡ Q 9 8 4 2
◇ J
♣ 8 6 5

RHO
♠ K 10 9
♡ K J 10 7 5
◇ 8 2
♣ K 9 7

Shoe
♠ 8 6 5 2
♡ A 6 3
◇ Q 10 6 5 4
♣ 4

At this point, LHO, who was the Shoe's landlord Don "Moo" Cowan, sensed a profitable save and decided to introduce a little sand into the machinery with a jump to three diamonds (natural). In addition to everything else, this or a spade would have been the only lead to beat six clubs, assuming Shoe and Bozo reached this inferior slam.

Playing penalty doubles, Bozo had a genuine problem. If three diamonds was legitimate, he might well be collecting about 500 into a grand slam in clubs. Finally, he decided to introduce the club suit. A more experienced player might have passed (forcing). The club bid had several disdvantages, including moving the bidding to the four-level.

On the actual hand, the Shoe had to decide what to bid. Was four diamonds natural or a cuebid? Did he really want to cuebid four hearts with a minimum response and a singleton club? After RHO passed, the Shoe decided to bid four spades as the least of evils and the Moo now introduced five hearts. This was a transparent auction, easy to figure out, wasn't it? Certainly, it was. Both Bozo and Shoe knew the Moo had been operating, but Bozo thought that five notrump now might be a grand slam force in spades and he was really worried that, since he hadn't penalty doubled three diamonds, six diamonds couldn't be natural. Bozo opted to pass, the most encouraging auction.

Over on his side, the Shoe could not really introduce six diamonds when Bozo had not penalty doubled. There were many other inferences to be had on this hand, but inevitably, the contract became five hearts doubled down four into the laydown grand slam in diamonds.

Shortly afterwards, Bozo retired from serious competitive bridge to take up teaching and raising a family, although he claimed he had intended to do so all along. The Shoe continued playing serious events with Colonel Bulldozer as his new victim. Bulldozer is perhaps the only player in the world who can disrupt entire tournaments by laughing with pleasure, no matter which side got the great result. The Colonel turned out to have the happy knack of playing better under pressure and he carried the Shoe to his first win in a Regional. Playing against a professional team undefeated in the fourth round, they posted a blitz with little nuggets like this:

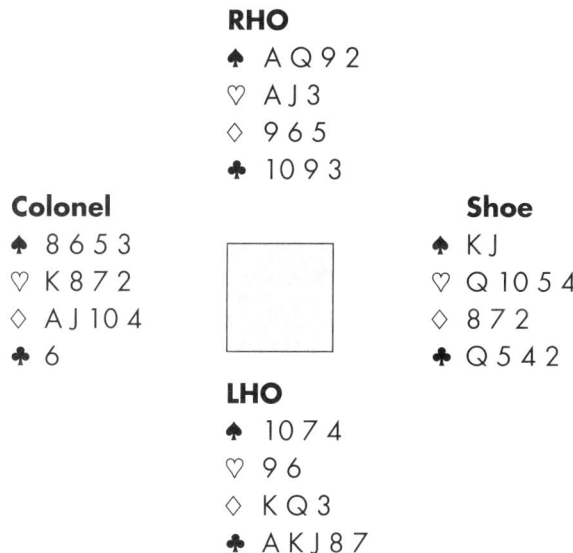

RHO
♠ A Q 9 2
♡ A J 3
◇ 9 6 5
♣ 10 9 3

Colonel
♠ 8 6 5 3
♡ K 8 7 2
◇ A J 10 4
♣ 6

Shoe
♠ K J
♡ Q 10 5 4
◇ 8 7 2
♣ Q 5 4 2

LHO
♠ 10 7 4
♡ 9 6
◇ K Q 3
♣ A K J 8 7

The opponents bid their way to the dizzying heights of a vulnerable two clubs. The Colonel led the ♠3, taking the view that MUD leads did not extend to four-card suits. Declarer opted to duck in dummy and the Shoe won his jack and shifted to the ◇8 to the king and ace.

A further spade was ducked as the Shoe won the king. Declarer rose with the ◇Q on the diamond switch and belatedly worried about the spade ruff by cashing the ♣A and ♣K. This was no great success, as the Shoe was able to win the third club, cross to partner's ◇10 and score a spade ruff. Two tricks in every suit but hearts produced the improbable one down, +100. At the other table, partners played three clubs doubled with an overtrick, +870.

Winning the Regional confirmed an affection that the Shoe had held for the Colonel for many years. It all dated back to a hand Bull-dozer had played with his wife, Mrs. Four-Notrump. It had been one of those great results you couldn't explain that started the Shoe on his everlasting search for wrong plays that came at the right time. Not vulnerable against vulnerable opponents, Bulldozer held:

♠ J 10 9 8 6 3 2   ♡ 7   ◇ A K 9   ♣ 8 5

The Colonel's LHO opened one club and Mrs. 4NT overcalled one diamond. RHO cuebid two diamonds and the Colonel doubled to show his diamonds, prompting LHO to contribute two notrump with-out a diamond stopper. Mrs. 4NT chose to introduce a bid of three hearts, doubled smoothly by the cuebidder and Bulldozer decided to mention his spade suit 'on the way' to four diamonds. When that was doubled, he changed his mind and decided to play there, hav-ing recently been converted to the Shoe's theory that hands played one or two tricks better from his side. With spades breaking 3-1, this contract was one down for -100. Why was this such a good thing? For all this modest bidding, Mrs. Four-Notrump held:

♠ 7 4   ♡ 10 9 4 3   ◇ Q 8 7 6 4 2   ♣ 10

The opponents were not just cold for game, they made a small slam in hearts or clubs. Of course, the actual -100 even beat the pairs who had languished in partscore.

The disadvantage of playing with the Colonel was that he was decidedly uncomfortable with the System. In the subsequent Cana-dian team trials, I know better than to miss showing up to kibitz, so the Winning Butterfly is plentifully in attendance, though I am forced to watch auctions that take place in mundane Standard American. That includes watching the ill-humor that Standard American engenders in the Shoe, all the while watching Bulldozer laughing happily as though nothing bad can happen.

The Shoe certainly needed the Winning Butterfly. Shoe thought he was in his element early as he picked up an opening one notrump bid:

♠ A Q 4   ♡ A Q 5   ◊ J 6 2   ♣ K 9 8 3

You could just see him getting pretty comfortable. Even his RHO's opening bid of one club did not disrupt his notrump plans, so he overcalled one notrump. LHO passed and Bulldozer contributed a cuebid of two clubs, from the days before 'systems on' was invented. RHO was unimpressed and contributed a bid of five clubs. The Shoe produced a firm double: he wasn't going to let people push around his notrump overcalls, especially if they proposed to do it at the five-level in his longest suit. Bulldozer removed to five hearts, which became the final contract. This was the entire deal:

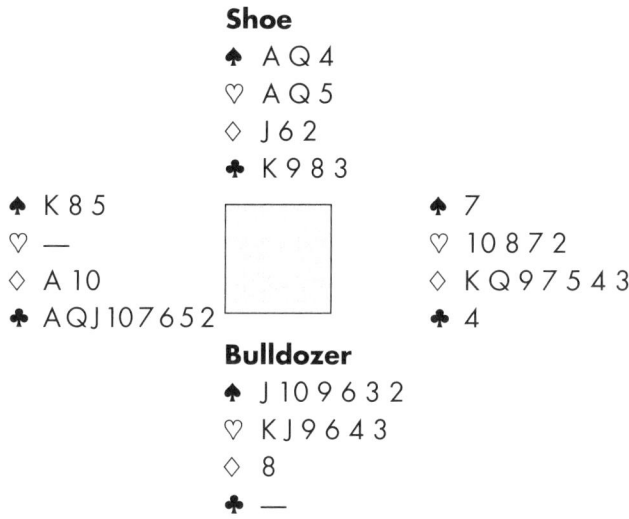

Shoe
♠ A Q 4
♡ A Q 5
◊ J 6 2
♣ K 9 8 3

♠ K 8 5
♡ —
◊ A 10
♣ A Q J 10 7 6 5 2

♠ 7
♡ 10 8 7 2
◊ K Q 9 7 5 4 3
♣ 4

Bulldozer
♠ J 10 9 6 3 2
♡ K J 9 6 4 3
◊ 8
♣ —

With the spade finesse onside, slam was cold. The other side didn't get to slam even after the Colonel's hand opened the bidding in first chair with one spade. However, in the post mortem, I am forced to assert myself by asking the Shoe if he would have found the diamond lead and diamond continuation that are necessary to lock out the dummy and set five clubs.

A little later in the event, the Shoe opened a mundane one diamond at unfavorable vulnerability holding:

♠ J 5   ♡ Q 10 9 3   ◇ A K Q 9 6 5   ♣ Q

LHO overcalled one spade and Bulldozer contributed a negative double. RHO raised spades and Shoe had to bid three hearts or risk losing the suit forever. No one had passed so far. LHO continued with a jump to four spades and the Colonel bid five hearts. RHO continued to five spades. The whole auction hadn't taken twenty seconds and still no one had passed.

The Shoe claimed later that he had discussed this very auction with the Bambino in the car on the way to the game. At this vulnerability, if you bid smoothly to six hearts, how can the opponents fail to take a save? Even Mrs. Whaley would take the save. Yet six hearts was passed out smoothly and the opponents cashed their major-suit aces for one down, as Bulldozer's hand was:

♠ 7   ♡ K J 7 6 5   ◇ J   ♣ A J 7 5 3 2

That was -100 at both tables. Bulldozer, laughing heartily, announced that it was another failure for theory.

After four of six matches, the Shoe's team was well below average and Bulldozer was enjoying himself as much as ever. A blitz was necessary or qualification for the next round was impossible. The Shoe gave me a sarcastic Bungalow remark that included reference to the Winning Butterfly. He picked up this little beauty:

♠ A   ♡ 3   ◇ K 4 3   ♣ A K 10 9 8 6 5 2

Nobody was vulnerable. The Shoe was dealer and was probably happy that the bidding hadn't reached the five-level by the time it got around to him. He opened an innocent one club and the first round was equally innocent: one diamond on the left, one spade by Bulldozer, pass on the right.

In the post mortem, the Shoe explained his reasoning (for which read, the reasons for his mistakes). "Years of playing against little old ladies should have taught me that you always bid four clubs on these hands and await developments. However, there was no way back to three notrump from four clubs. Also, I was thinking about the need for a blitz and the other possible bids. All diamond bids showed a spade raise: two diamonds a good hand, three diamonds a splinter with a singleton and four diamonds a splinter with a void. It occurred to me we had too many ways to raise spades.

"I rejected three clubs because I immediately pictured being passed out there when partner had:

♠ J x x x x   ♡ x x x x   ◇ A x   ♣ Q x

"On the same theory, I couldn't really bid three notrump and go down when six clubs makes. I also gave fleeting consideration to an effort to make the headlines by reversing into my singleton heart, and this might indeed be the bid that gets me information, but Bulldozer would not picture my 8-1 shape and I might have to play with Bulldozer again.

"After a brief pause of five or six minutes, I settled for a bid of five clubs, as it was the most likely game to make and partner might figure out to bid slam with both red aces, or a red ace and the trump queen."

The logic was sound, but Bulldozer still passed holding:

♠ Q J 5 4 3   ♡ A Q 6 2   ◇ A 9 8   ♣ 3

This hand is an example of a basic rule for would-be world champions: play the contract you are actually in, not the one you wish you were playing. The Shoe reacted in a fairly undignified way, proving he was not yet ready for prime time. He pointedly asked the Colonel what he thought he would need to bid on to slam in this auction. Bulldozer never lost his benign expression while he declined comment. The Shoe stayed aggravated, observing that the grand slam is on little more than a trump pickup.

He began the play of the hand by winning the opening diamond lead in the closed hand with the king with RHO contributing the deuce, an obvious singleton, then cashing a high trump. When LHO showed out, a squeeze would have to be for making five. Obviously, the hand was cold if the opening lead had been won in dummy and Shoe took the safety finesse in trumps when an honor did not appear. This had been the entire deal:

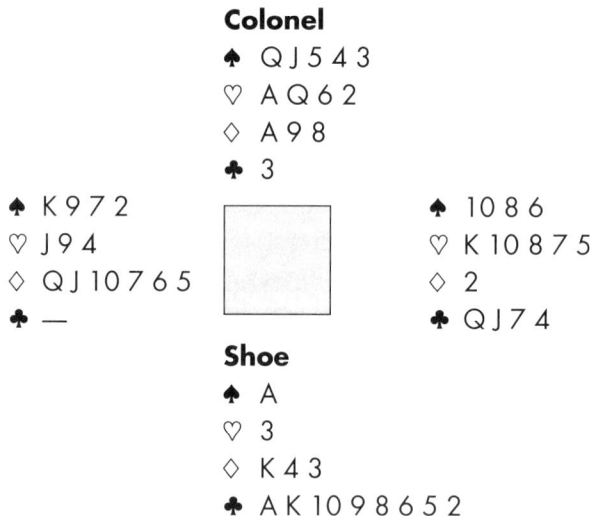

Colonel
♠ Q J 5 4 3
♡ A Q 6 2
◇ A 9 8
♣ 3

♠ K 9 7 2
♡ J 9 4
◇ Q J 10 7 6 5
♣ —

♠ 10 8 6
♡ K 10 8 7 5
◇ 2
♣ Q J 7 4

Shoe
♠ A
♡ 3
◇ K 4 3
♣ A K 10 9 8 6 5 2

Now of course, the Shoe was too embarrassed and despondent to figure the hand out and to play it correctly. All this when he should have been delighted that the slam might not make. Shoe continued with the king and another trump. RHO correctly cashed his second trump winner and LHO encouraged with the ♠9. Shoe won the ♠A, cashed a trump and then played a heart to the ace and ruffed a heart, coming to this position:

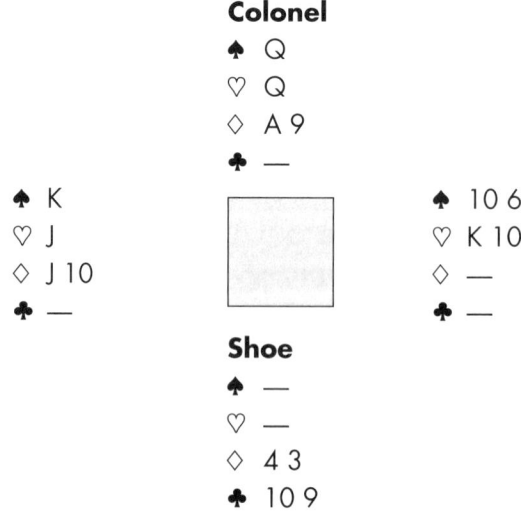

Colonel
♠ Q
♡ Q
◇ A 9
♣ —

♠ K
♡ J
◇ J 10
♣ —

♠ 10 6
♡ K 10
◇ —
♣ —

Shoe
♠ —
♡ —
◇ 4 3
♣ 10 9

From the Shoe's point of view, LHO's major-suit cards were unknown. When he cashed the second last trump winner, LHO could surrender if he held both major-suit kings. On the actual hand, he produced the ♡J and Shoe had to guess which major-suit king LHO had. He chose to believe LHO's encouraging signal and pitched dummy's ♡Q. Then on the cash of the final trump, LHO was genuinely squeezed in spades and diamonds.

It turned out everything had been the same at the other table: same simple auction, same play at Trick 1, same comments about partner's sanity, same misplays at Trick 1 and Trick 3. However, team-mates had the foresight not to signal encouragement in the spade suit. Declarer had guessed to play the heart-diamond squeeze instead of the spade-diamond squeeze. Win 10 IMPs. Win a blitz. Qualify for the next round.

The Shoe is almost humble in the post mortem, announcing that he played five clubs like an amateur. We tactfully skip the implication that he is usually a professional. He proceeds to ruin another Fran's tablecloth by writing out the eleven-card ending that remains in five clubs after he mistakenly wins the opening lead in the closed hand and cashes a high trump:

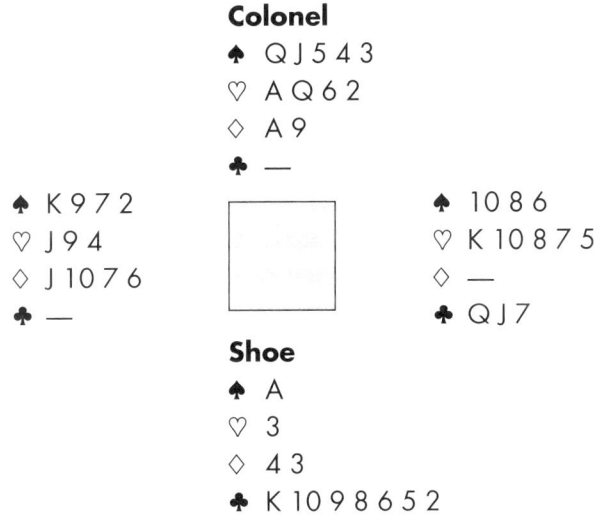

Colonel
♠ Q J 5 4 3
♡ A Q 6 2
◇ A 9
♣ —

♠ K 9 7 2
♡ J 9 4
◇ J 10 7 6
♣ —

♠ 10 8 6
♡ K 10 8 7 5
◇ —
♣ Q J 7

Shoe
♠ A
♡ 3
◇ 4 3
♣ K 10 9 8 6 5 2

Shoe challenges everybody to find the second mistake but people are more interested in their second beer, so it's hardly fair. After a decent interval, he pontificates only slightly.

"It is not necessary to guess anything if I just play half decently, even after my horrible mistakes at Tricks 1 and 2. We know that

RHO's play at Trick 1 showed a singleton diamond, so he is now out of diamonds. At Trick 3, I have to cash the ace of spades. Then, when I lead the ten of clubs, being careful not to pitch a spade from dummy, RHO is caught on his first endplay. He can't lead clubs or hearts without giving up a trick and he has no diamonds, so he must lead a spade, which I ruff. Now king and another club (pitch a heart and a diamond from dummy) endplays RHO again. RHO must lead another spade, which I ruff again. If RHO has no more spades, he's endplayed into giving me a heart trick for a diamond pitch. If, instead, LHO has no more spades, the ruffing finesse is on and I have two red aces in dummy for the entries. In all other cases, spades were 4-3, so I can travel to dummy with a red ace, trump a fourth round of spades and claim with the other red ace and a good spade for a diamond pitch.

"So what have I learned from all this?" he concludes. We are all seriously doubting that the Shoe has ever learned much of anything outside bridge. "I've learned that I can't fix anybody's mistakes except my own." As we are all hoping this statement might become true, we all nod sagely, except Bulldozer, who laughs happily. Shoe adds that there are far too many books written about squeezes.

14

More Squeezes

Nevertheless, the Shoe continued to be fascinated by squeeze play. So often, it came back to the Bambino's rule: "If I run my long suit, maybe something good will happen." The Shoe's horrible bidding did occasionally come back to haunt him, especially when he was desperately trying to keep the Half Bee off play. This was a perfect example, the Shoe held:

♠ 9 5 3   ♡ A 4   ◇ A 10 8 3 2   ♣ Q J 5

The Half Bee opened one club, which in the Forcing Diamond system meant any hand with no five-card major or notrump opener, under 17 HCP. East overcalled one heart. The Shoe jumped to two notrump, obviously from the wrong side with hearts out of position and no spade stopper. The Half Bee raised to three and the ♡8 was led on this layout:

Half Bee

♠ A 7
♡ J 9 3
◇ K Q 9 5
♣ A 10 6 3

♠ Q J 10 8 4 2   ♠ K 6
♡ 8 2   ♡ K Q 10 7 6 5
◇ 7 6   ◇ J 4
♣ 9 8 4   ♣ K 7 2

```
      N
  W       E
      S
```

Shoe

♠ 9 5 3
♡ A 4
◇ A 10 8 3 2
♣ Q J 5

It was immediately obvious that the Shoe, in his rush to keep the Half Bee off play, had bid off more than he could chew. Three notrump from the Half Bee's side would get the ♡K lead, won in Shoe's hand, and declarer could safely take the losing club finesse to make ten or eleven tricks. It was looking a lot like down a few from the Shoe's side, but I did not become number one kibitzer, inventor of the Winning Butterfly, by being content with such analysis.

The Shoe appeared unperturbed. He tried the futile ♡9 from dummy and won the ten with the ace. Then, in accordance with the Bambino's Rule, he rattled off five diamond tricks, pitching a heart from dummy. East had to come down to seven cards, including at least four hearts. (If East keeps fewer than four hearts, the losing club finesse becomes safe.) The other three cards were a singleton spade and the guarded ♣K, easy to diagnose when West made a wild series of spade pitches followed by a small club. East had been stripped of his safe exits and Shoe proved he had been paying attention by cashing the ♠A and exiting with a heart. The eventual club endplay produced nine tricks, only one trick worse than the Half Bee would have gotten in his sleep. The Shoe advised that this had been a strip squeeze. "Nicely played," said the Half Bee and I in unison.

There is no doubt that the Shoe landed in a few atrocious contracts, not invariably because of wild bidding. It was always interesting, in these situations, to watch him thank partner politely and then pull some rabbit out of the hat to make the hand. The most interesting deals were those where the rabbit was real, not just an illusion. I remember that he stumbled into six notrump with the Tree, famous for her excellent dummies, on this layout:

Tree
♠ K Q 5 2
♡ A 6 5
◇ Q 10
♣ K Q J 4

Shoe
♠ A 8
♡ K 10 4 2
◇ K 8 3 2
♣ A 9 6

Anyone could see there were only ten obvious tricks. It looked as though it was going to be necessary to finesse the ◇10, just for starters. Sure enough, on the opening club lead, the Shoe went through the ritual of thanking the Tree, won the club lead with the ace, and fired a diamond to the ten. That lost to the ace and the club return went to the dummy. Dummy's minor-suit winners were cashed, clubs first, discarding a heart from the closed hand. RHO discarded a diamond and a heart while LHO showed in.

On the ◇Q, LHO contributed the jack. Now both the Shoe and I were wondering if he could have been so lucky as to buy ◇J9x with LHO. A spade was led to the ace and the cash of the ◇K revealed the bad news: both LHO and dummy discarded a heart, leaving RHO with the ◇9. The Shoe went into a rare long huddle because he was pretty sure he could squeeze RHO, but what was RHO's other suit? Finally, from the discards, Shoe decided it was more likely that LHO had four or more hearts and therefore RHO had the spade stopper. The ending therefore became something like this, one round of spades having been played:

Tree
♠ K Q 5
♡ A 6
♢ —
♣ —

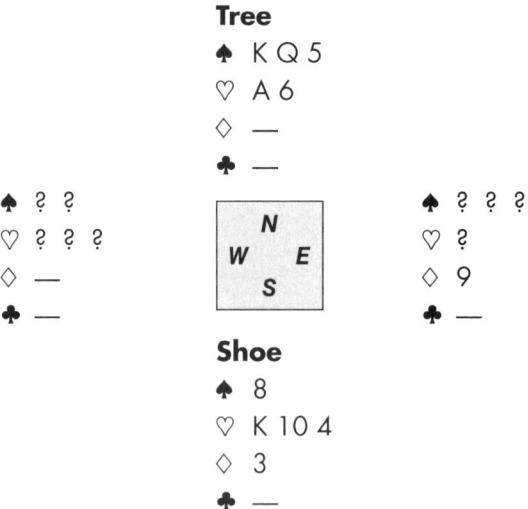

♠ ? ?   ♠ ? ? ?
♡ ? ? ?   ♡ ?
♢ —   ♢ 9
♣ —   ♣ —

Shoe
♠ 8
♡ K 10 4
♢ 3
♣ —

The Shoe cashed the high hearts ending in the closed hand, and RHO had to keep the good ♢9, so he was forced to pitch a spade. That created three spade winners in dummy. "Of course," the Shoe said to me, "if RHO had the hearts, I had to cash spades first to operate the heart-diamond squeeze on LHO."

"Of course," I replied.

"Of course," added RHO.

Sometimes, there were even good contracts. At another post mortem over beer at Fran's, the Shoe drew out a hand on which he and Bozo reached slam on this layout, after a spade preempt by East:

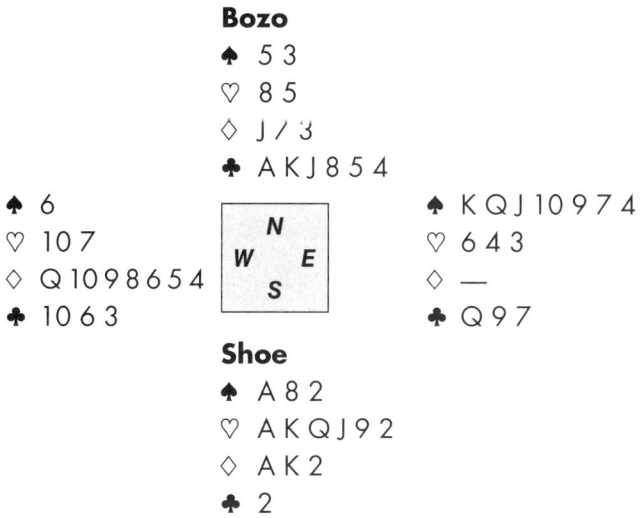

Bozo
♠ 5 3
♡ 8 5
◇ J 7 3
♣ A K J 8 5 4

♠ 6
♡ 10 7
◇ Q 10 9 8 6 5 4
♣ 10 6 3

♠ K Q J 10 9 7 4
♡ 6 4 3
◇ —
♣ Q 9 7

Shoe
♠ A 8 2
♡ A K Q J 9 2
◇ A K 2
♣ 2

"Obviously, six notrump makes on a simple double squeeze after a spade lead and spade continuation," announces the Shoe, with emphasis on the word 'simple'. "Having rectified the count by ducking the first spade, a high diamond would reveal the diamond situation. On the cash of all the winners, ending with hearts, I come down to four deuces. Dummy would keep the three of diamonds and the ace-king-jack of clubs. The ace-king-four would do just as well. On the cash of the deuce of hearts, West must keep a diamond and therefore only two clubs. Dummy then pitches its diamond and East must keep a spade over my deuce, also reducing to two clubs. Clubs divide 2-2 for the last three tricks.

"Unfortunately, we were in six hearts, doubled by East. I couldn't duck the opening spade lead, nor could I rectify the count as there was nothing to duck later except a spade, in which case East could cash two spade winners. This was a serious problem. It sure looked as though I'd need a club finesse. While I thought about it, East began to berate his partner for failing to give him a ruff. The little light went on in the 'idea' department. I drew trumps, making sure to keep all my diamonds in dummy. West had showed up with one spade, two hearts and a hypothetical seven diamonds and, therefore, at most three clubs.

"I love this hand! I cashed the ace and king of clubs, pitching my king of diamonds. Then I ruffed a club back to my hand and exited with ace and a diamond. West had to give me the dummy."

Bozo was no fool about squeezes, either. On this deal, Bozo and the Shoe defended seven notrump:

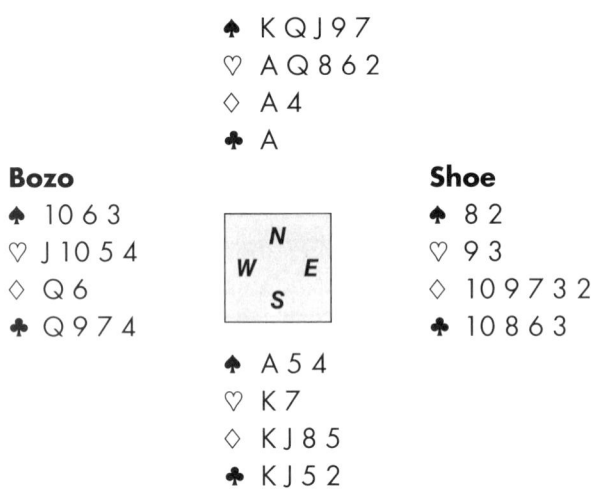

♠ K Q J 9 7
♡ A Q 8 6 2
◇ A 4
♣ A

Bozo
♠ 10 6 3
♡ J 10 5 4
◇ Q 6
♣ Q 9 7 4

Shoe
♠ 8 2
♡ 9 3
◇ 10 9 7 3 2
♣ 10 8 6 3

♠ A 5 4
♡ K 7
◇ K J 8 5
♣ K J 5 2

Declarer won the spade lead in dummy and played three rounds of hearts to discover they did not split. Then, ♣A, spade to the ace, ♣K. The run of the spades produced this ending:

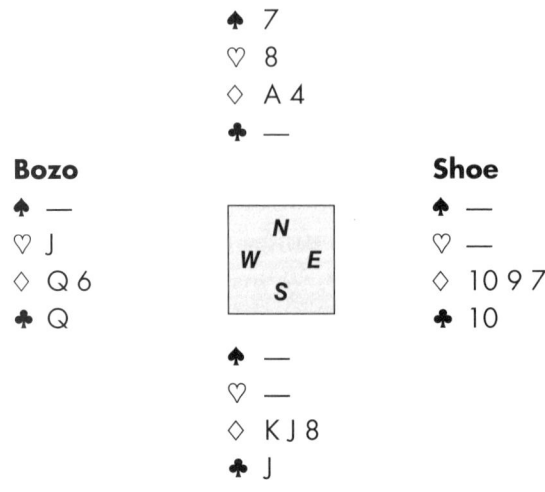

♠ 7
♡ 8
◇ A 4
♣ —

Bozo
♠ —
♡ J
◇ Q 6
♣ Q

Shoe
♠ —
♡ —
◇ 10 9 7
♣ 10

♠ —
♡ —
◇ K J 8
♣ J

On the cash of the last spade, the Shoe pitched the ♣10, declarer the jack and Bozo the queen. Shoe was now known to hold three diamonds from an initial five-card holding, while Bozo had two diamonds plus a good heart. Bozo had brilliantly bared the ◇Q by bo ing dealt a doubleton before the squeeze began. The Shoe followed with the nine and ten to the ace and small diamond from dummy. Declarer had lots of good reasons to misguess and did, two down. The boys had been very lucky that hearts did not split and that Shoe hadn't been dealt the ♣Q or the ◇Q.

As soon as the opponents were out of earshot, Bozo suggested an artistic alternate line of play that avoids the agonizing guess. His line was to cash the ace and king of both minors. If a queen falls, as in this case, the hand is over. If nothing good happens, run the spades. If one player has four or more hearts and either minor-suit queen, he will be caught in a double Vienna Coup on this ending:

♠ 7
♡ A Q 8 6
◇ —
♣ —

♠ —
♡ K 7
◇ J 8
♣ J

On the cash of the last spade from dummy, declarer can afford the ◇8, keeping two minor-suit jacks. Anyone with a heart stopper and a minor queen must come down to three hearts to keep the minor queen, so hearts will run for four tricks. Not only will you make the hand, you will get your name in the newspaper as well. Of course, if hearts were 3-3 all along, they are still 3-3 and you also get the necessary heart tricks, but not as much applause.

Another intriguing contract was the hand where Colonel Bulldozer reached seven spades after Shoe opened and East overcalled three hearts, both vulnerable. Bulldozer launched into Blackwood as he had been trained to do, and the end result was a contract of seven spades doubled by West and redoubled by Bulldozer. West led a high club, and this was the deal:

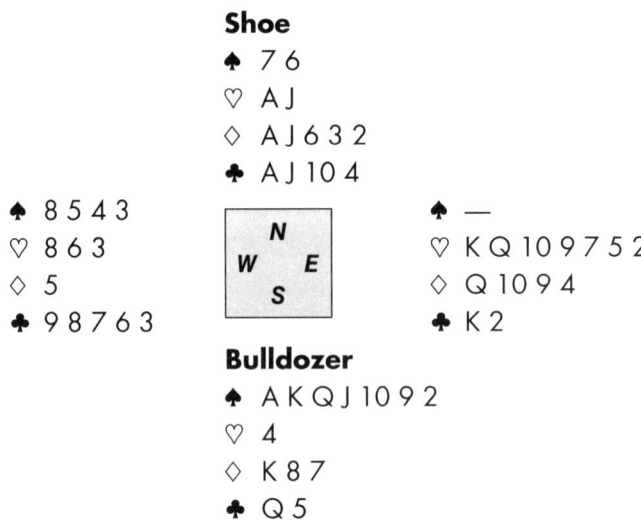

Shoe
♠ 7 6
♡ A J
◇ A J 6 3 2
♣ A J 10 4

♠ 8 5 4 3
♡ 8 6 3
◇ 5
♣ 9 8 7 6 3

♠ —
♡ K Q 10 9 7 5 2
◇ Q 10 9 4
♣ K 2

Bulldozer
♠ A K Q J 10 9 2
♡ 4
◇ K 8 7
♣ Q 5

If the double hadn't been enough, East's spade void suggested that East had the ♣K *and* a diamond stopper. Bulldozer played accordingly, winning the ♣A and running the spades to produce this six-card ending with one spade trick to go:

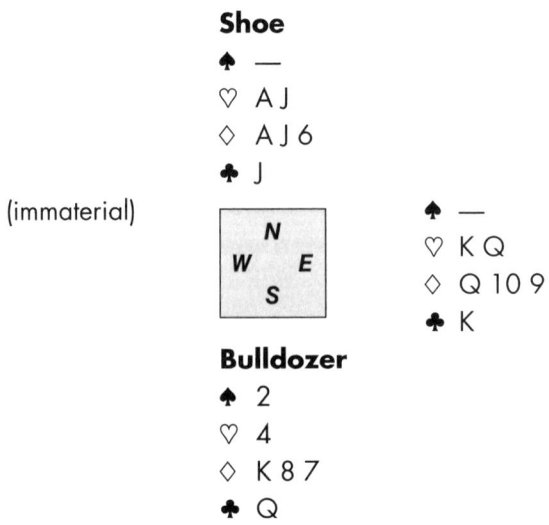

Shoe
♠ —
♡ A J
◇ A J 6
♣ J

(immaterial)

♠ —
♡ K Q
◇ Q 10 9
♣ K

Bulldozer
♠ 2
♡ 4
◇ K 8 7
♣ Q

On the cash of the final spade, dummy let go a club and East had no winning options. A heart or a club pitch would repeat the squeeze. East did his best with a diamond, but Bulldozer was up to the unblock of the ◇J on the second round of diamonds so that he could win the third round of diamonds in the closed hand. That way, the Vienna coup repeated in clubs and hearts.

The Shoe had a soft spot for squeezes on defense, especially in mundane contracts. Here is a hand where it looked for all the world like he would be declarer:

♠ K J 6 2   ♡ 3   ◇ A J 10 9   ♣ A Q 8 2

RHO opened one club and the Shoe was losing by enough that he violated his system, which would have demanded a pass, by bidding one spade. LHO made a negative double and RHO converted to one notrump, which became the final contract. Stuck for a lead, the Shoe tried the ◇A. This was the deal:

LHO
♠ A Q 5
♡ A 10 8 4
◇ 6 4 3 2
♣ 7 5

Shoe
♠ K J 6 2
♡ 3
◇ A J 10 9
♣ A Q 8 2

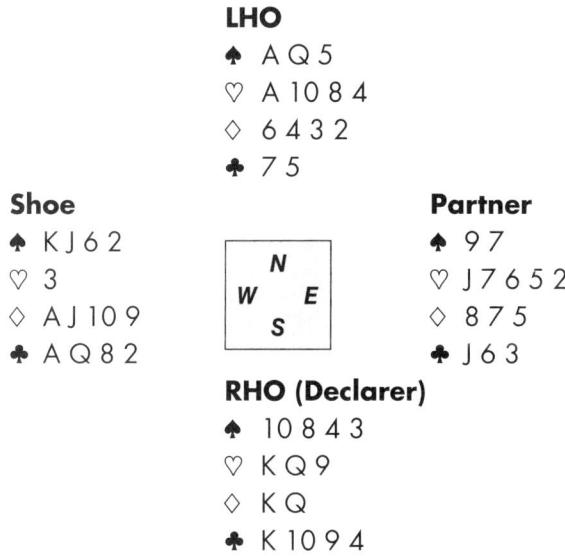

Partner
♠ 9 7
♡ J 7 6 5 2
◇ 8 7 5
♣ J 6 3

RHO (Declarer)
♠ 10 8 4 3
♡ K Q 9
◇ K Q
♣ K 10 9 4

After the ◇A caught the queen, the Shoe cleared the diamonds. Declarer won and finessed the ♠Q. Then he tested hearts and got the bad news on the second round, Shoe discarding the ♣2. Now came the ♠10, covered, to the ace. Declarer forgot to notice that East showed in. Next, he tried a club down. Partner valiantly tried the jack, which went to the king and ace. The Shoe cashed the diamonds, producing this ending with one diamond to go:

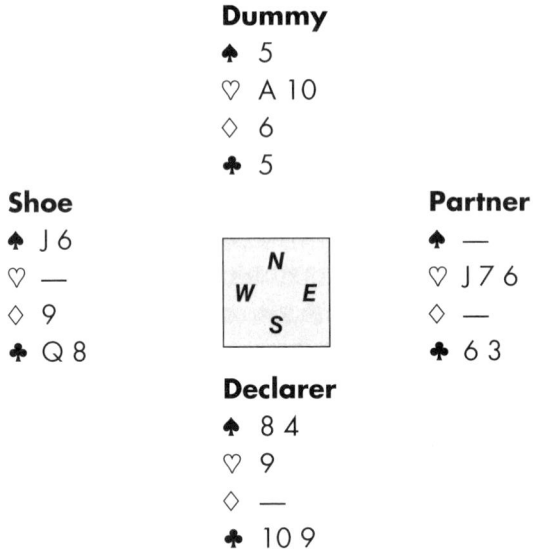

Dummy
♠ 5
♡ A 10
◇ 6
♣ 5

Shoe
♠ J 6
♡ —
◇ 9
♣ Q 8

Partner
♠ —
♡ J 7 6
◇ —
♣ 6 3

Declarer
♠ 8 4
♡ 9
◇ —
♣ 10 9

On the cash of the last diamond, declarer could not afford to part with a black card, so he had to pitch the ♡9. Now locked out of the dummy, Shoe produced queen and another club, forcing declarer to lead from the ♠84 into Shoe's ♠J6. A strip squeeze on declarer for one down. That was worth 1 IMP, since at the other table, partners had obtained 2200 defending two hearts redoubled. But it was worth it.

However, it took the Victim and his instant table presence to teach the Shoe that you could actually defend against a squeeze. It is often a thing of beauty when declarer is an expert who notices things and the Shoe is on defense with someone equally bent. Oops, I meant to say, of a similar bent. In the auction, that would be the Bambino, but on defense, it was unquestionably the Victim.

On this deal, they were playing a detail-oriented expert who made note of everything and used 90% of both pairs' allotted time to do it. He was also a player with a nose for getting his name in lights for the spectacular play. The Victim and the Shoe long ago reached the agreement that they would use extra time forced upon them by slow declarers to study their assumptions about the hand, rather than sitting there self-righteously steaming. The auction went:

Victim (West)	Dummy	Shoe (East)	Declarer
			1♠
2◇	pass	pass	3♠
pass	4♠	dbl	rdbl
all pass			

This was the deal:

Dummy
♠ 10 8
♡ Q J 8 6 4
◇ K 8 2
♣ 6 4 3

Victim
♠ —
♡ 10 9 7 2
◇ A J 10 9 5 4
♣ 9 8 5

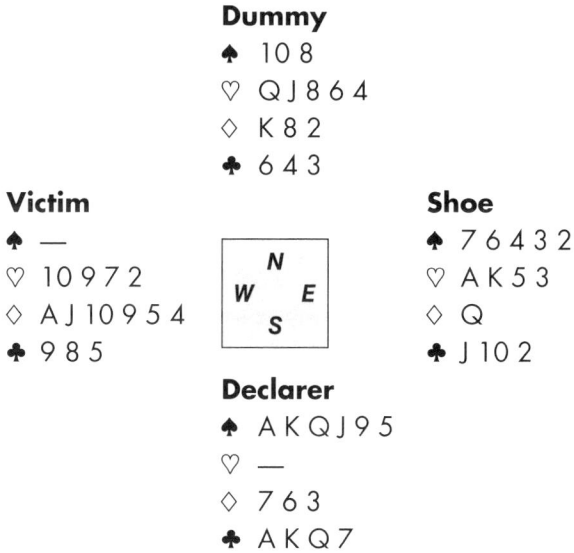

Shoe
♠ 7 6 4 3 2
♡ A K 5 3
◇ Q
♣ J 10 2

Declarer
♠ A K Q J 9 5
♡ —
◇ 7 6 3
♣ A K Q 7

The Victim led the ◇A, Shoe playing the queen. The ◇J was continued, king from dummy, ruffed by the Shoe with the ♠2 and a trump
was returned.

Declarer went into a very long study. The Victim was not playing preemptive jump overcalls and occasionally bid very light. The
Shoe would not double without outside cards, holding no trump
tricks. Declarer reconstructed the hands by allocating the Shoe four
or five hearts to the ace and king. If four hearts, clubs were 3-3. If five
hearts, clubs were 4-2 and something brilliant would be required.
During all the time it took for this analysis, the Shoe and the Victim
were working along the same lines.

Ultimately, declarer won the ♠8 in dummy and led the ♡Q, king
from Shoe, ruffed high, seven from the Victim. Back to the dummy
with the ♠9 to the ten to lead the ♡J, covered and trumped as the
Victim played the ♡9. This looked like ♡1097 with the Victim, so he

had the four clubs. Declarer now drew the rest of the trumps, assuming the Victim had to keep all four clubs and a high diamond. Sure enough, on the last trump, the Victim let go the ♡10, establishing the ♡86 in dummy.

Declarer now cashed the ♣A and noted the fall of Shoe's ten. He led the ♣7 and claimed triumphantly when Shoe won the jack. Unfortunately for declarer, Shoe produced the ♣2, having picked up on the 'hide the deuce' motif when the Victim had concealed the deuce of hearts for three rounds. That left declarer hand-locked with a diamond loser when clubs had been 3-3 all along. The Shoe innocently observed, at the table, of course, that this defense could never have worked against a player who didn't pay such careful attention to the spots.

15

Tomorrow, the World

After Bozo retires from serious bridge and Colonel Bulldozer balks at playing the System, Shoe enters the doldrums. He is rescued in an unlikely fashion. He begins to be stalked by a bridge player from Montreal who has heard all the Shoe-related horror stories from the likes of Eric Kokish and assorted other Montreal bridge luminaries. This guy bears an uncanny resemblance to Big Bird, without all the yellow feathers. Out of kindness to Big Bird, the Shoe dubs him 'The World's Largest Rookie', TWLR for short.

At this point, the Shoe is renting the third floor apartment over an entertainment agency run by the Moo Cow, the very player who beat him with all the slams in 1975. One day, the Shoe and I are heading out to Kate's when TWLR shows up and announces he's rented a room on the second floor. The good news is, now he can learn the System and discuss it with the Shoe every day. The other good news is that he brings a giant television set and a sound system the size of a room.

The Shoe agrees to play with him, and the rest, as they say, is agony. The Shoe and TWLR play various serious events and I am ordered to bring the Winning Butterfly. Over time, TWLR becomes too complicated as a nickname. Inevitably, 'Big Bird' prevails.

Big Bird turns out to be amazingly gifted at difficult bridge hands, though not quite as steady on the ordinary boring stuff. The following is an example from the System in action and also of the Big Bird on defense. With no one vulnerable, Big Bird picks up:

♠ Q J 5 ♡ K J 10 2 ◇ A K Q 9 ♣ 10 6

The Shoe starts the proceedings with one club (17+ HCP, forcing, asks controls) and Big Bird shows his four controls by bidding one notrump, forcing to game. Shoe continues with two clubs natural and Big Bird's RHO steps in with an ill-conceived two hearts. Big Bird doubles for penalties and everyone passes. Just as though it was perfectly normal, Big Bird's opening lead is the ♡2! The whole deal was:

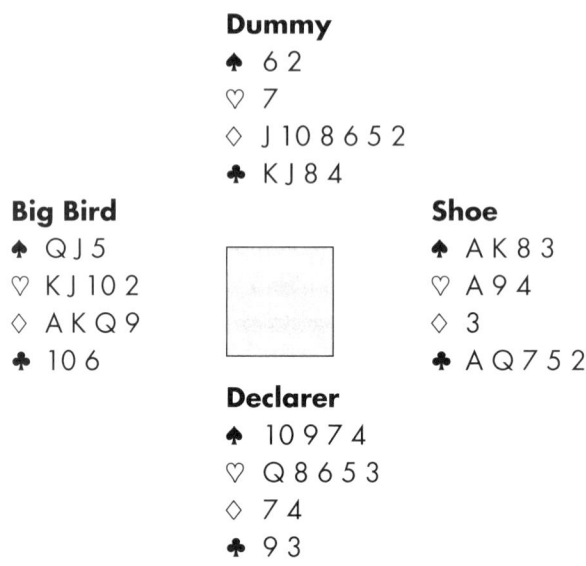

Dummy
♠ 6 2
♡ 7
◇ J 10 8 6 5 2
♣ K J 8 4

Big Bird
♠ Q J 5
♡ K J 10 2
◇ A K Q 9
♣ 10 6

Shoe
♠ A K 8 3
♡ A 9 4
◇ 3
♣ A Q 7 5 2

Declarer
♠ 10 9 7 4
♡ Q 8 6 5 3
◇ 7 4
♣ 9 3

Trumps are drawn and the defense collects four hearts, four spades and two tricks in each minor. Even using old math, this is +1300, more than a small slam. No one bids the grand slam that needs the heart pickup and the club finesse.

One of the first serious outings for the new partnership was the pairs trial to qualify for the World Championships in Monte Carlo. The Shoe already had the press release drafted for when they qualified: "This pair are new arrivals on the international bridge scene. The Shoe's career as a bridge humorist is underscored by his theories of bidding. It has been said his partner, Big Bird, plays the dummy like Lizzie Borden plays the axe. The Shoe insists this is not so, as Lizzie Borden played the axe quite well. They will be chaperoned by their designated kibitzer, 'Bungalow' Bill Miller."

After one session, things were proceeding as planned: they had 453 matchpoints and the second place pair had 411 on a 25 top. In the second session, they extended their lead to nearly three full boards. The generous carryover formula cut their lead to a single board without the need to play a single card. When they finished four boards below average in the third session, they were now a board and a half below average after being eight boards above the day before. The event was over, but it was not without its educational hands.

My favorite was one where Big Bird and the Shoe reached four spades after an opponent had interjected an overcall of clubs. You may recall that the System involves the canapé style of opening bids, where the four-card suit is bid before the five-card suit. This was the auction:

LHO	Big Bird	RHO	Shoe
			1♠
pass	2♠	3♣	3♡*
pass	4♠	all pass	

The entire deal was:

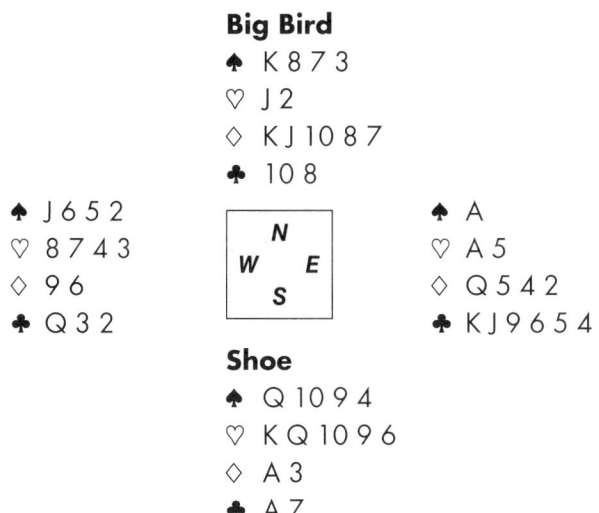

Big Bird
♠ K 8 7 3
♡ J 2
◇ K J 10 8 7
♣ 10 8

♠ J 6 5 2
♡ 8 7 4 3
◇ 9 6
♣ Q 3 2

♠ A
♡ A 5
◇ Q 5 4 2
♣ K J 9 6 5 4

Shoe
♠ Q 10 9 4
♡ K Q 10 9 6
◇ A 3
♣ A 7

On a small club lead, Shoe won in the closed hand and travelled to the ◇K, LHO contributing the nine, to lead a trump from the board. RHO had no choice but to win the ace. He cashed a high club and it was pretty obvious that the Shoe had begun with a 4-5-2-2 distribution. After much thought, RHO produced the usual expert rhetorical question, something to the effect of: what can it hurt to give a ruff and discard? So he did.

The Shoe knew that the long spades were going to be on his left, so he trumped in the closed hand. The cash of the ♠Q confirmed the 4-1 split. The Shoe announced that he was reduced to a heart attack. The favorable lie of the heart suit meant that even with best defense (a duck on the first round of hearts, winning the second round and returning a diamond to the ace), Shoe could pitch the remaining two diamonds from dummy. Two had already gone on diamond leads, and one was pitched on the ruff and discard.

In the actual case, RHO continued with a second ruff and discard; again Shoe trumped in the closed hand and again a diamond was discarded from dummy. Now the Shoe just ran hearts until LHO ruffed in, when he overruffed, drew trumps and claimed. Everyone took for granted the brilliance of the two ruff and discards and admired the way the Shoe had overcome this defense.

It was only later at Fran's Restaurant that the Shoe gave this defensive problem to the local experts. They all found the ruff and discard: given that Shoe was marked with 4-5-2-2 and both minor suit aces, 'there's no harm in it'. Perhaps a trump trick would be promoted for partner.

The Shoe admonished them for reading too many bridge books: there *was* harm in it. RHO not only had the count on the Shoe's hand, but also on his partner's. Partner was 4-4-2-3 and you need his spades headed by at least the jack or the ten-nine, or for declarer to misplay the hand by drawing too many rounds of trumps. Any better holding was a natural trump trick and the defense was irrelevant.

If RHO had returned a simple diamond, the declarer would have to leave two trumps outstanding when he dislodged the ♡A. Drawing all the trumps would leave the hand in notrump with all the clubs running. Drawing all but one would leave no communication when RHO forces declarer to trump a third round of (low) diamonds with his last trump while partner pitches a heart. So, when RHO gets in with the ace on the *second* round of hearts, the ending with RHO on lead, as the Shoe diagrammed on the tablecloth, becomes:

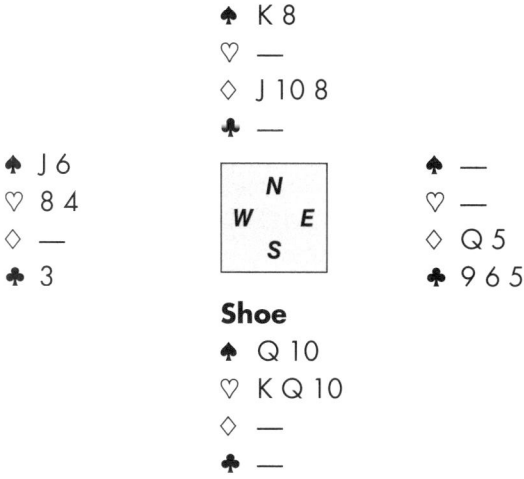

♠ K 8
♡ —
◇ J 10 8
♣ —

♠ J 6
♡ 8 4
◇ —
♣ 3

```
    N
 W     E
    S
```

♠ —
♡ —
◇ Q 5
♣ 9 6 5

Shoe
♠ Q 10
♡ K Q 10
◇ —
♣ —

Now the lead of another diamond finishes declarer: he has to lose an overruff right now or trump with the ♠Q while LHO discards a heart. Now the dummy is left with a diamond loser if LHO trumps low at the earliest opportunity, as declarer can't draw the last trump by returning to his hand. Of course, nothing works if partner's trumps were headed only by the nine or ten, as declarer is still able to have the queen and jack of trumps in the ending (with the ten outstanding that meant he had to float the nine of trumps to draw the second trump at some point). The important thing is to realize what your task actually is, pontificates the Shoe. The ruff-sluff never promotes a trump trick that wasn't there in any event, while the continuous diamond plays promote a trick if partner has the jack, or the ten-nine, or maybe just the ten.

The next year Big Bird and the Shoe were back at it in the Canadian teams championship. Early matches weren't looking so great by the time this board rolled around. The Shoe's hand was:

♠ A K 4 3   ♡ Q J 4 3   ◇ —   ♣ A K 7 4 2

Big Bird opened the bidding one diamond and after the Shoe responded two clubs, removed the Shoe's double of two hearts to three clubs. Shoe gave him one chance to escape by bidding three notrump, but when Big Bird removed to four clubs, he strung him up in six clubs. This had been the entire auction:

LHO	Big Bird	RHO	Shoe
	1◇	pass	2♣
2♡	pass	pass	dbl
pass	3♣	pass	3NT
pass	4♣	pass	6♣

This was the dummy:

Big Bird
♠ 9 8 6 5
♡ —
◇ A K 8 7 5 4
♣ 10 8 6

Shoe
♠ A K 4 3
♡ Q J 4 3
◇ —
♣ A K 7 4 2

The opening lead was the ♡A. Usually, the less the Shoe complains about the dummy, the worse are his chances, and he made comment here. You should know that the System permits opening one of a suit with weak one-suiters with defense, provided that you don't canapé into another suit, which shows a 'real' opening bid (11+ HCP).

Prospects were not good. The Shoe could see that even with all the suits splitting, he would need the ruffing finesse in hearts. Unless LHO had overcalled a mere five-card heart suit, LHO would have to cover the first high heart led from the closed hand, so that the other small heart could also be ruffed in dummy. In addition to all that, there would be a shortage of hand entries, so Shoe would have to guess LHO's three-card side suit and it had better not be clubs.

The early play was easy because there were no choices. Trump the opening lead as RHO contributes the deuce and cash two high diamonds pitching the spade losers from the closed hand. LHO played the deuce-six and RHO the three-jack. Travel to a high spade and lead the ♡Q, covered as requested. Back to the other high spade: nobody ruffs. Trump the small heart with dummy's last trump.

Now came the hard part, but Shoe decided to return to the closed hand by trumping a diamond based on the number of cards outstanding and also on the fall of the cards. This had been the entire deal:

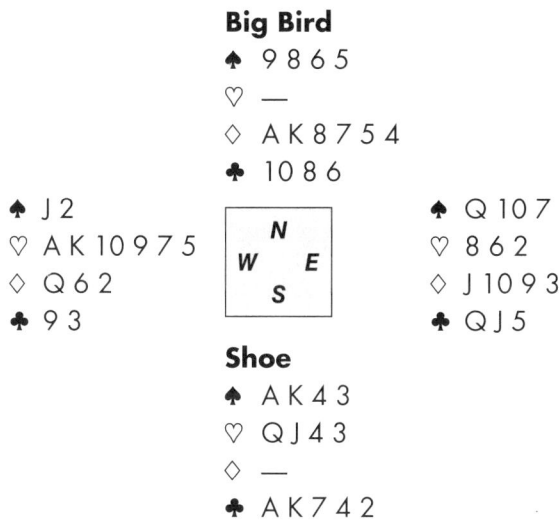

Big Bird
♠ 9 8 6 5
♡ —
◇ A K 8 7 5 4
♣ 10 8 6

♠ J 2
♡ A K 10 9 7 5
◇ Q 6 2
♣ 9 3

♠ Q 10 7
♡ 8 6 2
◇ J 10 9 3
♣ Q J 5

Shoe
♠ A K 4 3
♡ Q J 4 3
◇ —
♣ A K 7 4 2

The diamond ruff succeeded and the clubs split. The boys chalked up +920, winning 14 IMPs as somebody forgot to make three notrump at the other table. Big Bird nodded sagely and added, "You had to be there." The opponents had not been strong on defense but with the 14-IMP pickup, the boys won the match by four.

The Shoe, who was beginning to show a disturbing tendency to reanalyze hands, noted that the hand was actually Shoe-proof. Even if LHO does not cover the ♡Q, the hand will make after he lets it ride. Then the third heart is trumped in dummy and a spade is led back to the hand. RHO can overruff the fourth heart with his natural trump trick, but there is no uppercut as only one round of spades and two rounds of diamonds have been led.

The weak hand with diamonds proves to be an omen, as the Shoe later picks up, vulnerable against not:

♠ 8 5 2   ♡ 4 3   ◇ A K J 10 4 2   ♣ 6 5

In the System, Shoe opens the 'automatic' one diamond. LHO bids a preemptive two hearts. There are a lot of points left over for the other two hands. Big Bird cuebids three hearts and RHO contributes four hearts. Shoe passes, as does LHO, and Big Bird, never timid, bids Blackwood, then six diamonds. This is the deal:

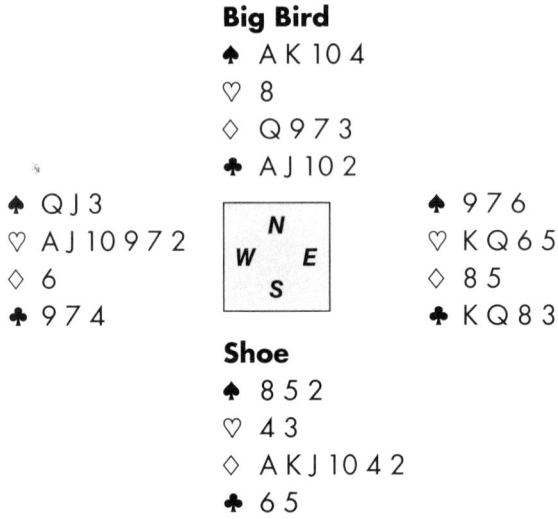

Big Bird
♠ A K 10 4
♡ 8
◇ Q 9 7 3
♣ A J 10 2

♠ Q J 3
♡ A J 10 9 7 2
◇ 6
♣ 9 7 4

♠ 9 7 6
♡ K Q 6 5
◇ 8 5
♣ K Q 8 3

Shoe
♠ 8 5 2
♡ 4 3
◇ A K J 10 4 2
♣ 6 5

LHO leads the ♡A and shifts to the ♠3. The Shoe calculates his monumental odds: a 3-3 spade break into the heart preempt, with the ♠QJ onside. There is no other play that can succeed, so Shoe inserts the ♠10. When that wins, six diamonds comes rolling home. LHO, it can now be revealed, was Bill Milgram, playing bridge the way it should be played with the excellent low spade shift. He continues playing bridge the way it was intended, congratulating the Shoe on his fine play. The Shoe says there was no other option and Bill continues in the same gracious vein that many players would not have found it.

Probably in deference to all this sportsmanship, Shoe waits until the Milgrams have left the table before he adds, "You actually have to go down in five diamonds. In five, the percentage play is to take the double club finesse to pitch a spade. Weird hand. Cold for six diamonds, can't make five."

Big Bird and the Shoe begin to chalk up a long series of good showings in Canadian championships, but there are, as yet, no victories. Even so, there are signs of improvement. Although Big Bird and the Shoe are refining the System, their good results continue to happen in non-System situations. Late in one event, with first place already hopelessly out of reach, the Shoe picked up an automatic one notrump bid:

$$\spadesuit K Q \quad \heartsuit A Q 8 7 \quad \diamondsuit J 10 7 \quad \clubsuit A 10 4 2$$

Big Bird treated him to Gerber, so Shoe showed his two aces and a king, and Big Bird settled in seven notrump. LHO was a solid, reliable player and RHO was the Hummingbird. With little to go on, LHO showed genuine concern over the opening lead, presumably eliminating clubs as the Bird had missed two opportunities to double those. He finally emerged with the ◇2 and the Shoe bought the following single-dummy problem:

Big Bird
♠ A 3
♡ 9 2
◇ A K Q 8 5
♣ K J 9 6

Shoe
♠ K Q
♡ A Q 8 7
◇ J 10 7
♣ A 10 4 2

Even without the duplication of the spades, the grand slam was ambitious. The Shoe let the diamond run around to the ten, Hummingbird showing in. On the continuation of the diamond, the Hummingbird pitched the ♡3. On the next two diamonds, the Hummingbird contributed the ♠2 and then the ♠4, while the Shoe dumped a heart. Now, Shoe took the unavoidable heart finesse which won, both opponents following small. The ♠K was followed by the queen to the ace while everyone showed in, LHO playing low-nine. On the final diamond the Hummingbird and the Shoe pitched small hearts and LHO the ♠J.

The Hummingbird had shown four low spades and he must have the ten and maybe a sixth spade: LHO would have led a spade from ♠J109. The Hummingbird also must have five hearts, as he would never have made an early heart pitch from four to the king. That left one diamond and at most two clubs for the Hummingbird, three or four clubs for LHO.

In the old days, that's where the analysis would have ended, but this was the new Shoe, king of reanalysis. What was going on here? If the Hummingbird 's early count in spades was accurate, LHO was *trying* to look like a guy with three spades and therefore four clubs, when he actually has three spades and three clubs. Also, would LHO have had such a big lead problem from:

$$♠ J \, 9 \, 8 \, (5) \quad ♡ \, 10 \, 4 \quad ♢ \, 9 \, 6 \, 4 \, 3 \quad ♣ \, Q \, x \, x \, (x)$$

Furthermore, the Hummingbird was never forced to pitch an early heart to tip off the five-card heart suit, so he was revealing his short-ness in the key suit voluntarily. He should have been pitching all spades, at least at the beginning, and especially if he had six of them. Would the Hummingbird have pitched the extra heart, rather than a spade loser, if LHO had the ♣Q? Wouldn't he try to look like a man with five spades and four hearts, and therefore three clubs? The Hummingbird is good: he notices stuff like this. So, in addition to the problem on opening lead, the Shoe became very suspicious of that heart pitch at the first opportunity. He concluded that the Humming-bird had the missing ♣Q. It turned out that he did have it, doubleton, and that was making seven.

Quite accidentally, the Shoe and Big Bird developed a sort of spe-cialty at torturing George Mittelman, at that time one of Canada's most successful players in various world championships, with med-als to his credit. No one quite knows when this began, but it was probably right around the time that the Shoe out-analyzed George on this hand:

```
     ♠ J 8
     ♡ A K 10 8 5 4
     ◇ 3
     ♣ J 10 9 4

          ┌─────────┐
          │    N    │
          │ W     E │
          │    S    │
          └─────────┘

     ♠ K 5
     ♡ Q 6 3 2
     ◇ A K Q 10
     ♣ Q 8 5
```

Naturally Shoe opened the South hand one notrump and became declarer in four hearts after a transfer auction. After the opening lead of the ♣2, George won the ace and shifted smoothly to a low spade. It is true that 'everybody' knows about the underlead of the ♠A in that situation and that a lead from the queen rates to give a trick away. After what for the Shoe was long deliberation, he played low! That forced the ace. George, never shy about discussing his feelings, let fly with a string of unprintable adjectives, all modifying the word 'Shoe', then added the observation that "no one guesses this situation." The Shoe volunteered to give George bridge lessons for a modest fee. The board was no swing, as the other table, without the benefit of a transfer auction, received a low spade lead from East, making the guess pretty much automatic.

In the hotel bar after the game, everyone including George had to know about 'the guess'. The Shoe was happy to oblige, even without a modest fee or a free beer: "LHO was obviously making an aggressive lead and he succeeded. The club had to be from a three-card suit because no one was trying for a club ruff, so George had ace-third. Why had LHO chosen a club lead from king-third rather than a spade? The only sensible reason would be because he had the ace of spades, and maybe even the ace-queen. I was lucky to find George with the queen of spades, but George couldn't have the ace."

George's displays of frustration led the Shoe to search for ever-greater atrocities when he was at George's table. This was one, neither vulnerable:

♠ J 9 8 6 5 2   ♡ 7   ◇ J 10 9 8 7   ♣ 10

George, on Shoe's right, opened one heart and the Shoe volunteered a Michaels cuebid. That didn't seem to produce the desired result, as Big Bird vaulted to three notrump. The Shoe converted to four spades, which ended the auction. This was the entire deal:

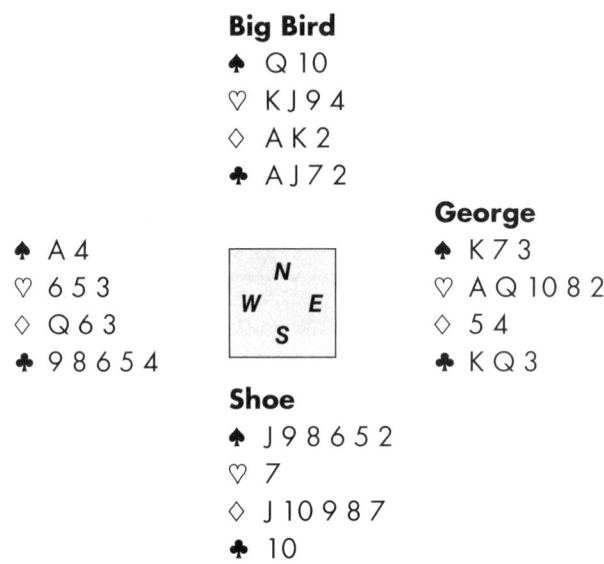

Big Bird
♠ Q 10
♡ K J 9 4
◇ A K 2
♣ A J 7 2

George
♠ K 7 3
♡ A Q 10 8 2
◇ 5 4
♣ K Q 3

♠ A 4
♡ 6 5 3
◇ Q 6 3
♣ 9 8 6 5 4

Shoe
♠ J 9 8 6 5 2
♡ 7
◇ J 10 9 8 7
♣ 10

LHO led the ♠A and shifted to a small heart. Shoe took a mini-pause and played low from dummy. George won the eight and tried to cash the ♡A. When that was trumped, George expressed a tiny amount of frustration by throwing the rest of his hand against the wall. Once the hand had been retrieved, the Shoe drove out the king of trumps and as a grace note, played ♣A and ruffed a club, discovering the ♣KQx with George. Eventually, he took the diamond finesse to make the contract. He explained the hesitation on the heart suit by noting that he was looking for the best play for two diamond pitches, in case LHO had four diamonds. A single pitch was useless. The Shoe observed gratuitously that George's throwing away the hand ruled out the possibility of his holding the ◇Q, although it had, of course, been ruled out already by George's failure to open one notrump.

It was in that same year that the crowning atrocity on the George-o-meter occurred and I sensed strongly that the boys might finally win a Canadian championship. To go with his penchant for reanalysis, the Shoe had developed a little paranoia about the opponents peeking into his hands. As a result, he had begun to memorize his hand and then fold his cards face down on the table for the auction. With the use of screens, this method could not be observed by Big Bird, which meant there were never any objections from the opponents. In first chair, Shoe picked up:

♠ K 6 3   ♡ K 8 7   ◇ A Q J 2   ♣ 10 7 3

Putting his cards face down on the table, he opened one diamond and Big Bird ran away with the auction. He responded one heart, raised to two by the Shoe. Big Bird now bid two spades, ostensibly a help-suit game try, and the Shoe signed off in three hearts. When Big Bird now went on to four clubs, two spades was converted to a slam try. The Shoe signed off in four hearts and Big Bird made one more slam try with Blackwood. Discovering one ace with Shoe, he felt constrained to venture the slam. The Shoe now picked up his hand again and discovered to his horror that the king of spades had disappeared! This was the whole deal:

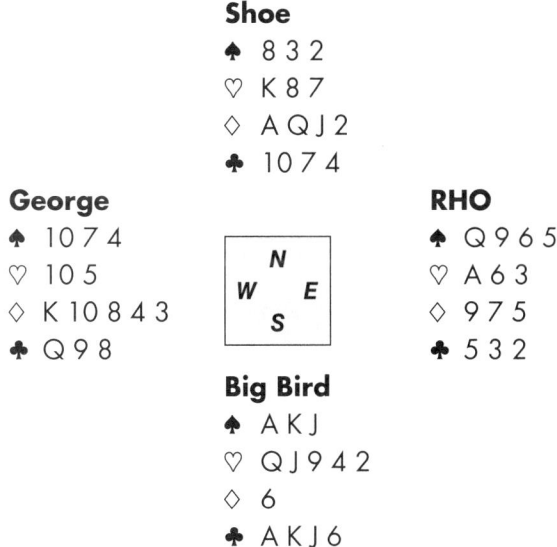

Shoe
♠ 8 3 2
♡ K 8 7
◇ A Q J 2
♣ 10 7 4

George
♠ 10 7 4
♡ 10 5
◇ K 10 8 4 3
♣ Q 9 8

RHO
♠ Q 9 6 5
♡ A 6 3
◇ 9 7 5
♣ 5 3 2

Big Bird
♠ A K J
♡ Q J 9 4 2
◇ 6
♣ A K J 6

George, on Big Bird's left, led a small spade to the queen and ace. This was another hand with few choices: a low heart went to the king and ace. RHO, a very good player, went into a long, long huddle. He finally emerged with... another huddle. Not the problem of a man who held the ◇K. In fact, he looked awfully like a man with no club or diamond stopper who desperately wanted to return a diamond into the jaws of dummy's ◇AQJ in order to break up the club-diamond squeeze on George. His problem was that he wasn't sure he had a defense to the post-mortem if George had found the killing spade lead and there was a spade to cash, while declarer had the ◇K. At long last, he returned a spade.

Big Bird was attuned to the inferences, so he won the spade lead and ran everything. With six cards to go, George had made the early club discard so that he would not appear squeezed. This was the ending:

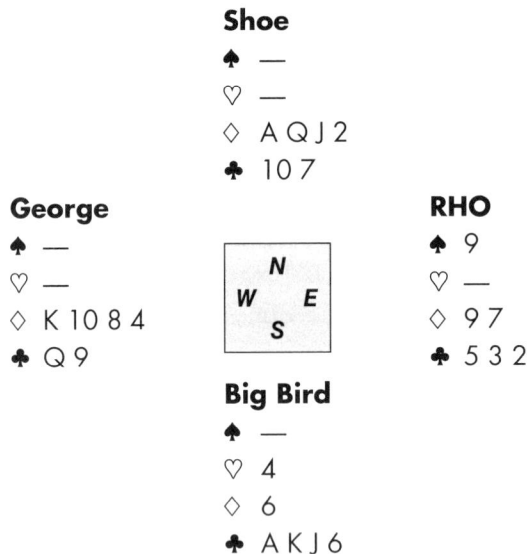

Shoe
♠ —
♡ —
◇ A Q J 2
♣ 10 7

George
♠ —
♡ —
◇ K 10 8 4
♣ Q 9

RHO
♠ 9
♡ —
◇ 9 7
♣ 5 3 2

Big Bird
♠ —
♡ 4
◇ 6
♣ A K J 6

On the last trump, George did not have to consider coming to a singleton club because partner's play of the lowest outstanding diamond marked Big Bird with a singleton in that suit. He was able to part with a diamond. Big Bird proved he had been awake by cashing the ♣A and ♣K, claiming without a finesse when the queen fell.

George turned to him and pronounced, "Big Bird, you asshole!" The Shoe, who could not afford to have George barred from the event, advised pleasantly, as if astonished by such language, "George! ...only I get to call the asshole an asshole." Clearly, they were ready.

The finals of the Canadian team championships provided confirmation. Early in the final, the Shoe and Big Bird missed a slam against George that only required that they pick up Kxxx opposite AJxxxx for no loser. George held the three outstanding trumps, Q10x, behind the ace-jack. More bad language and 13 IMPs in the bargain, an undeserved 26-IMP swing. An omen, for sure.

The killer hand came against Mark Molson and Boris Baran in the second quarter of the final. Mark, the black sheep of the wealthy beer dynasty in Montreal, was one of the nicest guys on the Canadian bridge scene, which was ideally suited for playing with the intense Boris. Together, they formed an effective and dangerous partnership. Everyone was under minor time pressure because fire alarm testing was scheduled almost exactly when the second quarter was due to end. Big Bird and the Shoe had had a healthy lead after the first quarter and it was likely to increase; they hadn't dropped anything, but had been on the right side of two vulnerable game swings, one that might have made that they set, and one they had made when it could have been set. On the second last board, the Shoe picked up, at favorable vulnerability:

♠ J 9 3   ♡ 5   ◇ K Q J 8 7 5 2   ♣ 6 5

As dealer, he opened four diamonds. Molson went into quite a huddle and finally emerged with a double. Big Bird, never shy, and alive to the hesitation, raised to seven diamonds. He had:

♠ Q 10 2   ♡ 10 4 3   ◇ 10 9 4   ♣ Q 10 8 2

Just then, the fire alarm went off, probably causing Baran to choose a forcing pass with seven hearts to the ace, queen, jack and the ◇A. With the alarm still ringing, Molson opted for seven spades and Baran converted to seven notrump. This was the deal:

Molson
♠ A K 8 6 4
♡ K 9
◇ 6 3
♣ A K 7 4

Shoe
♠ J 9 3
♡ 5
◇ K Q J 8 7 5 2
♣ 6 5

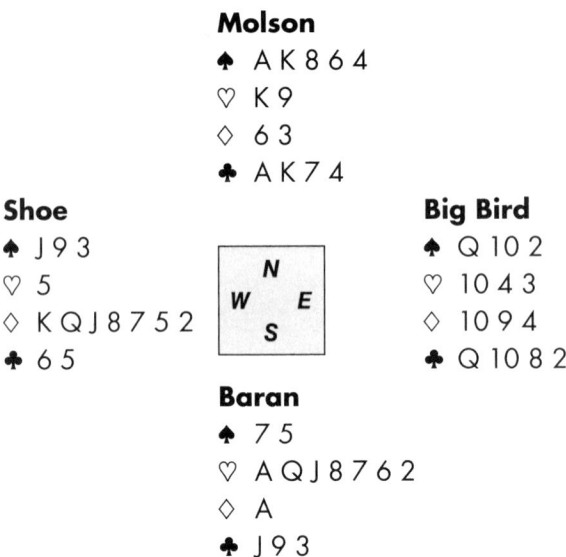

Big Bird
♠ Q 10 2
♡ 10 4 3
◇ 10 9 4
♣ Q 10 8 2

Baran
♠ 7 5
♡ A Q J 8 7 6 2
◇ A
♣ J 9 3

You can see that the ♣Q didn't drop and the Vienna Coup failed because the Shoe had a spade stopper. One down in 7NT was a 17-IMP pickup, on a board where they should have lost 13 IMPs since partners only reached six hearts rather than seven. At the half, their lead was up to 86 IMPs. The last two quarters were a mere formality. In fact, the Shoe went for a nap while the other two pairs finished up. He awoke to the post-game celebration.

This time it was real: they were headed to Mexico City for the three-country playoff to become a North American team in the Bermuda Bowl!

16

The World at Last

The Shoe woke up as Canadian Teams Champion for 1986. It had been a runaway win. Naturally, I was at the celebration, violating my healthy regimen by accepting a glass of champagne. In this respect I was massively upstaged by David Turner, a lifetime teetotaler, who was preparing for the three-country playoff in Mexico City by standing on a table holding aloft his glass of champagne and calling for 'altitude training'. The three excellent pairs on this team consisted of David partnered with Greg Carroll, Marty Kirr with Arno Hobart plus, of course, Big Bird and the Shoe. Everyone was playing some variation of the System. The three-country playoff with Mexico and Bermuda, for the right to represent North America in the Bermuda Bowl, was scheduled for February 1987.

Unfortunately, neither my health nor my budget permitted such travel on my part. The Shoe made various consoling Bungalow noises, including the promise of a full report. George Mittelman became non-playing captain, a popular, excellent choice. In Mexico City, the Shoe was much too caught up in the excitement. You won't want to hear about the team's lack of success in locating a racy nightclub. Arno, in particular, had instructions that he could commit any indiscretion he wished, as long as he was wearing a diving suit. The rest of the story was similarly incongruous. Because of the ever-present paranoia about water quality, the Shoe drank only beer. Because he was acting in a strictly disciplined manner, treading the high wire between concentration and relaxation, the Shoe limited his intake to one beer per six hands.

There was a long round robin involving Mexico, Bermuda and Canada, with the top two teams to survive for an extra day with full carryover. When playing the Mexicans, NPC Mittelman assigned the Shoe to be screen-mate of George Rosenkrantz, a multi-millionaire from his research on birth-control pills, and now a full-time bridge player. In the early going, the Shoe made various aggressive bids at favorable vulnerability: a psychic two-over-one in clubs, a four-level diamond preempt and others of the same ilk. Rosenkrantz and partner fielded everything perfectly, and the Shoe posted a succession of minus 700 numbers (old math) for four down doubled. This was no great harm as partners could make twelve tricks in a major for 680 each time, so each number rated to be a 1-IMP loss since the slams were not likely to be bid. Greg and David, however, were such good teammates that they bid two of the slams and twice won 12 IMPs, making the Shoe look competent. The combination of the numbers and the beer led to Rosenkrantz approaching Big Bird at tournaments for years to come, always to ask, "How's your buddy with the beer?"

Canada got lucky because they were leading Mexico but trailing Bermuda at the cut. Mexico reached the final against Canada after the tie-break (IMP quotient), so a potential negative carryover became a positive one without the turn of a card. After the third quarter, the Canadian lead had grown to 50 IMPs, comfortable but not conclusive. Big Bird and the Shoe played a very fast final quarter, emerging a full hour ahead of Marty and Arno. They weren't telling many stories except to say they had zigged and zagged fantastically well. When pressed, the Shoe sketched out one example:

♠ J 3   ♡ A K 9 7   ◇ A K Q 10 3 2   ♣ 10

The Shoe opened a vulnerable forcing club and Big Bird responded one heart, which did not promise hearts, but showed 6 or more HCP and two or fewer controls. The Shoe rebid two diamonds and his LHO doubled for takeout of diamonds. This came back around to the Shoe. Blessed with the knowledge that neither hearts or diamonds rated to break and that diamonds, in particular, were going to break horribly, and further, that they were off too many controls for slam, the Shoe passed. That made four, +580. Four hearts could in theory be made double dummy.

When the scores were finally compared, Canada had picked up another 50 IMPs to win by a tidy 100 IMPs. Two diamonds doubled was worth 12, as four hearts went down in the other room. The Canadian team was headed for the Bermuda Bowl, scheduled for Ocho Rios, Jamaica, in October 1987.

Of course, the Shoe was crying on my shoulder all the time, now that he had safely achieved his lifetime bridge dream. In September, one month before the event, reality set in as he received a five-pound package which contained the convention cards and system notes of the thirty or so pairs playing in the event. A third of them played Ferts, one-level bids that showed a very weak hand, usually 0-6 HCP. The ACBL had barred such bids, so they were heading into a world championship essentially as novices in regard to the bidding methods of a third of their opponents. The Shoe gave thanks for his early education at Hart House and the Metro Club, but thought a team meeting to discuss defenses might be in order. Apparently, Big Bird was bowling in a league and indicated that he would be too busy to participate. I was the Shoe's obvious victim as he had to vent to someone about this outrage.

Big Bird continued to display the same singular lack of dedication. On the flight to Jamaica, in those halcyon days when liquor on an airplane was free, he snagged the bottle of cognac from the stewardess and began serving the passengers. This didn't help much with the last-minute systems discussions. They arrived two days before play was to begin and were shown to a hotel room where the carpets had just been installed, leaving them with the unenviable choice of sniffing glue or negating the air conditioning by living with the windows open in the 90 degree heat. Big Bird opted to avoid the whole thing by renting jet skis and acquiring a world-class sunburn. In fairness, I must add that the Shoe's account also mentioned that none of this appeared to affect any of the results at the bridge table.

The event was to be an eight team, double round robin, with the top two teams to qualify for the semi-final round. The American team and the European Champions, Sweden, already had byes to the semi-final. The teams in the round robin were England, Pakistan, Brazil, Taipei, Venezuela, New Zealand, Canada and the host Jamaicans.

Big Bird played one of the really nice hands of the entire event in the first match against Jamaica. The Shoe had:

♠ J 10 9 8 3 ♡ K Q 2 ◇ A K Q 3 ♣ 5

With the Jamaicans passing throughout, Big Bird opened one club, showing 17+ HCP. The Shoe responded 1NT (artificial, four controls) and the bidding went naturally: Big Bird 2♣; Shoe 2♠; Big Bird 3♡;

Shoe 4◇ (undiscussed, but what could it be?). Big Bird tried special-ized Blackwood 4NT and the Shoe's response of 5◇ showed an ace and two kings. Big Bird sensibly signed off in six diamonds and the Shoe, even though he had his best diamonds possible, talked himself into the possibility that this was a grand slam try and naively, as the ensuing play will show, converted to six hearts. That went all pass.

The whole deal was:

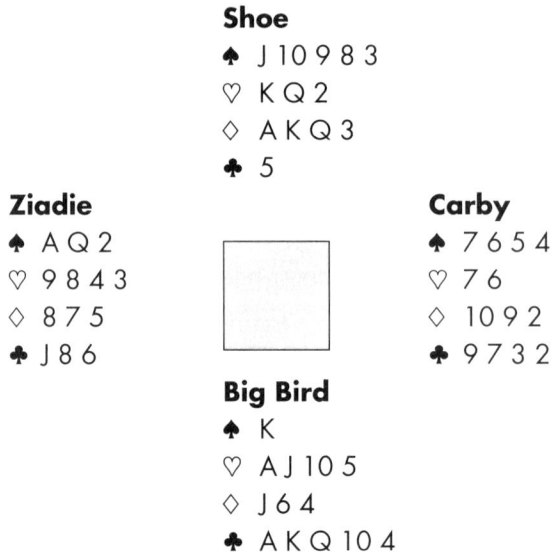

Shoe
♠ J 10 9 8 3
♡ K Q 2
◇ A K Q 3
♣ 5

Ziadie
♠ A Q 2
♡ 9 8 4 3
◇ 8 7 5
♣ J 8 6

Carby
♠ 7 6 5 4
♡ 7 6
◇ 10 9 2
♣ 9 7 3 2

Big Bird
♠ K
♡ A J 10 5
◇ J 6 4
♣ A K Q 10 4

Ziadie had listened to a graphic auction and, holding four trumps, wisely led the ♠A in an effort to tap declarer. This was hugely suc-cessful when the ♠K dropped. Big Bird had no choice but to trump the ♠Q continuation.

Undeterred, Big Bird cashed three high clubs, pitching two high diamonds from dummy. That was followed by two rounds of dia-monds, ending with the jack in the closed hand. When the low ruff of the third diamond survived, Big Bird could claim on a high crossruff. Even if Ziadie had been able to ruff the diamond in front of dum-my, Big Bird could cash one spade to come to twelve tricks. For this to fail, Ziadie would have had to have begun with 2-6-2-3 shape, in which case six diamonds would also go down. In the result, Canada won two slightly tainted IMPs for +980 versus +920.

This hand got written up in the *Daily Bulletin*. It was only justice, claims the Shoe, that with all the pre-game aggravation he had suffered from Big Bird, that the Bulletin listed the Shoe as declarer.

The Winning Butterfly seemed to go on vacation whenever Canada played New Zealand. In the first round robin, the pivotal hand had Big Bird on lead against seven notrump doubled. These guys were playing Ferts and a relay system. None of that mattered much in the outcome, except that Reid became declarer. This had been an all-relay auction:

West	North	East	South
Big Bird	Crombie	Shoe	Reid
	pass¹	pass	2♣²
pass	2◇	pass	2♡
pass	2♠	pass	2NT
pass	3♣	pass	4♣
pass	4◇	pass	6♣
pass	7NT	dbl	all pass

1. Forcing (shows an opening bid or better).
2. Shows diamonds.

Big Bird had to lead against seven notrump doubled armed only with the knowledge that the Shoe would never make a frivolous double in this situation: the double was supposed to help to set the hand by calling for an unusual lead, whatever that was. Big Bird's hand was

♠ 4 3   ♡ J 10 9 8   ◇ J 6 4 2   ♣ 7 5 2

After the first round, the remaining bids were relays that showed nothing about North's hand, but South had shown 2-3-6-2 distribution with six controls (ace = 2, king = 1). He had furthermore promised two of the top three honors in spades, hearts and diamonds, with one top honor in clubs. Assuming this was the explanation on the other side of the screen before the Shoe doubled, what would you lead?

Presumably, a spade was the safest lead and must now be ruled out. Dummy's 'first bid' suit is diamonds, though they were actually shown by declarer. Who has ever discussed this situation, let alone whether dummy's first bid suit has anything to do with an unusual lead in grand slam? The most unusual lead is obviously a diamond, but the other genuine consideration is that if the opponents are really off the rails, how will they make thirteen tricks without declarer's six-card suit? Couldn't a diamond lead give away the whole suit? These are the kind of sugar plums that dance through your head as you opt for the safe heart lead. At the post-game reception, so did all but two people among the assembled competitors. This was unfortunate, as the whole deal was:

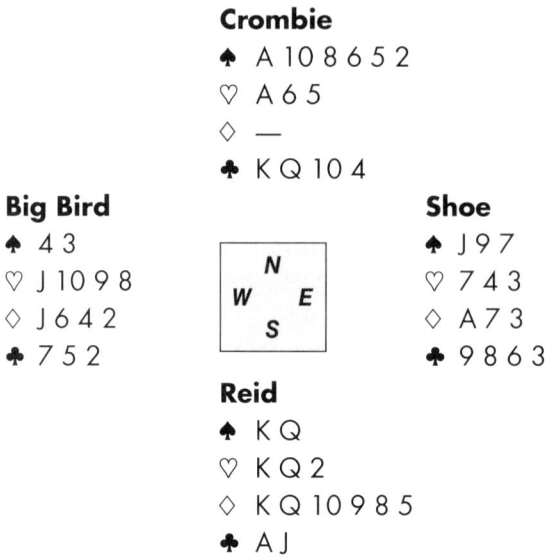

Crombie
♠ A 10 8 6 5 2
♡ A 6 5
◇ —
♣ K Q 10 4

Big Bird
♠ 4 3
♡ J 10 9 8
◇ J 6 4 2
♣ 7 5 2

Shoe
♠ J 9 7
♡ 7 4 3
◇ A 7 3
♣ 9 8 6 3

Reid
♠ K Q
♡ K Q 2
◇ K Q 10 9 8 5
♣ A J

After the lead of the ♡J, spades behaved for six winners and Reid conveniently held the ♣J, so that was thirteen tricks. There was something like a sheepish explanation: the response for five controls was 3NT and Reid was afraid partner would pass. It did not seem such a disastrous result until partners missed seven spades in the other room.

Canada blitzed the leading Taipei team, then proceeded to bid more slam hands against England, both of whose pairs were playing Ferts. This was a deal that contributed to the 34-IMP Canadian win:

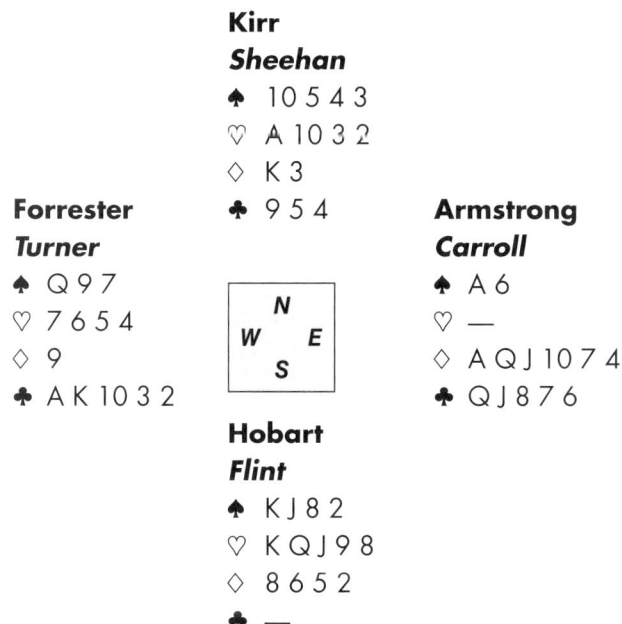

Kirr
Sheehan
♠ 10 5 4 3
♡ A 10 3 2
◇ K 3
♣ 9 5 4

Forrester
Turner
♠ Q 9 7
♡ 7 6 5 4
◇ 9
♣ A K 10 3 2

Armstrong
Carroll
♠ A 6
♡ —
◇ A Q J 10 7 4
♣ Q J 8 7 6

Hobart
Flint
♠ K J 8 2
♡ K Q J 9 8
◇ 8 6 5 2
♣ —

At the first table, Kirr passed and Armstrong, East, kicked off the proceedings with a forcing pass, over which Hobart and Kirr played 'systems on'. Hobart therefore overcalled one spade, the equivalent of a canapé style one spade opening bid. Forrester doubled to show cards, and Kirr introduced as much aggravation as possible by bidding two diamonds, ostensibly natural. Armstrong doubled and when this came back around to Kirr he corrected to two spades. Armstrong jumped to four clubs and everyone was bid out after Forrester raised to five clubs.

At the other table, Sheehan opened a club Fert with the North hand. Carroll overcalled one diamond, Flint bid one heart and Turner made a negative double. North raised preemptively to three hearts and Carroll correctly evaluated his heart void and bid four hearts. When Turner came out five clubs, rather than some number of spades, Carroll raised to six. Even with clubs 3-0, the hand made seven. The Canadian team won 13 IMPs where they could have lost 13 IMPs had England bid the grand slam.

In the fifth round, Shoe is on VuGraph with Pakistan. He and Zia compare in the same seat. Even if the hero of the piece turns out to be David Turner, it doesn't get any better than this! Zia had been heard before the event to counsel his teammates against playing too much machinery and the pivotal hand provided a dramatic illustration. Here is the whole deal:

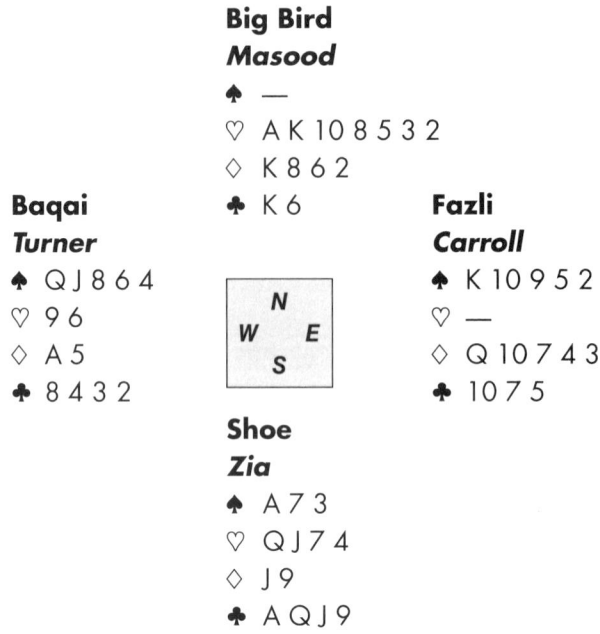

Big Bird
Masood
♠ —
♡ A K 10 8 5 3 2
◊ K 8 6 2
♣ K 6

Baqai
Turner
♠ Q J 8 6 4
♡ 9 6
◊ A 5
♣ 8 4 3 2

Fazli
Carroll
♠ K 10 9 5 2
♡ —
◊ Q 10 7 4 3
♣ 10 7 5

Shoe
Zia
♠ A 7 3
♡ Q J 7 4
◊ J 9
♣ A Q J 9

At both tables, East-West were silent. At his table, the Shoe began with 1NT (14-17) and Big Bird transferred to hearts. After the Shoe bid 2♡, Big Bird carried on to 3♣, a retransfer to diamonds. The Shoe jumped to 4♡, which showed a minimum with good hearts. Then came cuebids: 4♠ by Big Bird, 5♣ by Shoe, 6♣ by Big Bird. The Shoe subsided in 6♡. All this machinery had wrong-sided the hand and the cuebidding had pinpointed diamonds as the weakness, though the 6♣ cuebid by Big Bird, bypassing a 5◊ cuebid but committing to slam, must surely have shown exactly second-round control of diamonds. Nevertheless, Baqai led the mundane ◊A, and that was +980 for Canada.

At the other table, the auction was, if anything, more scientific but sillier. Zia opened 1♣ and Masood jump shifted to 2♡, raised to three by Zia. Masood splintered in spades, Zia cuebid 5♣ and Masood raised to 6♣. Given the spade splinter, Zia took this as natural and passed! The good news was that the trumps in the 4-2 fit split 4-3. This only happens if you are Zia. Note that the Pakistanis lacked the machinery to reach 6♡ from the wrong side, but the jump shift could have been huge clubs and the splinter bid let them make the bogus identification of clubs as the trump suit, enabling them to reach six *clubs* from the wrong side.

This opportunity was not lost on David Turner, who knew there was no future in either black suit or in hearts. He unerringly led the *five* of diamonds from ace doubleton! After the misguess, that was one down, plus 50, 15 IMPs to Canada. Canada won the match by 8 IMPs.

The final match of the first round robin was against Brazil, who would win the Bermuda Bowl two years later. The Canadians scored up a massive blitz, winning by 95 IMPs and effectively eliminating Brazil. This deal was typical:

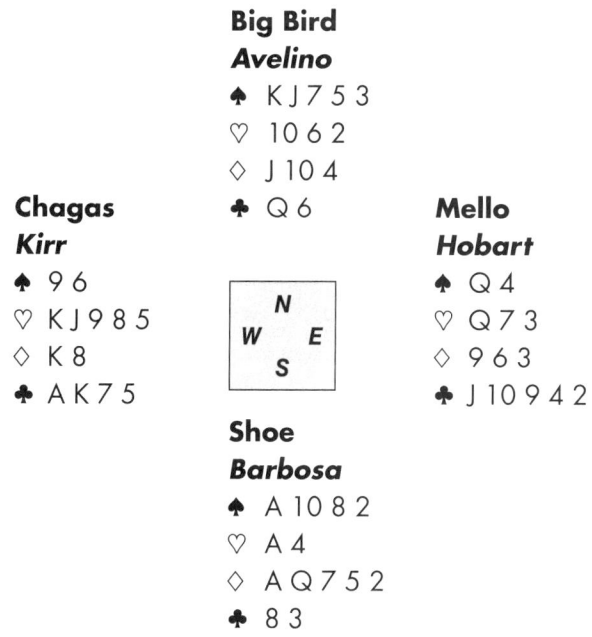

Big Bird
Avelino
♠ K J 7 5 3
♡ 10 6 2
◇ J 10 4
♣ Q 6

Chagas
Kirr
♠ 9 6
♡ K J 9 8 5
◇ K 8
♣ A K 7 5

Mello
Hobart
♠ Q 4
♡ Q 7 3
◇ 9 6 3
♣ J 10 9 4 2

Shoe
Barbosa
♠ A 10 8 2
♡ A 4
◇ A Q 7 5 2
♣ 8 3

At the first table, Shoe opened 1♠, canapé style. Chagas, one of the world's great players, overcalled two hearts, which would have gotten Mello off to the right lead. Fortunately for the Shoe, the canapé opening had right-sided the spades. Big Bird raised to two and then continued to 4♠ after the Shoe showed his diamond canapé. Chagas started by cashing the two top clubs and then, proving that even good players can have a bad day, did not see the possibility that two of dummy's hearts would disappear on declarer's fourth and fifth diamonds. He shifted to the non-bruising trump, making the hand Shoe-proof. At the other table, four spades was reached but played from the other side, so the diamonds were in plain view. Hobart led the ♣J to the king and Kirr shifted immediately to a heart. That ensured one down.

Aside from the miscue by Chagas, the Shoe considered this hand to be evidence that the play in this world championship was not all that great. Almost every declarer went down in four spades, but not a single declarer had gone two down as he should have. Most of the auctions would have gone 1◇ - 1♡ - 1♠ - pass, or maybe as at his table 1♠ - 2♡ - 2♠ - pass. After the cash of two clubs and a heart shift, declarer knows that East has three hearts to the queen. He also needs East to have the ◇K to make the hand. Surely East cannot also have the ♠Q and have failed to raise hearts? Really good players would start with the ♠A and then take the (losing) spade finesse against the queen.

Canada finished the first round robin in second place. The Jamaicans held a special reception for the Canadians and Pakistanis, the only teams that did not consist of professional players. Big Bird graced the event in a towel and his bathing suit, not a thing of beauty at the best of times. The misunderstanding was eventually remedied and the Shoe was able to emerge from his hiding place behind one of the couches.

The second round robin was seeded according to the results of the first round robin, so Canada began against the seventh place team… Brazil. They suspected the result of the first match might have been overkill. Early on in the rematch, the Brazilians bid a 15% grand slam in one room while Big Bird and the Shoe languished in game in the other. Unfortunately, the grand slam made.

The atmosphere remained positive, however. Big Bird had Chagas as his screen-mate, and Chagas was making small orations about how he had never been so unlucky in his whole life. On the first board the Shoe misplayed one notrump, which induced a misdefense by Chagas that permitted the contract to make. Later, we discovered that everyone else at every table went down. The pace of the complaints about bad luck picked up to the extent that the Shoe thought that George Mittelman, his NPC, had developed ventriloquist skills.

Inevitably, there was one of those pivotal hands. The Shoe picked up:

♠ K Q 10 9 8 5   ♡ A Q J 3 2   ◇ 5   ♣ A

Mello opened three diamonds on the right and the Shoe opted for a double. Chagas passed and Big Bird jumped to five clubs. The Shoe removed to five hearts, Chagas continued to mumble about his luck and this apparently goaded Big Bird into stringing the Shoe up in six hearts. These were the two hands:

Big Bird
♠ A J
♡ 7 5
◇ 2
♣ K Q 9 7 6 4 3 2

```
      N
  W       E
      S
```

Shoe
♠ K Q 10 9 8 5
♡ A Q J 3 2
◇ 5
♣ A

This slam certainly ranked among the most miserable of all slams. The Shoe needed Mello, with the preempt, to have exactly three hearts to the king. He also had to have at least two spades for the trips to the dummy, and, after an opening diamond cash and a club switch, no club void. When that all happened, the slam came rolling home and the flap on the screen was lowered. I have it from a reliable source that at this point, the Shoe reopened the flap, stuck his head into the gap and advised Chagas: "*Now* you've been unlucky." That result was win 11 IMPs toward a Canadian win of the rematch by 12 IMPs total.

The ninth match was New Zealand again. Both Hobart-Kirr and Carroll-Turner produced some huge results and nothing seemed too bad, but the end result was another loss, this time by 12 IMPs. The valuable victory points had begun to slip away, although in the next round Canada produced a near blitz against Jamaica. The amazing number of slams continued, with Hobart and Kirr doing very well under pressure on this deal:

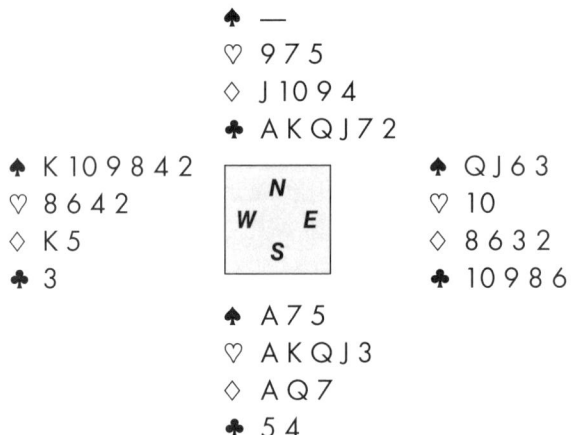

♠ —
♡ 9 7 5
◇ J 10 9 4
♣ A K Q J 7 2

♠ K 10 9 8 4 2
♡ 8 6 4 2
◇ K 5
♣ 3

♠ Q J 6 3
♡ 10
◇ 8 6 3 2
♣ 10 9 8 6

♠ A 7 5
♡ A K Q J 3
◇ A Q 7
♣ 5 4

At the Shoe's table, West never entered the auction after South opened two notrump. The Jamaicans reached a pedestrian contract of six clubs, making seven. At the other table, with North-South vulnerable, the auction went:

West	North	East	South
Chuck	*Kirr*	*Tai Ten Quee*	*Hobart*
			1♣*
3♠	4♣	pass(!)	6♡
pass	7♡	all pass	

We can only assume that Tai Ten Quee had seen Chuck's preempts before, as he declined the non-vulnerable save, which should have gone about five down against the vulnerable grand slam. Even in new math, that's only 1100, a profit against any kind of slam at the other table.

The eleventh round was England, who had been fifth in the first round robin and were playing all the top seeds first. They were mounting a charge and, as Canada was finishing against the top seeds, this match rated to be critical. The first half was a virtual tie. Things actually looked promising as Big Bird elected to open only three vulnerable hearts against vulnerable opponents, holding:

♠ 7 6 ♡ K J 9 8 6 5 4 2 ♢ K 10 ♣ 7

The Shoe raised to four hearts with:

♠ A J 8 5 3 2 ♡ Q 10 ♢ Q 6 ♣ A 8 4

After this start to the auction, it was difficult for fourth hand to step in vulnerable holding:

♠ 9 ♡ 7 ♢ A J 9 7 2 ♣ Q J 10 6 5 2

and four hearts made easily for +620. At the other table, Forrester chose the more aggressive four heart opening and Kirr balanced with four notrump. That led to five diamonds undoubled, two down, -200, win 9 IMPs.

Then the wheels began to come off very quietly for a Canadian team that had been playing extremely well. In the first room, the Brits had missed a cold four hearts and had scored +170. In the other room, Armstrong opened a weak notrump on 11 HCP and the auction developed:

West	North	East	South
Hobart	Armstrong	Kirr	Kirby
	1NT	dbl	2♠
3♣	pass	3♠	pass
4♡	pass	5♣	all pass

This was the deal:

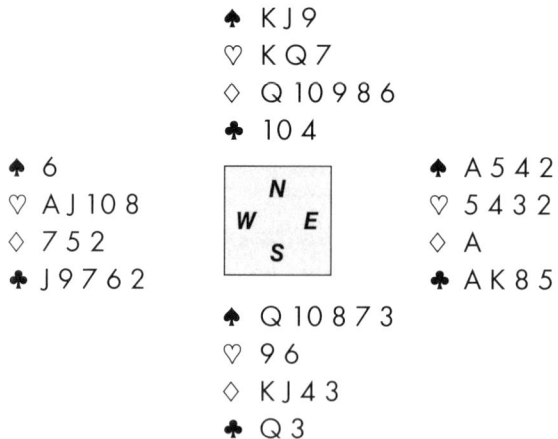

```
                    ♠ K J 9
                    ♡ K Q 7
                    ◇ Q 10 9 8 6
                    ♣ 10 4
♠ 6                                      ♠ A 5 4 2
♡ A J 10 8          ┌──────────┐         ♡ 5 4 3 2
◇ 7 5 2            │    N     │         ◇ A
♣ J 9 7 6 2        │  W   E   │         ♣ A K 8 5
                    │    S     │
                    └──────────┘
                    ♠ Q 10 8 7 3
                    ♡ 9 6
                    ◇ K J 4 3
                    ♣ Q 3
```

With two heart losers, already not so lucky, Hobart opted to play the notrump bidder for ♣Qxx or ♣Q10x. The debate still rages whether he could ever make five clubs unless clubs were 2-2, given that he needed two diamond ruffs in dummy. Anyway, that lost 6 IMPs instead of winning 6 IMPs, and in the end, Canada lost by 30 IMPs. With the schedule that remained, Canada was in trouble.

The twelfth round was against Pakistan, who put the Shoe and Big Bird under intense pressure by opening a weak notrump every time the Shoe had a forcing club bid. They responded admirably, making the right decisions every time. This deal was the most intriguing example of the bunch:

Big Bird
Masood
♠ 5 3
♡ 9
♢ A Q J 5 3 2
♣ 10 7 6 5

Munir
Turner
♠ 9 7 2
♡ 10 7 5 4 2
♢ 7 6 4
♣ Q 4

```
      N
  W       E
      S
```

Nisar
Carroll
♠ Q J 10 8
♡ K Q 8 3
♢ K 10 8
♣ J 2

Shoe
Zia
♠ A K 6 4
♡ A J 6
♢ 9
♣ A K 9 8 3

At the Shoe's table, Nisar opened 1NT as East and Munir chose to run from the double by bidding two diamonds. He was heavily punished when Big Bird opted to double for penalties and the Shoe removed to a cuebid of three diamonds. Big Bird deemed his hand unsuitable for notrump and bid four clubs. The Shoe correctly inferred that this must show a real club suit and distribution to bypass three notrump. He casually strung up Big Bird in the small slam. This made seven for +940 when the clubs behaved.

At the other table, the auction proceeded:

West	North	East	South
Turner	Masood	Carroll	Zia
		1NT	dbl
redbl*	2♢	pass	2♠
pass	3♣	pass	3NT
all pass			

Maybe two diamonds did not show values or maybe three clubs didn't necessarily show a real suit. In any event, Zia opted for three notrump. That made five, losing 10 IMPs. At the half, the Canadians led by 18 IMPs. In the second half, we made one of the Pakistani players an honorary Canadian for passing one spade redoubled making two, a plus of something like 1120 for our side when there was no game. Even so, the Pakistanis made a strong comeback in the second half to win by 6 IMPs.

Round 13 was Taipei, the leaders. Another good chance slipped very quietly away. You hold:

♠ A 7 6   ♡ K J 3   ◇ 10 7 6 5 4 2   ♣ 7

The auction proceeds:

LHO	Partner	RHO	You
		1♣*	1◇
1♠	pass	2♡	pass
3◇	pass	4♣	pass
4◇	pass	4♠	pass
4NT	pass	5◇	pass
6♣	all pass		

You are on lead, hearts and clubs bid on your right, spades on your left. One might simply opt to cash the ♠A and wait, hoping for a heart trick. As it happens, that beats the slam and all other leads permit it to make. Partners were in five clubs, so setting the slam wins 12 IMPs, while permitting it to make loses 13 IMPs. The ♠A was not led and Canada lost this 25-IMP swing to lose the match by 8 IMPs.

The thrilling conclusion was: with one match to go, Canada had dropped to fourth, a fraction behind Pakistan and a little further behind second place England. To get to the all-important second spot, Canada needed to win a blitz, plus there had to be no more than a close win by England and no blitz by Pakistan. Canada could equally well be knocked out of the top half of the field, as they were playing the fifth place Venezuelans. The Shoe and Big Bird were on VuGraph and a blitz seemed a realistic possibility until this hand came along. Fittingly, it was another grand slam. The Shoe held:

♠ Q 10 2   ♡ A 10 9 8 6   ◇ K 8 6   ♣ 4 3

As North, he began the proceedings with a pass. East, Caponi, opened 2♠, a preempt in either minor. In this situation, Big Bird and the Shoe played various gadgets, but the important one was that they would not trap pass with more than 16 HCP. Big Bird passed and West, Hammaoui, did not have the presence of mind to pass also, as the Shoe, a passed hand, would be unlikely to balance. Shoe would, in fact, have passed. Instead, Hammaoui bid 2NT to discover opener's minor, Shoe passed and Caponi bid 3♣. Big Bird went for the limelight with a bid of 6◇. The Shoe, who figured he had *three* losers covered, one in each suit but clubs, raised to 7◇ and slid the board under the screen. The board reemerged about two seconds later with double from Caponi and pass from Big Bird. This had been the whole auction:

West	North	East	South
Hammaoui	Shoe	Caponi	Big Bird
	pass	2♠*	pass
2NT	pass	3♣	6◇ !
pass	7◇	dbl	pass
pass	?		

The Shoe was unhappy that Big Bird had passed the double so quickly. Surely he had to consider seven notrump as an alternate contract if he had the ♣A? The Shoe hesitated for quite a while, but finally decided that a very slow redouble would be even worse than Big Bird's fast pass: surely it had to ask partner to bid seven notrump if the club control wasn't a void. The Shoe passed, sadly. After some hesitation, Hammaoui led a low spade, the flap went up, Big Bird saw the lead and announced "Wrong!"

This had been the deal:

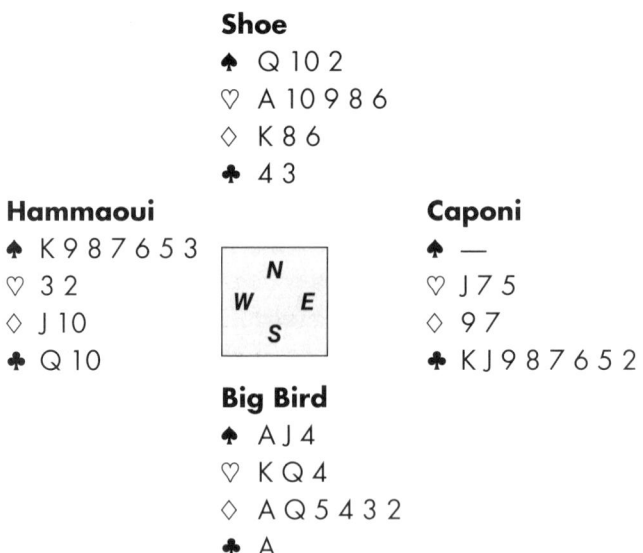

Shoe
- ♠ Q 10 2
- ♡ A 10 9 8 6
- ◇ K 8 6
- ♣ 4 3

Hammaoui
- ♠ K 9 8 7 6 5 3
- ♡ 3 2
- ◇ J 10
- ♣ Q 10

Caponi
- ♠ —
- ♡ J 7 5
- ◇ 9 7
- ♣ K J 9 8 7 6 5 2

Big Bird
- ♠ A J 4
- ♡ K Q 4
- ◇ A Q 5 4 3 2
- ♣ A

The Shoe reports that in Caponi's position, even had he held a spade, after Big Bird made his announcement, he would have trumped the opening lead. In the event, that drastic step was not necessary for Caponi, who had the void and trumped. Big Bird changed his announcement to an expletive even shorter than "Wrong!" though perhaps with more exclamation marks.

In the end, none of the disappointments late in the event changed the outcome. Both England and Pakistan posted blitzes, so could not have been caught. Venezuela came back to beat Canada, but not by enough to pass them in the standings. The Canadians finished a very respectable fourth, where they had had overall wins against all three teams that had finished ahead of them: 162-160 against Pakistan; 131-127 against England and 164-112 against the leaders, Taipei.

The Shoe continues to hold forth to a larger than normal audience, though it's at the Royal York Hotel lobby bar rather than Fran's. "Bungalow," he says, "the Winning Butterfly just got tired. He wasn't accustomed to going 14 rounds. But I'm really proud of having gotten to go and I'm really proud that not one member of our team was out of place or, for that matter, out of line. And of course, I made it to the Bermuda Bowl, just as I promised twenty-five years ago at Hart House."

All this puts me in mind of a hand from Hart House, recounted to me by a player who went on to ruin his bridge career by becoming a judge of the Ontario Court of Appeal. It involves the hereafter, where there are an infinite number players, using an infinite number of suits, each with an infinite number of cards. The Shoe is the new guy, in on probation, playing with Bungalow. You guys are all kibitzing. The Devil, holding:

A K K K K K K K...

and so on and on, one card in each suit decides to test the new guy with a psychic bid. He opens all but one of the second highest suit. Bungalow bids all but one of the highest suit and an infinite number of passes later, it comes around to the Shoe, who holds:

— A A A A A A A A...

and so on and on, with a void in the highest suit.

How bad can it be? The Shoe decides to bid all of notrump. An eternity later, the Devil doubles. Everyone passes. The Devil leads the ace of the highest suit and the Shoe is infinitely squeezed. He never does stop going down until the mercy rule is invoked.

After this result, no one in heaven or hell is willing to play with the Shoe, so his probation is revoked and the Shoe is sent back to earth to learn to play bridge properly. He wakes up sitting South at Table 1 in the Hart House Bridge Club, just as a guy walks in, introduces himself as Bill Miller and asks permission to kibitz.

Master Point Press on the Internet

www.masterpointpress.com

Our main site, with information about our books and software, reviews and more.

www.teachbridge.com

Our site for bridge teachers and students — free downloadable support material for our books, helpful articles and more.

www.bridgeblogging.com

Read and comment on regular articles from MPP authors and other bridge notables.

www.ebooksbridge.com

Purchase downloadable electronic versions of MPP books and software.